# Am

The door explo... ...a bullet train. I hear... ...e thugs waiting in th... ...ments of flying synthwood.

There were two other attackers awaiting me as I stepped out into the hall. I turned towards the ork and thrust my hands forward as though holding an invisible ball. Pale magelight flickered between them and the ork took a step forward, raising his gun. Then his eyes glazed and blood began to run out of his nose and ears as he toppled forward like a poleaxed cow.

I started turning towards the woman, but she was too fast. She brought her gun to bear and I started a protection spell, knowing I wouldn't be nearly quick enough. My attacker knew it too and gave me a nasty, feral grin that showed her sharpened canine implants just before tightening her finger on the trigger. . . .

# SHADOWRUN

## CROSSROADS

# Stephen Kenson

A ROC BOOK

ROC
Published by the Penguin Group
Penguin Putnam Inc., 375 Hudson Street,
New York, New York 10014, U.S.A.
Penguin Books Ltd, 27 Wrights Lane, London W8 5TZ, England
Penguin Books Australia Ltd, Ringwood, Victoria, Australia
Penguin Books Canada Ltd, 10 Alcorn Avenue,
Toronto, Ontario, Canada M4V 3B2
Penguin Books (N.Z.) Ltd, 182–190 Wairau Road,
Auckland 10, New Zealand

Penguin Books Ltd, Registered Offices:
Harmondsworth, Middlesex, England

First published by Roc, an imprint of Dutton NAL, a member of Penguin Putnam Inc.

First Printing, April, 1999
10  9  8  7  6  5  4  3  2  1

Series Editor: Donna Ippolito
Cover: Mike Evans

**RОC** REGISTERED TRADEMARK — MARCA REGISTRADA

To Christopher, for everything.

There are many people who helped in the creation of this book whom I would like to thank. Thanks go to everyone from the Sprawls amateur press association, where Talon saw his first adventures; to Sean Johnson, for the use of Boom; to Jak Koke, for his loan of Jane and Ryan Mercury; to Lou Prosperi, for his advice and comments; to Donna Ippolito, for her editorial work under pressure; to my family and friends and to everyone at FASA Corporation who help to bring the Sixth World to life and keep it moving. Thanks, everyone, I couldn't have done it without you.

# NORTH

CIRCA 2060

TSIMSHIAN

ATHABASKAN COUNCIL

Edmonton

ALGONKIAN-MANITOO
COUNCIL

Saskatoon

Vancouver

SALISH-SHIDHE
COUNCIL

Calgary

Regina

Pacific
Ocean

Seattle

Spokane

Winnipeg

Portland

Salem

Helena

SIOUX
NATION

Fargo

Duluth

Butte

Bismarck

TIR
TAIRNGIRE

Boise

Billings

St. Paul

Idaho Falls

Sheridan

Rapid
City

Minneapolis

Eureka

Sioux Falls

Reno

Salt Lake
City

Cheyenne

Des
Moines

Provo

Boulder

Denver

Omaha

San Francisco

UTE
NATION

Colorado
Springs

Kansas

CALIFORNIA
FREE STATE

Bakersfield

Las
Vegas

Pueblo

Topeka

Wichita

Santa
Barbara

PUEBLO
CORPORATE
COUNCIL

Los Angeles

Santa Fe

Amarillo

Tulsa

San Diego

Albuquerque

Oklahoma City

Little
Rock

Tijuana

Phoenix

Tucson

Roswell

Ft. Worth

Dallas

El Paso

San Angelo

Shreveport

Pacific
Ocean

Austin

San Antonio

Houston

Chihuahua

Corpus
Christi

AZTLAN

Monterrey

La Paz

Culiacan

Durango

Ciudad
Victoria

# AMERICA

UNITED CANADIAN AND
AMERICAN STATES (U.C.A.S.)

CONFEDERATED AMERICAN STATES (C.A.S.)

### North America

- National Capital
- City
- International Boundary
- State Boundary (U.S.A. circa 1990)

Kilometers
0    200    400    600
0    200    400

Miles

# Prologue

*October 2060*

The sprawl is a beast that never sleeps. Even in the dark hours of the early morning the lights of the city change the course of nature to bring day where it is needed for people to continue about their business, heedless of the course of the sun, sheltered in their tall towers of glass and steel. Deep in the heart of the city, the subways rush like caged creatures mindlessly running the course of a maze over and over again without purpose, always moving, but never resting or reaching their destination.

Anton Garnoff considered these things as he watched the dark walls of the tunnel rushing past through the dim reflections on the subway window. The night was a special time, when the sunlit world passed away and another took its place, a world of dark shadows and bright neon that could only exist through the genius of humanity. There was nothing like the unique world created by nighttime in the city, save perhaps nightfall in the jungle, which was the closest thing to the sprawling riot of city life that existed in nature. But Anton Garnoff was not interested in nature, and his errand on this particular night was in no way natural.

He kept careful track of the subway stops, ticking them off in his mind in a kind of mantra as the train passed through each one and brought him closer to his destination. There were only a few other passengers in the subway car with him, each of them sitting behind a personal wall of silence, careful not to allow a misplaced look or unusual sound to open their walls and draw attention to themselves. Like prey frozen in the undergrowth waiting for a predator to move on. Garnoff wondered idly if he should kill any of them.

An old ork woman sighed quietly and licked her lips as she shifted uncomfortably in her seat. Her dark skin was heavily seamed with lines and wrinkles that made her face look like a raisin beneath a rumpled mass of dark hair. The tusks protruding over her upper lip were yellowed and chipped, and she worried slightly at her lip with them as she sat, quietly mumbling to herself. She wore a tiny gold cross on a chain around her neck. Garnoff wondered if she really thought it would protect her against the creatures he knew were lurking in the shadows of the city.

Several seats further down a young man, human, sat listlessly looking out the window. But his eyes were focused on nothing anyone else in the car could see. A thin cable ran from the chrome jack behind his left ear to a small box cradled in his lap. The boy was lost in a fantasy world of someone else's making, reliving the scripted emotions of another person through a playback in his neural pathways. Living a life he'd already decided he could never have, that no one, in fact, could have, since it existed nowhere but in the mind of the person who had written and engineered it. Garnoff wondered how long the boy had been riding the train and how it was he knew when he reached his destination. He concluded that such a person really had no destination and didn't really care, one way or another.

The few other people on the train were in similar sorry states, each wrapped in their own meaningless little worlds. No, Garnoff thought, these pitiful souls would not do. They were too *dry,* too drained of life. The city had already drawn the most pleasing juices from them, leaving only husks to walk about the streets and ride on the trains in the dead of night. *He* needed far better than this sorry lot. He needed energy: emotion pure and strong and undiluted by the minutiae of daily life in the sprawl. He needed it desperately.

The train hummed to a stop, the doors hissed open, and Garnoff's new victim stepped into the car. He spotted her at once, a young woman, in her mid- to late-twenties, dressed in a smart black coat, collar turned up against the slight autumn chill in the air. Her hair was a lustrous brown, cut short and styled fashionably. She wore black leather gloves, and gold gleamed from her ears. Dark stockings and suede boots clad a pair of shapely legs. She quickly found a seat in the car and took a small datapad from her coat pocket. As the doors hissed shut and the train began to move, she settled back to read.

*She is the one,* Garnoff thought. She seemed ideal, provided she met all the other criteria. Settling back in his seat, anonymous behind his dark glasses, Garnoff allowed his gaze to roam over the young woman, taking her all in. He opened his awareness to the astral plane and observed the colorful play of light in her aura. It was bright and strong, without any blemish to indicate illness or artificial implants. Not like the poor, tired things taking up the other seats. This aura was clean, energetic, perfect for his work. Yes, she would do nicely. With a slight smile, Garnoff allowed his vision of her aura to fade from his sight and stood up.

Moving across the shifting floor of the subway car like a sailor crossing the deck of a swaying ship, he approached the young woman casually. She didn't even look up from her reading until Garnoff settled into the seat next to her. She glanced over at him for a moment, barely a flicker, then again, a bit longer this time, then returned to her reading.

Garnoff paused a moment to savor the experience, then gathered his will and focused on the woman before him.

"Excuse me," he said in a low voice, barely audible above the screech and grind of the subway's progress through the tunnels. The young woman looked up at him, an expression of quizzical concern on her face, and Garnoff struck. The force of his will surged across the short gap between them and she was his. The struggle was over before it even began, and the quizzical look was quickly replaced by one of shock, then fear, then a blank and vacant stare. The mage's spell took hold and Garnoff almost laughed out loud at the ease of it all. His power truly was growing. Just as he was told it would.

With a corner of his awareness, he directed the young woman to return to her reading and she did so. She was completely under his control. The effort of the spell hardly drained him at all. In fact, it left him feeling almost giddy from the warm rush of power at his command. He could hardly wait to feel it again.

When the subway hissed to a halt at the proper stop, Garnoff was pleased to make his leave. The sad scene of these pitiful people disappointed him. He could not imagine how they could choose to live like such sheep when they knew deep within themselves that they were doomed for doing so. He could see it in their eyes, the dull acceptance of animals being led to slaughter. They had surrendered themselves to the inevitable. It was sad that so few people in the world were capable of being anything more than victims, and most of them weren't even worthwhile as that. As he stood, he touched the woman gently on the arm.

"Time to go, my dear."

She looked up at him with a blank expression, but her body moved to obey him. She rose and allowed herself to be led from the train. To anyone watching, the two were simply a handsome couple out for a late evening. Not that anyone on the train had the slightest interest in anyone else's business. That wasn't a healthy occupation.

The platform of the subway station was all but abandoned. Only a few people stood in protective groups awaiting the next train. Somewhere out of sight a man was loudly muttering and cursing to himself, and the people gathered at the edge of the platform looked nervously in his direction from time to time.

Garnoff suspected they had little to fear. The man doing the cursing was likely where the boy on the train would be before too long, once he'd been compelled to run ever more outlandish and daring fantasies through his abused neural pathways to satisfy the void created in him by his empty world. Eventually he wouldn't be able to handle the sensory input his fantasies demanded and would be quite rudely thrust back into the real world he thought he'd left behind forever, a useless burnout. Pitiful.

Garnoff made his way to the edge of the platform, too quiet and unalarming within the cloak of his own thoughts to be noticed over the fears of the people who stood nearby, fears more real to them than the flesh and blood around them. He guided the young woman to walk in front of him, and they followed the edge of the platform into the tunnel. Garnoff paused to let his eyes adjust to a dimness broken only by the flickering lights embedded in the ceiling, then touched the woman's elbow and guided her on.

"What is your name, slave?" he said casually.

"Elaine, Elaine Dumont," she replied in a hollow voice.

"Well, Elaine, you're a prize catch," Garnoff said, almost to himself. "You should be able to help me nicely. You want to do that, don't you, Elaine?"

"Yes," she said, then added, "Master." Garnoff smiled to himself. So easy.

In short order, they arrived at a juncture between the present and the past. An old tunnel entrance lay off to the side of the main line, closed over like an old scar in the underbelly of the city when the underground system had grown and expanded long ago. Garnoff turned and made his way through the darkness of the tunnel with the ease of familiarity and continued for some time in the blackness, needing almost no light to guide his steps. Elaine walked at his side, Garnoff guiding her with a grip on her mind like an invisible leash.

A muffled creak echoed quietly through the tunnel, like the sound of an old rocking chair or a ship at sea. It was a rhythm with which all the other small sounds in the passageway seemed to harmonize, from the dripping of rusty water to the scurrying of unseen things in the shadows. Garnoff pulled his heavy overcoat closer around him in the chill dampness. Even his steady footfalls had begun to unconsciously synchronize with the steady rhythm of the creaking. He quickened his pace with anticipation as they neared the end of the tunnel.

A cursory examination of the stone wall sealing off the end of the tunnel revealed that all was as it should be. With a smoothness born of repetition, Garnoff drew a slim white wand from one of the many pockets of his coat and used it to sketch symbols in the air in front of the wall, leaving faintly glowing traceries behind as it moved. A low, whispered chant began under his breath and seemed to follow in time with the tunnel sounds and the steady, dull creaking. After a moment Garnoff lowered the wand and turned to Elaine with the mockery of a courtly bow.

"Ladies first," he said. Without question, the entranced woman moved toward the wall, as if she would walk right into it. Another step forward and she passed through the dark stone as if it weren't even there, then disappeared from sight. The illusion was perfect. Even someone closely inspecting the wall wouldn't imagine it was nothing more than a magical trick of light and shadow. Garnoff pocketed the wand and stepped through the wall himself, disappearing from view. The dark stones swallowed up his form like a heavy fog and the tunnel again grew silent.

Before him hung a figure from the rusting pipes overhead. It swung gently from side to side, like a pendulum, despite the fact that it was utterly limp and unmoving. The dull creaking of the heavy rope looped around its neck was louder here than in the tunnel. The only other sound was that of Garnoff's footsteps as he entered and moved deeper into the room to look up at its permanent occupant.

The hanging figure seemed very old, its skin withered and yellow like dry parchment beginning to peel at the edges. Dark, brittle hair hung lank around a face contorted in pain. The whiteness of bone peeked out in spots on the figure's face, its eyes bulging and mouth open in a silent scream. The head hung at an unnatural angle, and thin limbs hung slack below. The figure was dressed in a jacket of black synthleather, cracked and discolored with age. It also wore a T-shirt, blurred and threadbare, and a pair of jeans faded and worn with holes in places. Stained and dirty sneakers covered the limp feet. The clothing hung on the skeletal frame like garments on a scarecrow. Parts of them looked scorched and burned as if by a great heat.

Garnoff stood silently looking up at the gently swaying figure. The corpse's bulging eyes shifted to look down at him, and Garnoff suppressed a shudder at the fire of hatred gleaming in those blue orbs.

The dry rope creaked relentlessly as it sawed against the heavy metal pipe. Even though it had been doing so for years, the strong hemp showed little sign of fraying or weakness. The lone, limp figure had long ago blocked out the endless, maddening sound from its consciousness. Its presence was more like a whispering, subconscious reminder of its imprisonment.

*Once, time had no meaning for me,* it thought, *but years of waiting, locked in this dry, dead shell have taught me much about the suffering of isolation and the endless, drawn-out boredom of the slowly passing years as they tick by, minute by minute, second by second. I have watched each grain of sand fall in the hour glass of time. I have learned my lessons well. Soon the world will know just how well . . .*

A stirring at the base of the scaffold alerted Gallow to his servant's presence. The servant's stylish suit and overcoat were in stark contrast to the ancient and decayed surroundings. Behind him, near the entrance to the chamber, stood a young woman, held in the grip of Garnoff's spell like a trapped animal. Gallow could sense her life force, bright and strong, like a thirsty man scenting water on the desert wind. Below the outward calm imposed by Garnoff's spell, he could sense her terror welling up, like sweet nectar. Although Garnoff concealed his fear well, Gallow could sense it radiating off him in waves as well. He drank deep of that heady brew for a moment before acknowledging Garnoff's presence.

*"Well?"* he said in a whispery, dry voice that crawled through Garnoff's mind.

Garnoff swallowed once and mastered himself enough to answer. "She has escaped, and she is on her way to him."

*"Good. Very good. And she will bring him to us."*

"Are you sure? She may just disappear into the shadows, try to lay low. There are other reasons she might have gone to DeeCee . . ."

*"Do not be concerned, Anton. All is proceeding according to our design. The girl will bring him to us and then no one will be able to threaten us. She is the perfect tool. She will find him and he will want to help her. I know his nature. I know it very well. They will come here. Then we will deal with the both of them. Do not be concerned,"*

Garnoff bowed his head in respect to the swaying corpse. "As you say."

*"Tell the barukumin to prepare for the ritual. The time grows near and I want to be ready."*

Garnoff bowed again and a slight smile tugged at his lip.

*"Even the power of our rituals is nothing in comparison to what will soon be yours, my friend. Now go and make ready."*

The mage turned and walked to the stone wall. He passed through the solid stone and then out into the tunnel again, quickening his pace as he made his way back to the platform. As he hastened to inform his own servants to prepare for the night's working, he listened to the muffled creaking recede behind him. It seemed now to sound very much like a low, dry laugh.

Elaine Dumont's first thought as she slowly made her way back to consciousness was to wonder why her grandmother's rocking chair was creaking away all on its own. She had a dream that granny had come and spoken to her as she often did when Elaine was little, taking her granddaughter in her lap to rock her gently to sleep. The dull, relentless creaking seemed to pound into her brain and prevent any attempt at going back to sleep. Elaine stirred a bit and started to wake up.

When she realized she couldn't move, a memory sparked in her mind and she was suddenly wide awake, only to discover that the waking world was the true nightmare.

She lay on a dry wooden surface, worn silvery gray with age. Its surface was covered with painted symbols and designs and surrounded by a ring of candles that cast the only light in the room. Plastic ropes bound her arms and legs to the platform, and dark shapes moved in the flickering light just at the edge of her vision. Elaine looked straight above her and let out a scream that echoed in the chamber and brought titters of laughter from the shuffling shadows.

Hanging above her was a corpse suspended by a rope around its neck. The creaking was coming from the rope as the grisly form swayed gently back and forth. Elaine struggled and thrashed against the ropes in a mad effort to get away from the horrible sight, but the ropes held firm. Finally, the skin on her wrists and ankles rubbed raw and bloody, she stopped and went limp, gasping for breath and shivering in terror.

She looked around and saw a number of dark-clad figures standing outside the ring of flickering candles. One figure detached itself from the group and moved into the circle of golden light. He was an older man, wearing a long black robe made of some velvety material. He had dark hair, graying at the temples, and a salt-and-pepper beard. He looked rather like someone's kindly uncle, except for the long knife he held, its razor edge gleaming in the light. Elaine recognized him as the man from the subway, the man who spoke to her before everything went blank and she found herself here.

As the man approached, Elaine shrank away from him as much as the ropes would allow. He smiled warmly, like he was comforting a scared child. She noticed a murmur that began in the shadows outside of the circle, a rising chant that kept time with the steady, creak, creak, creak of the swaying body above.

The chant grew louder and louder, and the man reached out to stroke Elaine's hair gently. She wanted to scream, to struggle, but she couldn't move, couldn't think. All she could do was listen to the echoing chant, the dull, creaking rhythm, and watch the dark-haired man smile silently at her. His eyes were strange, like he was looking right through her, past her flesh into her very soul. Elaine wondered for a moment if he really saw her at all. He never said a word, only continued to stare and smile as the chanting built all around them, higher and higher.

When Elaine Dumont's blood stained the front of his

robe bright crimson and the lingering power of her life filled his veins with a warm rush of power, Anton Garnoff was still smiling, and the swaying corpse seemed to smile with him.

# 1

I hate bugs. I always hated them, even as a kid. I think there's just something hardwired, deep in the human brain, that says bugs are *wrong* somehow. Just looking at them creeps me out. So, naturally, there I was inside the rusting corpse of a factory complex some fifty kilometers outside the Federal District of Columbia, facing down a guy in charge of some bugs bigger than me. *Not* a nice feeling, let me tell you.

I flattened myself against a support girder along one of the upper walkways of the dimly lit complex and tried to still the sound of my own breathing so I could listen. I heard a distant humming echoing through the large open space above the maze of machinery quietly rusting away on the floor of the factory. It was broken up by random clicks and tapping noises. I tried to ignore it and focused instead on closer sounds that might give away the presence of my quarry.

I heard a faint rattling of the catwalk behind me and to the left and a muffled cry that was just as quickly cut off. I spun around the support girder and leveled my Ares slivergun across the open space toward the opposite wall and fired off a shot. It went wide of the mark, but I wasn't actually trying to hit anything. Gunfire would endanger the person I'd come here to save, and I had more precise weapons to use than a gun. The slivergun's plastic flechettes smacked against the ferrocrete wall with a loud crack as the dark figure on the other side waved his hand and called out in a harsh language of clicks and buzzes not mean to be spoken by a human tongue.

I ducked behind the girder again and heard a spattering and a loud hiss. A terrible stench filled the air as the acid began to eat away at the corroded metal, dissolving it. I spun and took a couple of quick steps back to stay out of the small puddle of greenish-yellow liquid that dripped from the edge of the catwalk, taking the liquefying remains of the top of the girder with it as it began to quickly evaporate.

"Give it up, Crosetti!" I called across the open space. "There's nowhere for you to run. You're trapped. Give up the girl and you might be able to walk away from this." Fat chance. Like I was going to let a total wacko like this one actually walk away, but I had to try and reason with him. As long as he had the girl, he was dangerous. Mocking laughter, high and shrill, answered me.

"You should be the one begging for mercy, Talon. You are in *my* domain here." The two of them had reached a staircase leading down to the factory floor. Crosetti had the girl in front of him like a shield, clasped protectively to him, with one arm clamped over her mouth to keep her from screaming. The other hand was empty, but I knew that a mage as powerful as Victor Crosetti was never truly unarmed. He began guiding her down the stairs, keeping his eyes on me. I was running out of options. The girl looked up at me with pleading eyes and I considered the fate that awaited her down below.

Victor Crosetti was a shaman, one of the people blessed

(or cursed, maybe, in his case) with the Talent. Since the Awakening some fifty years ago, one out of every hundred people developed the ability to use magic. Crosetti was one of the unlucky few whose magic was more than his sanity could handle. Shamans had totem spirits that guided them, animals like Bear, Fox, and Raven. Crosetti's totem was Ant, and contact with such an alien intelligence drove all insect shamans mad. But it also gave them great power. So, here was a lunatic with the power of a master wizard at his command and obsessed with Mary Beth Tyre, age fifteen.

Mary Beth had disappeared from her home when she was only six. She had been through some of the worst horrors imaginable since then: neglect, abuse, even slavery. I'd just spent nearly three months in some of the worst hell-holes I could imagine all along the eastern seaboard helping to track her down, and I sure as hell wasn't going to allow some nutcase to kill her when I was so close.

"Just let the girl go," I said in what I hoped was a firm, yet calm voice.

Crosetti laughed at me again. His balding head and his big eyes, combined with his tall, gangly body, made him look like some kind of humanoid ant standing on two legs. His voice was high and nasal, touched with a bit of hysteria. He really was on the edge.

"Oh, I don't think so," he said. "She's to be my queen, you see, my beautiful, beautiful queen. I've been waiting for so, so long, but now the time is right. Together we will rule over our people, our loyal subjects . . . won't we, my love?"

Mary Beth flinched away from Crosetti's touch and thrashed against him, but his grip was too strong and she was too weak. I had to do something.

Narrowing my eyes, I focused my will on Crosetti's misshapen head. I gathered my anger toward him like a physical thing, bright red strands of fury shot through with black threads of disgust. I plucked out any shreds of pity and wove that pure anger into a weapon. It became the image of a magical spear, the embodiment of the emotions that let us—let me—kill without remorse or mercy when necessary. I saw Crosetti's leering face at the center of a reddish haze as I raised my hand and flung the invisible spear at him with all of my strength.

The powerbolt lanced across the distance between us at the speed of thought, only to splatter against an invisible shield of magical power that surrounded Crosetti and his victim like a cloak. Crosetti flinched as the power of my attack battered him, but it couldn't get through his shields.

Damn, he was powerful, more powerful than I thought. I started to worry for myself as well as Mary Beth Tyre.

"Is that the best you can do, Talon?" Crosetti sneered. "You cannot match the power Ant gives me. Your magic is weak. If you want the girl, you have to come and get her." With that, he dragged the struggling Mary Beth down the stairs and disappeared into the dark maze of machinery below.

I leaned heavily on the railing of the catwalk, gasping for breath. The effort of the spell had taken more of a toll on me than usual. I'd let my anger get the best of me again. I wanted to goad Crosetti into casting a few more spells so he might exhaust himself. I figured my own defenses could handle it, but instead I'd ended up falling for the same tactic I'd been using. Now both of them were down there with whatever Crosetti had brought into this world from the depths of the astral plane.

I listened to the humming and clicking for a moment

and tried to get a better look at what was down there, but it was too dark to be sure. I took a deep breath to steady myself, then vaulted over the railing and dropped toward the ferrocrete floor some ten meters below.

The force of my will reached out, slowing my fall as I bent the laws of physics with the power of my magic. I landed on the floor of the factory as light as a feather, then dropped the levitation spell, alert and ready for anything. The smell I detected up on the catwalk was much stronger down here. A kind of musty, dry, organic scent, with a sickly sweet tang to it.

I transferred the slivergun to my other hand and drew Talonclaw from its sheath at my waist. The edge of the dagger gleamed in the dim light, winking off the runes cut into the blade and the fire opal set into the hilt. I felt the chain-wrapped hilt almost come alive in my hand, a warm tingling that spoke to me of the dagger's magical power. It would likely be more use against whatever was down here than my gun, or any other mundane weapon.

With a few whispered words, I cast out with my magical senses, searching for Mary Beth Tyre. The atmosphere within the factory was thick with the putrid essence of Crosetti's magic, but I could sense Mary Beth not far away and began to move through the darkened rows of machines toward her. As I came around the corner of one of the huge presses, an ant tried to take my head off.

That was even stranger than it sounds. The thing was the size of a pony, standing nearly face to face with me. As I dodged to the side to avoid the snapping mandibles, a detached part of me took note of the incredible detail visible on so large an insect. How hairy was its rough hide, how large and reflective its eyes and, most of all, how sharp and powerful its jaws and pointed legs, looking

capable of ripping a human limb from limb. Ants are creatures capable of carrying thirty times their own weight, and
the one in front of me must have weighed a hundred and
fifty kilos, if it weighed a gram. It was more than capable
of crushing me. Had I been a mundane, that is.

The ant warrior lunged toward me with a high-pitched
chittering sound. I dodged to the side again and struck at
one of the flailing legs. My dagger connected, and the leg
fell to the floor in a pool of pale yellow goo. The ant spun
faster than anything so large had a right to and slammed
me across the narrow aisle into one of the machinery
banks. I managed not to drop Talonclaw, but my slivergun clattered across the floor somewhere.

There was no time to worry about it because the thing
was on me again in an instant. One leg struck me in the
chest like a baseball bat wielded by a troll, knocking the
breath from my lungs with a whoosh. Another tried to
crush my head like a melon, but I slid down the wall and
avoided it, bringing me close to the creature's thorax.
The leg punched a deep dent in the rusting side of the machine press behind me.

Focusing my awareness on the astral plane, I could see
the dark, shimmering aura of the insect spirit and the bright
gleam of my mystic blade. With a powerful lunge I stabbed
Talonclaw deep into the ant warrior's thorax, near the head,
striking not at its physical body, but at its spirit on the astral plane.

The ant spirit gave a psychic shriek of agony and stumbled backward, flailing wildly and thrashing its head. I
managed to retain my grip on the hilt, and the blade slid
out of the creature's body with a slight sizzling sound. The
ant fell heavily against one of the presses and lay still.

Ignoring my lost gun and the slightly twitching body

of the ant warrior, I moved quickly through the maze of machinery toward where I'd sensed Mary Beth's presence. No other bugs tried to block my way, which started to worry me. Crosetti was an Ant shaman of some power. He certainly must have more spirits serving him. Their number was limited without the aid of an Ant Queen, which he clearly wished to summon, but it had to be more than a single warrior drone. If they weren't out here looking for me, I was afraid I knew where they were. As I moved, I whispered words of power under my breath, reaching into the depths of the astral plane, sending out the call. I had reinforcements of my own.

In the heart of the factory was an open area between the massive presses where heavy loads could be moved through. Crosetti had converted it into his lodge, the ritual place where he could summon his totem spirit to the physical world. Strange spirals and geometric designs in rust red and dun yellow decorated the gray floor, and a choking smell like warm yeast filled the air.

Nestled against some of the heavy machines were pale white cocoons, like giant grubs. They held Crosetti's other victims, people in the process of being possessed by ant spirits so they could serve as host bodies, a gateway to allow the spirits to live in the physical world. In the center of the circle Crosetti and five other ant spirits were preparing Mary Beth Tyre for the same fate. Crosetti turned toward me, a twisted look of hatred on his face as he pointed at me with a bony finger.

"Kill!" he shouted to the ant spirits, and they began to move toward me. I spoke the final words of invocation, a sound that echoed through the astral, and twin pillars of flame sprang up, flanking me. Within the white-hot depths of each, you could see a vague humanoid shape.

"Okay, guys, you know what to do," I said and the two fire elementals sprang into action, attacking the ant spirits as I made a run for Crosetti. Flames engulfed the two closest ants, creatures that were a weird melding of human and insect. They were flesh-forms, not like the spirits I'd fought earlier. They were mortal bodies possessed by ant spirits, making them fast, strong, and tough, but not as immune to harm as a true spirit. The flesh-forms shrieked in pain as the flames burned and charred their twisted bodies.

Crosetti saw me coming and gestured tightly with one hand. His dark eyes seemed to bug out even more, gleaming in the light of the burning ant soldiers, and I was sure I could see a faint impression of antennae and mandibles on his face. A shimmering wall of light sprang up between us and I nearly ran right into it. An astral barrier spell. Crosetti tittered as I stopped dead in front of the translucent wall of crackling energy.

"You've lost your gun, Talon," he said with a malicious sneer. "And no magic can pierce this wall. Try to destroy it in the astral, if you want, and my loyal spirits will rip you apart. Now you get to watch as my Queen comes and takes her rightful place at my side." He began to turn back to Mary Beth.

"Don't do this, Crosetti! We can help you!" I shouted. There had to be some way through the barrier. I could try to break through with a spell, but the effort could exhaust me, leaving me no defense against Crosetti and his bug spirits tearing me apart. Already the ant warriors were beginning to overwhelm my two elementals. The smell of burning flesh was strong, and smoke was billowing through the open area.

"I don't need your help!" Crosetti screamed, flecks of

foam spraying from his mouth. "I need *her,* my Queen, my beloved Queen . . ." He raised his arms in invocation and began a humming, clicking chant.

I needed a mundane weapon, a way through the barrier, but all I had was my magic. I took a step back from the shimmering wall and threw Talonclaw with all my strength. The moment the magical blade left my hand, my aura no longer supported its enchantment. The dagger became nothing more than a normal piece of steel that flipped end over end right through Crosetti's barrier, intended to block only the passage of astral beings and magical forces. There was a meaty thunk as the blade embedded itself in his upper back. His chant broke off with a cry of pain and he crumpled to the ground, the shimmering wall fading. I rushed forward, a killing spell close at hand.

Behind me, the ant spirits faltered. Without the guidance of their master, they fled back into the astral plane. The fire elementals consumed the remains of the flesh-forms, then hovered in the air, awaiting my next command. I bent down near Crosetti and rolled him over, ready for anything. His eyes were wide and staring past me at something only he could see, his mouth still open in silent invocation to his beloved Ant Queen. His aura was dull and fading fast. I glanced over to where Mary Beth Tyre lay, too frightened to move, and all Hell broke lose.

Windows and doors shattered and burst in like an explosion as people rushed into the factory complex armed for bear. With near-military efficiency they covered the area in front of them and a voice called out, "All right, nobody move!"

"It's all right, Ryan. It's all over. She's safe!" I called back. I heard the sound of footsteps rapidly approaching

as I stood and spoke the words of dismissal to my elementals. They executed a graceful bow in the air and
flickered out like a candle in the wind, returning to their
astral home.

I turned to Mary Beth again and put on what I hoped
was my most comforting and reassuring smile.

"You're safe," I said. "Nobody will hurt you now.
I promise." She looked up at me with a pair of heart-
breaking blue eyes that started to fill with tears as a group
of armed shadowrunners came around the corner and took
in the scene. The smoldering remains of three flesh-forms
lay on the ground, giving off a charred odor and wisps of
smoke. Victor Crosetti lay at my feet, a small puddle of
dark blood spreading out from under him.

With a low-voiced command to the others, one of the
men walked toward me, heedless of the carnage. He was
Ryan Mercury, the leader of Assets, Incorporated. My
boss. Though clad in a dark jumpsuit covered with straps
and pouches that held various weapons and tools of the
trade, Ryan was a living weapon who didn't really need a
gun or a knife to take down an opponent; only the power
of his magic and his bare hands. He was one of the scari-
est guys I'd ever met.

"Talon," he said in a low, controlled voice, "what the
hell did you think you were doing? I told you to wait for
backup." I bent down and pulled Talonclaw from Crosetti's back before I replied, and Ryan glanced down at
the bloody blade and the dead shaman.

"I couldn't wait. Crosetti was getting ready to make
his move. I couldn't just stand by—"

Ryan cut me off with a curt swing of his hand, like a
knife. "So instead you risked yourself and the girl's life
by jumping in and playing hero."

"You're the one who told me this job was risky when I signed on," I said.

Ryan nodded. "That's right, and I also told you how important it was that we work together to make sure the girl stayed safe once we found her. 'Her survival . . .' "

" '. . . is critical.' " I finished for him. "Yes, I read what Dunkelzahn said, too. And I handled it. She's safe."

"You got lucky this time. Next time you might not be."

"I can handle myself," I said hotly. "I'm not Miranda."

Ryan winced at the mention of his friend's name like I'd struck him. Miranda had been the Assets mage before I came along. She'd died a few years ago during the messy business with the Dragon Heart, the same run that eventually brought me into the group. I knew when I mentioned her I'd made a mistake, but it was too late.

"No," Ryan said slowly, "you're not Miranda. She worked and died for this team and didn't play lone wolf when it suited her. If you can't handle the way we do things, then maybe you should think about why you're still here."

We stared at each other a long moment, and I realized that I'd been almost shouting. Everyone else was standing around, quietly watching us.

"Trust me," I said to Ryan. "I *am* thinking about it."

I turned and walked out of the heart of Crosetti's would-be ant colony. To their credit, nobody tried to stop me.

# 2

There was guilt in the brown eyes looking back at me from the rear-view mirror as I spun the Eurocar Westwind out of the overgrown parking lot of the factory complex. I glanced up at my reflection again as I turned onto the main road. *What the frag are you looking at?* I thought and sighed. It was late and there was no one out on the road. No one to vent at. I really had no idea why I blew up at Ryan like that. It wasn't his fault. It was me.

I ran one hand absently through my hair, brushing some short, damp strands back from my forehead. It had been a couple years already and I still wasn't entirely used to it. My hair used to be long, just past my shoulders, a style worn by all the wiz young magicians years ago. I'd cut it short a little less than six months after I joined Assets.

Ryan had taken one look at it and laughed. He said it made me look totally corporate. I glanced at myself in the mirror again and he was right. The only thing that broke the image was the silver hoop through my right ear, and even that was conservative enough for any corporate suit these days. Gods, what the hell had happened to me?

I used to be quite the wild kid, living on the streets, learning magic, becoming a shadowrunner. Now I'm thirty

years old, an age when most shadowrunners are either
dead or retired. Running the shadows was a young person's game. I knew deckers who were considered washed-
out by the time they were twenty, and wiz-kid mages
who'd given it up, or burned out, long before thirty. When
you started to slow down, you hoped to hit the big score
and get out of the game. Those who didn't usually ended
up dead sooner rather than later.

I was the exception. I'd hit the big time in a way I
could never have imagined. I joined Assets, Inc. for one
run because they needed a mage and because I had a
reputation in the shadows, one I'd built up with years of
some of the nastiest runs around. Assets warned that everything I'd seen before was nothing compared to the run they
were planning, but that didn't stop me. They were right.
Nothing on the streets of Boston, L.A., or Seattle prepared
me to take on elf wizards who claimed to be immortal, a
powerful spirit possessing a cyborg capable of taking out
a battalion, or saving the world from a threat from the
depths of astral space. It was like some kind of Hollywood
simsense production, a grand adventure, and I became
part of it.

Assets, Inc. was the big time. They were pros in the
truest sense of the word, the best shadowrunners I'd ever
worked with. They had friends in the highest of places
and the backing of an organization with the power of a
megacorp. I would have been a fool to turn Ryan down
when he offered me a permanent place on the team. It
was a chance to achieve all I'd ever wanted: to step out of
the shadows and into the light, to become legit without
really having to leave the action behind. The best part of
the deal was that we were the elite troubleshooters for the

Draco Foundation. It was like going from street scum to
high-class super-spy.

I lightly caressed the wheel of my sleek new Eurocar,
bought and paid for with the nuyen I'd earned working
with Assets. Driving it fast like I was slotting a simflick
that made me James-fraggin-Bond. It was a long way
from where I came from. So what the hell was I so mad
about?

The red icon of a bell interrupted my thoughts, flashing in the upper right-hand corner of my vision; an incoming call. That was another change I never expected:
the cyberware. When I was young and first working the
shadows, I would never in a million years have gotten
anything implanted in my body. Street samurai and other
muscle relied on the power cyber gave them. It made you
stronger, faster, tougher, but it also made you less human. Some of the street-muscle I'd known were more
machine than man.

If you were a magician, cyber had other consequences.
It was well-known that artificial implants of all kinds in-
hibited the use of magic, and most of us magical types
avoided it like the plague. But the streets are hard, and
time takes its toll. A lot of spell-slingers needed more of
an edge, so they got a little cyber to keep them on top.
When it weakened their magic, softened their edge, they
got a little more. Then a little more, and a little more, until they were burnt-out shells stuffed with machines and
their magic was gone. I used to look at burnouts like that
and feel pity for them. It was a sorry sight.

It's different with me. That's what I keep telling myself, anyway. After working with Assets for a while, I
picked up a little cyber. Nothing major. Just enough to
make life easier and, honestly, because I thought it was

chill. My magical abilities were as strong as ever, stronger even with all the practice and the new things I'd learned in the past three years. Like I said, Assets had friends in high places, and some of them knew magic like I'd never seen before. So, a cyberware virgin at age twenty-eight, I got a datajack. Then some memory chips to store data and download it into my head. A display link to project it onto the retina of my eye and a comm system to keep in touch with the rest of the team silently in my head, and finally some data software to manage it all. It wasn't much hardware, so it didn't really affect my magic that much, especially considering how much more magic I'd learned since joining Assets. The implants were just conveniences. They didn't make me all that different. Or so I told myself.

The red bell icon flashed insistently. I mentally keyed the channel open and heard a faint click as it connected. Suddenly I caught sight of a figure sitting in the passenger seat next to me out of the corner of my eye. I knew it was just an optical illusion, the result of tiny lasers hitting the retinas of my eyes, but at first glance it was very convincing. Jane's new toys and tricks were always impressive.

She was dressed entirely in tight red leather today, including a wickedly short miniskirt that I'm sure wouldn't have been possible if her appearance were bound by the laws of physics. I didn't bother looking over at her. It wasn't like she could see me anyway. The image was just for show, to give her some physical presence. She must have known I was in the car, otherwise the image would have appeared right in front of me, which would be a real problem on the highway.

"Hello, Jane," I said.

The image turned to look at me (nice touch, that). Her

red lips, matching the color of the leather, moved in perfect sync with the words I heard in my head through the subdermal speakers. "What's this I hear about you ditching out on the end of the Tyre run, chummer?"

"What's to tell? It was done. I did my job and now I'm going home, like a good little team member."

"Talon . . ." Her tone sounded like a parent who'd just caught a wayward child in a fib.

"Look, Jane, I don't really want to talk about it, okay?"

"No, it's not. Something's been bothering you for a while and I want to know what it is. I'm worried about you, Tom, and I'm not the only one."

I almost turned to look at her as I shifted lanes to get closer to the exit that was coming up. The Eurocar's scan-system wasn't picking up any police radar or laser scans along the highway, so I was making good time.

"Has Ryan said something to you?" I asked.

"No, he didn't have to. I heard you blew up at him."

"Not his fault. He was only doing what he thought was right." That's what Ryan always did.

"I didn't say it was, but you don't do something like that for no reason. You're too responsible for that, Tom. You're too professional."

"Maybe that's it," I said, as much to myself as anyone else. Having a conversation with Jane over my headlink was almost like talking to myself sometimes. "Maybe I'm just a little *too* professional these days. It just feels . . . confining. I've worked with teams before, but not like this. On other teams I was always the hotshot, the wiz-kid mage who knew how to handle anything. Now . . . now I feel like I'm out of my depth, Jane. All the things I've seen, all the things I know about what's out there . . .

Do you know I still have nightmares about all that drek involving the Dragon Heart?"

There was a moment of silence over the line. "No, no I didn't."

"I nearly died, Jane. Hell, I *did* die out there on the bridge, and Lucero brought me back from the other side. I don't know what the hell to make of that. When I was running the streets, I was sure I'd be history before I hit twenty-five. Then twenty-five came and went and I never thought I'd see thirty. Now, here I am. I used to think I knew how it all worked: life, death, magic, but now nothing makes sense."

Jane remained silent, so I continued. "It used to all be about making the next score; finding another run, another deal to make enough nuyen to get me through another few months. I didn't think about the future. It was all about keeping it together in the here and now. Now I *am* thinking about the future, and I don't know what I'm going to do. I'm not sure I can handle all of this."

"You're not giving yourself enough credit, Talon."

"Maybe not," I said quietly. "But you worked for Dunkelzahn, Jane, worked for a fraggin' great dragon for *years*. I never even met him. Hell, the only time I met a dragon before Assets, it scared the hell out of me. You were practically friends with one."

"Not friends exactly," Jane mused. "I don't think dragons really have friends like other people. But I do think Dunkelzahn appreciated us in a way other dragons don't."

*Yeah, like as something other than lunch,* I thought. "What I'm saying is you and Ryan and the others got used to all of this weirdness . . ."

"And you will, too. It just takes some time."

"How much time, Jane? Where do I go from here?"

"Wherever you want, chummer."

I thought about that for a long moment, watching the road zip past as I came up on the exit.

"I want to go home," I said. "Only I don't know where that is anymore."

I slid the Eurocar gently to a stop at the end of the ramp to wait for the light to change. I turned and looked at Jane's image. She was beautiful, one of the most beautiful women I'd ever seen. The virtual projection was something of a statement for Jane; one part fantasy and one part sarcasm, since in real-life Jane-in-the-Box looked nothing like the seductive she-devil in red I saw before me. She was a stellar decker and computer programmer. To her, everything was all light and shadow, bits that could be manipulated with the right programs, the right toys, to make it into anything she wanted. Right then, I envied her control and composure.

"How's the girl?" I asked, changing the subject. The light turned green, and I pulled out onto the street.

"She'll be fine. We're evacing her to a private clinic in Maryland. They'll take good care of her and we can make sure she's returned to her parents when she's ready." While we were talking, Jane must have been monitoring communications with the rest of the team, coordinating things with the clinic, and preparing data for the mission debriefing, all at the same time. Her ability to multitask was uncanny.

"That's good," I said. I didn't know what else to say about it. It *was* good. Mary Beth would soon be back with the parents who loved and missed her, but how would she handle being away for the last nine years? And how would her parents handle the almost-woman who would return to them in place of the little girl they lost?

"You know," I said to Jane, "she's just the sort of thing I'm talking about."

Jane paused a beat before responding. She was probably handling another call at the same time. Or else the cell-net was baffled for an instant by the masses of ferrocrete and metal as I cruised down the street.

"How's that?" she asked.

"Hundreds, hell, thousands of kids disappear every year, gone without a trace. Some of them get found, but most don't. They vanish into the sprawl and get swallowed up." *I was almost one of them,* I thought. "Most parents can't afford to hire shadowrunners to track them down. The only reason we looked for Mary Beth is because the dragon told us to. Dunkelzahn's last will and testament, the driving force of our existence."

When Dunkelzahn was assassinated following his successful bid for the presidency of the UCAS three years ago, Assets was left without an employer. The dragon was smart, though. He left a will, dividing up his vast fortune. His money set up the Draco Foundation and provided Assets, Inc. with enough resources to continue operating nearly forever. And his will left very clear instructions on what the dragon wanted done.

"The will said 'her survival is critical.' What the hell does that mean?" I asked. "What did Dunkelzahn know about Mary Beth Tyre? Why is she so important?"

"I don't know," Jane said, "but he had his reasons. Dunkelzahn usually turned out to be right in the end."

"Yeah? Then how come he's dead?"

Jane didn't have a reply to that. There was silence over the line for a moment.

"I'm sorry, Jane," I said. "I really seem to have a talent

for saying the wrong thing today. You knew Dunkelzahn, I didn't . . ."

"Null sweat," she said, her voice quiet. "Sometimes it seems like an age since he died. Other times, it's like it was yesterday."

"Look," I said, "tell Ryan that I'm taking some time off. I need to be alone for a while to think, just to get away from the whole thing and get some perspective."

"How long?"

"I don't know. A few weeks, a month, maybe more. I'll let you know."

There was another long moment of silence. "All right," Jane said finally. "I'll tell him, but I think you should talk to Ryan yourself before you go."

"I'm not sure I'd go if I did that. We can talk when I get back."

"*If* you get back, you mean."

"That too."

"Okay, Talon. If you need anything . . ." She left the offer incomplete. That was Jane, always playing the team organizer. It was more than that, though. I think I was one of the few people in the world whom Jane considered a friend. I felt honored by that. Jane didn't have a lot of friends. Neither did I.

"I've got the telecom numbers," I said and tapped the side of my head. "And I've always got access to a phone."

Jane couldn't see the gesture, but she got my meaning. "Take care of yourself," she said and broke the connection.

I glanced over to see the expression of sadness on the phantom figure sitting next to me before she faded out.

"You, too, Jane," I said to empty air. "You too."

# 3

I'm not much of a believer in premonitions, even though I'm a mage. But when I saw a woman sitting in my favorite beaten-up easy chair in my apartment, I just knew she was Trouble, with a capital "T." Granted, I had just finished a long and exhausting run and a fight with Ryan, and finding unauthorized persons in my home is generally unnerving, but there was something else about her that I found disquieting. Maybe it was the gun she was pointing at me.

She was rather small, actually, but the gun made her more than imposing enough. Her long, midnight hair was swept back and caught up in a ponytail that fell over her left shoulder onto the forest green of her shirt. Silver gleamed from the datajack behind her right ear and from the Celtic-style necklace she wore. Black pants, a short black jacket, and black boots completed the outfit. She wore no makeup or other complement to her somewhat pale complexion, and her hooded, deep blue eyes never wavered as she stared at me over the massive barrel of the Ares Predator. It looked like the end of a train tunnel from where I was standing.

"Hello," she said in a voice as calm and controlled as

the hands holding the unwavering gun. "You must be
Talon. I have some business I'd like to discuss with you."

Moving slowly away from the door I took off my broad-
brimmed black hat and hung it on the door hook with exaggerated care, gathering my thoughts, considering my
options. They were none too good at the moment.

"Most people call when they want an appointment,"
I said.

She smiled slightly, but it was a cold smile, without hu-
mor. I got the feeling that for all her outward calm, this
young woman was feeling cornered right about now. I
would have to handle things very carefully so she wouldn't
panic and do something that I would very much regret.

"This is a matter of some urgency," she said.

"So I see. Do you think you could stop pointing that
thing at me? I'm willing to talk reasonably, but it's a little hard to concentrate right now."

She shook her head slightly. "Not yet. At least not until we've gotten to know each other better."

Great. Just what I needed, a burglar with an insecurity
problem. I've had dates that went a lot like this, except
without the gun.

"Well," I said, "as long as you've got my undivided attention, why not tell me what this is all about?"

"It concerns a man you knew named Jason Vale . . ."

I took an involuntary step back as the memories returned in a rush of images and feelings.

"You did know him, didn't you?" she said and I hated
her right then for forcing me to remember.

"Oh, yes," I muttered. "I knew him."

How could I forget the night I met Jase, the night I was
certain I was going to die? Huddled in a dank corner of an
abandoned squat, I didn't really care whether I lived or

not, as long as the strange things I was seeing and feeling would stop. I didn't know it then, but my newly awakened astral senses were open to all the emotional impressions and ghosts lingering in the Rox, the worst neighborhood in Boston. The place where I grew up. I could sense it all, and I was sure I was going mad.

The images and sensations had been getting worse and worse. The bliss I took deadened things enough that I was able to ignore them, but I was coming down off my last dose and I'd used up all my meager nuyen to buy that. If I wanted any more of the drug—or anything to eat, for that matter—I would probably have to start selling myself down on the Strip or the Combat Zone, like some of the other street kids I knew. I was sixteen years old and completely alone in the world.

As the drugged euphoria faded, it was replaced by a dull, throbbing pain. I could see strangely colored shadows dart and flit through the debris, into and out of sight. A faint glow surrounded my body out of the corner of my eye. I felt sick and started to sweat, despite the late autumn chill blowing in through the cracked plastiglass window. It would be much colder soon enough, but the coming of winter was the least of my worries at the time.

A creak echoed through the squat. Someone was coming up the stairs. My hands fumbled for the rust-spotted switchblade in my pocket, but I couldn't seem to make them function because of the lingering euphoric high of the drug. It was most likely another squatter, looking for a place to sleep out of the wind, but it could be some chipped-out nutcase or worse. I'd heard, too, that ghouls sometimes came out of the Catacombs at night to hunt and scavenge in the squats and mostly deserted areas of the Rox.

The sound came closer, and I tried vainly to crawl over
to the nearest heap of refuse and hide myself. It was all I
could do to raise my head and try to look defiant. The
door creaked open and a pair of figures entered, silhouetted by the faint light from the hall. I was going to say
something to make them back off, but the after-effects of
the bliss made my throat so dry that all I could manage
was a croaking cough. It elicited a low grunt from one of
the figures, like a chuckle.

The figures shuffled closer, and I could just see them
through the faint neon and moonlight coming through
the cracked and dirty windows. They were both hairless,
dressed in rags, with scabrous, rough gray skin. Their
crooked hands were tipped with dark claws and their
mouths lined with sharp, pointed teeth. Their eyes were
dead-white and looked out onto nothing, but they moved
toward me with unerring accuracy, sniffing the air slightly.
Around each of them was a dark glow that sent waves of
emotion battering into me: caution, excitement, eager-
ness and, above it all, hunger, terrible gnawing hunger.
Ghouls. I was a dead man for sure.

They started to close in, splitting up to circle around
either side of me. I couldn't move. I just stared in horror
at them. The force of their feelings pinned me to the floor
like a mouse facing a snake. A dark tongue emerged from
the mouth of one and he licked his lips.

The figures approached and I tensed, waiting for a
ghoulish set of claws at my throat. Instead, I heard a voice
that rang out in the silence of the squat.

"STOP!" it shouted. "Leave him alone!"

I looked up and saw something that made me sure the
bliss was making me hallucinate . . . or that I'd finally
gone totally wacked. A glowing figure, robed in gar-

ments of light and carrying a long wooden staff, stepped through the wall of the room like it wasn't even there. His presence seemed to light up the room in a cascade of golden light. The ghouls shrank back from the glow and hissed.

"He is under my protection," the shining man said in a forceful voice. His features were like a marble statue, pure, refined, chiseled, and pale. Even his flesh seemed to glow from within and his eyes were like pits of green fire. He was beautiful. For a moment I recalled everything I'd been taught about angels by the Catholic Family Mission where I'd grown up. Right then and there, staring up at that shining figure, I was ready to believe they existed.

The ghouls were startled by the shining man's initial appearance, but they quickly recovered. They didn't intend to be cheated of their dinner, and they started moving toward the intruder. He calmly held his staff in front of him in both hands. I noticed that his feet didn't even touch the floor. He hovered about five or six centimeters above it.

With a strangled cry, one of the ghouls rushed him and the staff flashed out. The ghoul fell back, screaming in pain. The staff swung again, and again, tracing faint arcs of light in the air where it passed. With each swing the ghouls cried out and backed away from the figure, who glowed like an avenging angel.

"Out!" he cried, and swung the staff one more time. The ghouls broke and scurried away, whimpering and whining. I could hear the sounds of their retreat fade into the distance as I looked up at my shining savior with little or no comprehension of what had just happened. At that point, I still wasn't sure the whole thing wasn't just a bliss-induced hallucination.

A gentle hand touched my shoulder and I heard the stranger whisper, "Don't worry. It'll be all right. You're safe now." He started to sing in a low and quiet tone. As I tried to follow the tune, I drifted off to sleep, feeling very safe and secure.

I awoke with a start, sitting bolt upright in bed. Bed? I was in a bed, a real bed. There was a brightly colored Indian blanket thrown over me. The bliss hangover was gone and I was still weak and sore, but I felt better than I had in weeks.

I looked around the room. It was the main room of a small apartment. Most of the wall space was taken up by rows of bookshelves made of old bricks and scraps of wood and construction plastic. On those shelves were more books than I had ever seen in my whole life, dozens of them. Real hardcopy books, not just optical chips or CDs, although I saw a small stack of those, too, next to a small chip-reader.

The rest of the place was done in soothing tones of tan and brown and gold. There were a couple of chairs and a small table that looked like a desk. The bed where I sat looked like it served most of its time as a sofa.

I began to wonder how I had gotten here, then I remembered the shining stranger and the weird song he sang. I glanced over as the door swung open and a young man entered, carrying a steaming earthenware bowl on a tray.

He was in his early twenties, I'd say, with a thatch of unruly black hair. He had a pointed chin, an easy smile, and a small scattering of freckles across his straight nose that all hinted at an Irish ancestor. His eyes were a shade of sea green that made them seem to look right through you. He was wearing a pair of well-worn black jeans and a white T-shirt with something written in bold red Japanese characters on the front. Hanging from a black cord around his neck was a small five-pointed star within a circle, made of silver.

"Well," he said, "good to see you up. Try and drink some of this. It will help you get your strength back." He set the tray holding the bowl of steaming broth down nearby. I looked at him for a moment and wondered if I should trust him. He could be a pimp—someone who picked up squatter kids and then got them hooked so that they would work for him—but this place didn't look like the kind of doss where a pusher or pimp would live, nor did he really look the type.

"Don't worry. It's not spiked or anything," he said as if reading my mind. "I spent too much effort getting you clean just to try and hook you on something again." To prove it, he took a sip from the bowl and put it back on the tray. I took the broth and drank it slowly. It seemed like the best thing I'd ever tasted and it did make me feel better. The mysterious stranger just sat silently in a chair and watched me as I finished it off.

"Who are you," I asked, "and why are you helping me?"

He smiled and leaned forward, resting his elbows on his knees. "You don't recognize me, do you? But then you probably wouldn't. I looked somewhat different last night."

I stared closer at his face and I could see the shadow of the shining man. The hair had been a bit longer, and the face more refined, but it was definitely the same face. He wore different clothes and there was no staff. No halo of light surrounded him, but I was sure he was the same person.

"You saved me from the ghouls," I said slowly.

"Yes," he said, making a face. "I don't like ghouls in

general, but I especially don't like ones who hunt people in the Rox."

I sat up a bit more in bed and set the broth bowl on the table. "What's your name?" I asked.

"Names have power," he said sternly and I was taken aback. His expression softened and he smiled again. "It's not always polite to ask someone's name. Better to ask what they prefer to be called. They call me Jase. How about you?"

"Talon," I said. At his curious look I quickly added, "Er, Tommy. Talon is just sort of a nickname. I . . . I don't have a real last name."

"Okay, Talon," he said, not questioning me further. "As to why I'm helping you . . . let's say we're kindred spirits. I know you've been having a tough time with the awakening of your Talent."

"Awakening? Talent? What the frag are you talking about?"

He touched the star at his throat and said, "Magic."

I felt a chill go up my spine. I knew, just like everybody, that magic had come back to the world and that magicians, ghosts, and dragons were a reality. The native Americans, led by the Ghost Dance prophet, Howling Coyote, had used their magic to reclaim much of their lost land and form the Native American Nations. Magic was a reality, but few people ever saw a real magician. I certainly never had, until that moment.

"You're a . . . wizard?"

"It's as good a name as any, I suppose," he said. "Yes, I'm a magician, but don't be too impressed. As you'll learn, magic is more a state of mind than anything. Unless I miss my guess, you're a magician, too."

\* \* \*

I refocused my eyes on the black pit of the gun barrel and yanked my thoughts out of the past. The woman still regarded me coolly over the gun.

"That's how I knew Jason Vale," I said. "He saved my life when I first discovered my Talent and taught me how to use it."

She looked slightly surprised for the first time, and her gaze flicked from my feet to my face as if she were getting a second look.

The gun barrel dropped about ten centimeters. I decided to take that as an opening. "So tell me, what does all this have to do with Jase?"

"Someone wants to kill me, and maybe you, too. Because of him and something he was involved with."

"What?" I said.

She took a deep breath and started to explain. "I was hired by a Mr. Johnson to—" The crack of shattering plastiglass cut her off as a small, roundish object crashed through the window and tumbled into the room.

GRENADE!

Everything went into automatic as time seemed to slow to a crawl. I hit the floor and rolled behind the heavy steamer trunk I used as a coffee table. There was a dull "wumph" as the grenade went off, and a thick, white mist filled the room. Almost immediately my eyes began burning and I started coughing. Tear gas!

I crawled toward the door on knees and elbows and nearly bumped heads with my uninvited guest as she did the same. When she reached for the doorknob, I grabbed her hand and shook my head.

Holding the bottom of my coat over my nose and mouth, I choked out a phrase in Latin, extending my senses beyond the door and the walls of my apartment. Suspicions confirmed I stood up, eyes burning and streaming profusely now, and thrust my hand toward the door, palm out as I coughed out a single sharp word.

The door exploded outward like it was hit by a bullet train. I heard shouts of surprise and pain as the thugs waiting in the hall were struck by jagged fragments of flying synthwood. A gun roared and blasted chunks of wood and plaster from the ceiling as its startled wielder fell backward, clutching at the bloody piece of door protruding from his throat.

There were two other attackers awaiting me as I stepped out into the hall. One ork and a human woman who looked to be hyped up on something, whether drugs, magic, or wire, I couldn't say. The third guy was down and bleeding from the throat wound. I turned toward the ork and thrust my hands forward as though holding an invisible ball between them. Pale magelight flickered around them like heat rising off a summer highway, and the ork took a step forward, raising his gun. Then his eyes glazed and blood began to run out of his nose and ears as he toppled forward like a poleaxed cow.

I began turning toward the woman, but she was too fast. As she brought her gun to bear I started casting a protection spell, knowing I wouldn't be nearly quick enough. My attacker knew it, too, and she gave me a nasty, feral grin that showed her sharpened canine implants before tightening her finger on the trigger.

The smile vanished in a red mist as half her head exploded, sending bits of bone and brain splattering all over the hallway. I turned to see my recent guest standing back near the doorway holding the smoking Ares Predator that had been pointed at me only a minute ago. Her eyes were red and puffy and tears steamed down her cheeks as the gas slowly drifted out of the broken doorway. I picked my hat up from the ruins of the door and started dusting it off.

"Thanks," I coughed.

"You're welcome," she said. "For the time being, it seems like we need each other." I wasn't about the argue with her assessment right then. Especially since she seemed to be right.

"Looks like you were right about someone out to get one or both of us, and the fact that they hit us with a grenade says they probably have friends outside. Do you have any connections here in DeeCee?"

She shook her head numbly.

Frag. That figured. The security for my building was pretty decent, Assets saw to that, so the cops would be here any minute now. Right at the moment, I didn't feel like giving a long explanation to the authorities and testing out the strength of the legal identity Jane-in-the-Box had set up for me here in DeeCee.

"My car's around back," I told her. "We can try getting out that way. I know a place where we can go and finish our little chat."

I reached inside the apartment and grabbed the kit bag I always left sitting near the door. I made a habit of keeping all my "necessities" handy in case I had to book in a hurry. With Assets, there were always runs coming up at a moment's notice, and I wanted to be able to roll out just as fast. When you ran the shadows, disappearing was a habit you got into.

My guest ran back to the chair and retrieved a narrow case on a shoulder strap. I had hung with Jane-in-the-

Box and other deckers long enough to know it was a cyberdeck carrying case, which only made me more curious about what this lady knew.

I led the way downstairs to the back door. We didn't encounter any more muscle, and I was grateful for living in Rockville right then. The rest of the tenants knew enough to keep their doors closed and locked and pretend they didn't hear anything when the shots rang out earlier. They would wait for the cops to show before they poked their heads out, which was just fine by me. If I'd lived in a real high-class neighborhood like Ryan thought I should, the cops would already be all over the place. Of course, if I lived in a high-class neighborhood, people probably wouldn't be tossing grenades in my window, either.

The back parking lot was pretty dark. Fate had chosen last night for the local go-gang to shoot out most of the working lights, and the building superintendent hadn't bothered to fix them yet. As we moved over to my trusty steed I hit the remote control in my coat pocket to disarm the security system. I felt my companion come up short behind me.

"How's your driving?" I said.

"Why me?" she asked.

"Because I want to have my attention free in case somebody else wants in on this little party, okay? Doing magic can make it hard to concentrate on mundane things like staying on the road."

"*So ka.*" She popped open the driver's door and climbed in while I moved around to the passenger side. I paused for a moment to close my eyes and whisper a phrase under my breath, then got in.

"What was that, a prayer?"

"Something like that." I gave her the ignition code and

she punched it into the car's keypad, bringing the engine humming to life. She opened the small panel to the right of the steering column and pulled out a length of optical cable terminating in a connector, which she plugged into the chrome-lipped jack behind her ear. It gave her access and control over the car's auto-pilot and other systems. I didn't use it all that much, myself. Despite the hardware in my head, I preferred to do most things the old-fashioned way.

"It's not rigged," I said, though she already knew that. I didn't have the complex cyber riggers used to make themselves nearly one with the machines they operated. Aside from the fact that it would probably cripple my magic, the whole idea kind of frightened me. Merging that much with a machine just wasn't natural, if you asked me.

She nodded. "That's chill. I'm not wired for it." She threw the car into reverse and pulled out of the space. "But I think I can manage."

We moved out of the lot with the headlights off. When we reached the street, I directed her to turn right, then hit the lights when we had gone about a block. A Ford Americar appeared around a corner about three blocks behind us.

"Should we try and lose them?"

"Just a tick." I closed my eyes and traced a symbol in the air with my index finger like I had in my apartment. A strong impression of danger filled my mind.

"Gun it," I said. She hit the accelerator and we shot ahead, but the driver of the Americar compensated quickly and gave chase. Suddenly the chatter of automatic gunfire split the night, and the rounds sparked off the pavement as we took a corner.

I crouched down in my seat as a shot blew out the rear

window. Damn, now they were getting me mad. My doss was one thing, but nobody was going to shoot up my car! I focused my attention on the astral plane and spoke a short phrase as we took another corner. *Go get 'em!* I thought.

I was slammed against my safety harness as we screeched to a halt. I looked up and saw that the narrow side street we had turned into ended in a tall chain-link fence.

"Oh, frag," muttered the mystery woman. The Americar rounded the corner, and she reached for her gun, but I grabbed her wrist.

"What the frag are you . . ." she was starting to say when a hellish yellowish light flared in the alleyway. The windscreen of the Ford shattered as it careened out of control and skidded onto the sidewalk, crashing into the side of the building, sending loose bricks flying. Smoke and flames poured out of the broken windows for a moment, then the Ford went off like a bomb. An orange fireball boiled up to the sky in a cloud of black smoke as bits of car rained down over the area, pinging off the roof and hood of my Westwind.

She sat in stunned silence for a moment, staring at the flaming wreckage, then finally found her voice. "What . . . what the frag happened? Did *you* do that?"

I shrugged and tried not to look too smug. "I've had a fire elemental tagging along in astral space ever since we left the parking lot. I told it to get them off our backs. Fire elementals tend toward overkill sometimes."

She just looked at me for a moment, then back at the flaming wreck of the Americar, then back at me. "No drek," she said quietly. "By the way, we haven't really been introduced. I'm Ariel, but my friends call me Trouble and . . . what's so funny?"

I shook my head. I couldn't help but laugh.

Extending my hand to take the one she offered, I said, "M'lady, I knew you were trouble the moment I saw you."

# 4

After we drove around for a bit to make sure no one else was following, I asked Trouble to pull over into a darkened side street not far from the glowing neolux sign of a Stuffer Shack. It was getting late, and there was little traffic on the road. As we pulled over I popped my seat belt and opened my door.

"I think I should take it from here," I said. Trouble made no objection, just nodded. We both got out of the car, and I moved around to the driver's side while she slipped into the seat I'd vacated. Once the doors of the Westwind were shut again, I reached into the pocket of my long coat, pulled out a length of black silk, and started folding it carefully.

"What's that for?" Trouble asked, no doubt expecting some kind of magic trick. I clutched an end of the cloth in each hand and held out the folded strip to her. She glanced at it and gave me an incredulous look.

"You have *got* to be kidding."

I shook my head. "Nope. Before we go any further, you've got to wear this."

"A blindfold? Do I look stupid to you? There are people trying to kill me."

"Trying to kill *us*," I corrected.

"So we've got a reason to trust each other that's . . ."

"That's the only reason we're still here," I interrupted, "but I'm not the only one involved in this. I have friends, associates. As much as I don't want to involve them, right now I haven't got much choice. If I'm going to do anything that affects them, I have to protect their interests. So you can either wear the blindfold or we can part ways right now. I'll drop you off and we can call it quits. I've got more questions I want answers to, so I'd like to have your help. If you can't give it, I'll find the answers on my own, *so ka*?"

Trouble looked me in the face for what seemed like a good minute before she took the cloth from my hands and tied it snugly over her own eyes, brushing her hair out of the way to adjust it.

"Happy?" she said.

"I'm not happy about any of this, but thanks."

She nodded and I could see she understood the score. Loyalty in the shadows was all-important. You had to know who you could count on, and friends didn't betray friends. We both understood that. She wasn't happy about wearing the blindfold and I wasn't happy about doing it, but we understood why it had to be that way.

I also had to admit that the blindfold was only partially to keep the location a secret. I wanted to see how far she was willing to trust me. The fact that she was going along with the blindfold at all told me two things: first, she was most likely telling me the truth, and second, that she was in pretty dire straits to agree to something so dangerous.

Settling back in her seat, Trouble flashed a small smile.

"In another place and time," she said, "I could almost enjoy this." My snort of derision brought a peal of laughter from her as we drove off into the night.

The safe house owned by Assets, Inc. wasn't the Taj
Mahal by any means. It wasn't even as nice as my own
apartment (which was definitely going to need a new
door, if I ended up moving back there), but the little three-
room doss in a quiet and isolated part of town was still
nicer than all the places I'd lived before joining up with
Assets, and larger than most of them put together. It was
tucked away just across the border into North Virginia. It
had second-hand furniture, a small stash of food, weapons, and other gear, and a telecom unit rigged up by Jane
to be virtually untraceable, provided it didn't get used
too often. All the comforts of home for a shadowrunner
on the run.

I let Trouble remove the blindfold as soon as we were
inside. I took enough unnecessary turns along the way
that I was reasonably sure she hadn't a clue to where this
place was, even if she knew the DeeCee area well, which I
suspected she didn't. She made her way over to the threadbare couch and threw herself down on it, taking the whole
place in (which didn't take very long).

"Not bad," she said. "Is it yours or Assets'?"

It shouldn't have surprised me that she knew who I
worked for, but the question did catch me off guard a
bit. Deckers had an annoying tendency to know things
about people they shouldn't, kind of like mages, in fact. I
reminded myself that she'd been hired by someone to
look into my background, and wondered briefly what else
she knew.

"It belongs to Assets." No sense in lying about it. Knowing the truth didn't tell Trouble anything she hadn't already figured out. I didn't bother to ask how she knew. I
dropped my kit bag next to an overstuffed chair with a
couple of patched-up holes and settled into it.

"Now, then," I said, "before we were so rudely inter-rupted, you were telling me about something that involved me and Jason Vale." Trouble nodded and curled up on the couch, tucking her legs underneath her and resting her hands on her knees as she began to speak. I got up and walked over to check the windows before settling down again. I wanted to make doubly sure we weren't inter-rupted this time.

"I'm a decker," Trouble said. "I work out of Boston. Things have been busy since Fuchi broke up and Nova-tech came to town, with plenty of work to go around for someone who's good at getting the right data. I was hired by a Mr. Johnson to run a background jacket on Jason Vale, check into his known associates, activities, that sort of thing."

"Not an easy job," I said. "Jase was a blank, SINless." In the modern twenty-first century, everyone was tagged at birth with a SIN—a System Identification Number. It was used for record-keeping of all kinds, especially in the government databases. The only people who didn't have SINs were the have-nots, born in neighborhoods like the Rox in Boston or the Barrens of Seattle, or people who managed to find a decker skilled enough to wipe all traces of them from the world databanks. I was one of the former. I never found out which Jase was, but he'd told me he didn't have a SIN. Being outside the SIN system was vital for most shadowrunners. It made us virtually untraceable, ciphers, ghosts in the government record-keeping machine.

Trouble gave a knowing nod. "No, it wasn't easy, but the Johnson wouldn't have hired me if it was. There were no records on Vale in the state or federal systems, noth-ing in the public networks. That meant doing a lot more legwork and digging into more protected systems. All I had to go on was that he lived in South Boston ten years ago and that he was some sort of magician.

"So I started digging. One of the few things I turned up was a report by Knight Errant about Vale's death. I learned he was killed by a gang near the Rox. His only SIN was issued to him at the morgue and tagged Deceased. The number was connected with a police investigation, so it wasn't accessible from the public nets. I also found out you were with him when he died."

"Yes," I said, keeping my face expressionless.

Trouble studied me briefly, perhaps expecting me to elaborate, then shrugged and continued when I offered no further information. "You'll be pleased to know that you're just as tough to track down as Vale. I found out you went to MIT&T on a Mitsuhama corporate sponsorship after Vale died, and that you were expelled for cheating three years later. Then you disappeared into the shadows. I patched together some additional information on your activities over the past seven years or so, not very much, actually. I did manage to track you to DeeCee and crack the cover identity you're using here."

I figured as much, which told me she was a very good decker. I couldn't think of many who could crack IDs set up by Jane. I'd have to discard that ID and see about getting another one. Oh well, I could use a new place to live anyway. I didn't fancy explaining the thing with the door at the condoplex in the first place.

Trouble continued on. "After I got as much information as I thought I was going to, I made arrangements with my Johnson to make the trade—the complete jacket for the rest of the nuyen he promised." She paused, biting her lip. She had just admitted she was going to sell the

scan on me to someone else. Not exactly unexpected—
after all, that's what people hired deckers for—but it still
didn't make for a lot of mutual trust. I made no comment,
but simply let her go on.

"The meet was a setup. The Johnson sent some freak-
gangers instead of showing up himself. They said they
only wanted the chip with the data, but I could tell it was
more than that. There was no way the Johnson was going
to let me walk away from it. I was a loose end that needed
to be cut off. I'd been expecting something like that, so I
went to the meet prepared. I walked out, the freak-boys
didn't. But I knew I needed to find out why the Johnson
wanted me geeked and what was so important about the
information. It doesn't make any sense. It just doesn't
seem that important."

She had good reason to be worried. Johnsons didn't go
around scragging shadowrunners who did a good job. It
was one of the unwritten laws of the shadows. Employers who treated runners as disposable didn't remain employers for very long, just like shadowrunners who got a
reputation for double-dealing ended up unemployable.
Or floating face down in the nearest body of water.

"So you came to find out why your Johnson is willing
to kill you over a simple background jacket?" I said.

"That about sums it up. You're the only one of Vale's
associates who's still alive and the only one of any real
significance I was able to turn up. I had to get out of Boston while things cooled down, and you were my best bet.
I didn't think my Johnson would manage to track me here
so fast."

I shook my head. "Sorry to disappoint you, but I don't
have a fragging idea what this is all about. I was just a kid

then, and Jase was a street magician. Did you do a check on your Johnson's ID? Who is he?"

She made a face that said of *course* she had checked out the Johnson. Mr. Johnsons, people who employed shadowrunners, liked to remain anonymous. It was considered bad form to ask a Johnson too many questions about his (or her) real employer or interest in a run. Like Jase had told me, real names had power, and Mr. Johnsons preferred a mask of anonymity. Behind the scenes, of course, any good shadowrunner tried to dig up as much as possible on a prospective Johnson to know the angles and, maybe, gain a little more leverage where the Johnson was concerned. It kept me from being left to swing in the breeze plenty of times before.

"His name is Garnoff," Trouble said. "Anton Garnoff. He's a high-level mucky-muck wagemage with Manadyne."

I frowned a bit. Manadyne was a medium-size corporation in Boston, specializing in magical research and development, along with providing magical services to other corporations. I'd never worked for or against them. Honestly, they were too small and not involved in any of the stuff Assets was dealing with. They *did* receive some money in Dunkelzahn's will, as I recalled, but who the frag didn't?

"Doesn't ring any bells," I said. "I don't think I've ever heard of him. So what's Garnoff's stake in all of this?"

"That's just it," Trouble said. "I haven't a clue. Whatever it is, it seems to include taking one or both of us out of the picture."

"Well, then, I think we just might have to have a little talk with Mr. Anton Garnoff about that. Let me make a call and I'll see what I can do."

I didn't want to do it, but I used the telecom to patch in a call to Jane-in-the-Box. Jane had access to more comm lines than PacRimTelecom, so it wasn't hard to get through to her, and I knew the priority codes to get her attention from the dozen or so different things she and her various expert systems were probably overseeing at the moment. At least one was probably tracing my whereabouts, since I was sure news of what had happened at my condoplex must have reached Jane's ever-listening electronic ears by now.

The display lit up with an image of Jane's virtual self, all in tight leather (black this time), a total electronic fantasy girl. The concern and relief at seeing me written on the face of her electronic image continued to impress me with Jane's programming skills.

"Talon!" she said, "what the frag's going on? I've been trying to call your headphone . . ."

"Sorry. I turned it off," I said. "Things have been busy."

"What happened?" Jane asked. "I caught a police call about your apartment being broken into and shots fired."

I told her the story of Trouble's unexpected arrival at my condoplex and the subsequent uninvited guests who showed up. I didn't bother telling her where I was. Just calling from the safehouse telecom was enough to do that. The line was designed to be untraceable to standard countermeasures, but Jane knew ways around all of her own stuff. She probably knew my location the moment my call came in. There was no reason to clue Trouble in about our location right now. I also left out exactly why Trouble decided to show up on my doorstep, other than the fact that she was from Boston.

"Have the DeeCee cops managed to ID the goons who showed up at my place?" I asked.

Jane's virtual self nodded, and I admired her handiwork again. Probably keyed to respond even to her unconscious gestures and reflexes.

"They have. I pulled the data about twenty minutes ago. All small-time muscle-for-hire in the DeeCee area. All with modest rap sheets."

Not professional shadowrunners then. Runners didn't get rap sheets, at least, not good runners who managed to stay alive and in business for very long. That tended to imply the hit attempt at my place was planned quickly, drawing on whatever talent was available, or else the Mr. Johnson didn't have enough contacts down in DeeCee to get the best muscle.

Moving on to my next question before I even asked it, Jane said, "The interesting part is that all of them have some low-level connection with the local yakuza. Not *kobun* or even initiated members, mostly errand-runners. They were paid in certified credsticks, which pretty much dead-ends the trail. I'm checking into which bank issued it, but . . ." The electronic girl shrugged, another fantastically subtle gesture. Even for a decker of Jane's caliber, the data-trail on certified credit was colder than a Mr. Johnson's heart, particularly one Johnson I could think of.

"Don't worry about the data-trace on this one," I told her.

"What are you talking about, Talon? Of course I'm worried. Somebody just tried to ice you."

"This doesn't involve you, or Assets," I said. "It's personal."

"Talon," Jane said slowly, like she was trying to explain something to a child, "you're one of us. If someone attacks you, they attack Assets. That *makes* it my . . . our concern."

I shook my head as firmly as I could.

"No. This doesn't involve you, or Mercury, or Axler, or Grind, or anyone else. It's something I have to deal with myself. It's personal." I said it again like a magic phrase to try and make Jane understand.

"C'mon, Talon, don't pull that macho lone shadow-runner drek on me. I gave you credit for more brains than that. It doesn't matter what it is, you can use our help to handle it. We're a *team*, dammit! We stick together. Don't let some stupid pride start messing with your judgment." She paused. "This isn't about that blowup with Quicksilver, is it?" Jane used the code name for Ryan Mercury instead of his real name as I had just done. I blushed a bit at the unspoken rebuke and the memory of the argument.

"No, it's not that . . . exactly. Look, Jane, it isn't that I don't appreciate everything you're trying to do, you and Assets. This is seriously old business, long before I met any of you, long before I was even running the shadows. It's a path I have to walk alone and I can't bring anyone else into it. Do you understand? It's my karma, no one else's, and I'm the one who has to straighten things out."

There was a long moment of silence on the line. The features of the blonde bombshell displayed on the screen were an electronic mask, unreadable.

"All right," she said finally. "I'll talk to Quicksilver and tell him you're all right."

"Tell him I'm going to need some time to work this out."

"Take as much as you need," Jane said. "That's what he'll say."

I knew she was right. If Ryan couldn't help directly, he would tell me to do whatever I had to. That's the kind of guy he was.

Her voice took on a slightly different tone, quieter and less brisk. "Is there anything else I can do?"

I thought for a moment. Maybe Jane felt responsible for getting me involved in the whole business with the Dragon Heart that had led to my working with Assets, or maybe she really considered me a chummer. Good friends were rare in our line of work, and I was honored to think Jane might view me as one.

"Well," I said, "there is one thing, two things actually. I'm going to need a new cover ID for a trip to Boston, and I need you to compile a jacket for me on someone who works for Manadyne. A mage by the name of Anton Garnoff."

# 5

As I stared out the window of the plane, I thought about how soon we would arrive in Boston, the city of my birth, a place I never thought to see again. When I'd left the Hub ten years ago, I hadn't planned to go back, and yet, here I was, on a UCAS Air shuttle flight on my way there. Jane came through with the cover ID and flight reservations in a matter of hours. Meanwhile, I'd managed to catch a few hours' sleep before Trouble and I boarded the red-eye flight at Thomas Jefferson International.

Trouble had slept for most of the trip, which steadily improved my evaluation of her capabilities. She showed the good sense to catch some zees when she could. In the shadows you never knew when you might next get another chance to rest, and it had already been a long night. I was too caught up in my thoughts for sleep.

From what I'd heard, both from Trouble and from the shadowtalk recently, Boston was a very different city than the one I'd left behind. A lot of the city had been damaged in the earthquake that hit the East Coast years before I was born. Historic buildings that had stood for centuries were destroyed, along with plenty more modern structures. The metroplex was quick to rebuild, and it had the good fortune to become the new home of the East Coast

Stock Exchange. The same earthquake had also devastated New York City, leaving Wall Street a pile of rubble. But business went on, and Boston became the new financial capitol of North America. It made sense. There were already so many corporate and financial interests there. The damage from the quake gave them the perfect excuse to rebuild the city in their own image.

Boston became an ultra-modern metroplex filled with old-world money and attitude. While the city center and the outlying Route 128 sections had been heavily renovated and rebuilt to meet the needs of the growing sprawl, areas like the Rox and South Boston, where I grew up, were left to whoever wanted them. The corporations had no interest in rebuilding homes shattered by the quake or in reweaving social fabrics torn apart by the upheavals of the Awakening or the Ghost Dance War. Like every sprawl, Boston had its dark underside, filled with the forgotten and the outcast, who survived day to day as best they could. If it hadn't been for my Talent and Jase's help, I'd probably still be there—alive or dead.

When I lived in Boston, the city wasn't much of a place for shadowrunning. The corporations considered the Stock Exchange too important to mess around with, so security in Boston was tight and the corps kept up a "gentlemen's agreement" not to cause each other trouble in what amounted to a neutral ground for all of them. Or almost all of them.

The neutrality lasted until Fuchi Industrial Electronics split up, not too long ago. One of the megacorp's owners, Richard Villiers, was originally from Boston, and it turned out he had quietly been preparing for the split by buying up smaller companies in the city through fronts and shells. He was building his own little corporate empire for the

time when he would have to jump ship, taking a lot of
Fuchi's secrets and resources with him. When it came
down to it, the split was bloody, and people on all sides
decided to hell with neutrality.

Suddenly, Boston was a hot spot in the shadow biz.
Opportunities for shadowrunners sprang up everywhere
as all the other corps started getting in on the act. There
weren't enough runners in Boston to handle all of the
demand, so shadowrunners from other metroplexes got
called in, and the population of the shadows boomed. Local runners like Trouble got their shot at the big time.

All things considered, it was kind of surprising that I
hadn't been back to the Beanplex before this. Still, Assets didn't get involved in the kind of business going on
in Boston these days. The Draco Foundation had bigger
fish to fry than worrying about corporations fighting over
the remains of Fuchi's carcass or the presence of Villiers'
new Novatech corporation extending controlling tendrils
everywhere in the high-tech industry.

I pulled my kit bag out from under the seat in front of
me and took out my Tarot deck. I folded down the tray table and unwrapped the black silk cloth protecting the
cards, idly shuffling them while forming the questions in
my mind and blocking out all other distractions. *What's
going on here? What does this have to do with Jase? Why
now?* I projected my questions and thoughts into the cards,
letting my hands shuffle at random. When I felt ready, I
split the deck into four equal piles and flipped up the first
card of each one.

*The Magician.* No surprise there, since the magician
was the card I generally identified with myself. Could
also mean that, whatever the problem was, it had something to do with magic. Maybe another magician was

involved. It could have associations with Garnoff, and even with Jase. The card was upright, not reversed, so I took it as more tied to me. Magic—and clear thought— were going to help me out of this.

*The Nine of Swords.* Cruelty and betrayal. Was Jase betrayed by someone? Could he have betrayed someone? Was this revenge on the part of Garnoff or whoever else was behind this? Or was I being betrayed? It certainly occurred to me that this whole thing could be some kind of trap, but why? I had no involvement with Manadyne. Hell, the corp didn't even exist when I was still in Boston. Still, best to be on guard.

*The Queen of Swords.* A woman, Trouble maybe, or Jane, the only real women in my life. Or maybe a woman I was yet to meet. Someone who offered wisdom and assistance. Or might she be the betrayer? I got a sense she would be helpful to me, but not very much beyond that.

I turned up the last card.

*The Hanged Man,* reversed. Deception, power at great cost, sacrifice and suffering. Not a good ending. However it went, this business was going to turn out bad for someone. I frowned as I looked over the cards. I didn't much like the picture they painted, what there was of it that I could understand, that is.

"Penny for 'em."

I turned, startled out of my reverie, toward Trouble sitting in the seat next to me. I hadn't noticed that she was awake.

"What's that?" I asked.

"Just an old saying, 'a penny for your thoughts.' You seemed to be thinking a lot about something. Were you doing magic?" She bobbed her chin toward the Tarot cards.

I picked up the cards, squared them and started wrapping them up again before I answered. Trouble obviously didn't know very much about mages or she would have known never to interrupt one while he's working. I wasn't doing anything major, but I could have been, and with some magic a distraction can be dangerous. Of course, most mundanes didn't scan much about how magic worked, even shadowrunners.

"Nothing fancy," I said, "just a divination to try and get a better idea of what's going on. I'm afraid it wasn't very helpful."

"Oh. Too bad."

"Tell me some more about your Mr. Johnson . . . Garnoff, right?" I said.

"Sure, what do you want to know?"

"Did he tell you why he wanted a jacket on Jase?"

"Nope, but then I didn't need to know that. He just wanted me to check up on this guy and then on you. Ours is not to reason why . . ." *Ours is but to do or die.* She left the rest of the quote unsaid.

"Did he want you to keep checking on Jase, too?"

"Hmmm, no. When I told him I was sure that Vale was dead, he told me to concentrate on you."

"Because of my connection to Jase?"

"Hey, you said the guy was your teacher, right? Maybe Garnoff is looking for something that Vale knew that he might of taught you."

I thought about that for a second and shook my head. "Secrets of the ages? I doubt it. I didn't get much more than my basic magical training from Jase. I learned most of my real magical stuff at the Institute and afterward on the streets."

"How about something he owned?"

"Maybe. Most of Jase's stuff got sold or trashed after he died. I've still got a few things, mostly books, but none of them are worth anything really. They're not rare or anything like that."

"Maybe something he didn't tell you about?"

I shrugged. "Anything's possible, but if that's the case, then Garnoff is going to be pretty disappointed, because I don't know what he could be after." I put away my Tarot deck and folded up the tray table with a sigh, then resumed my staring out the window.

"I remember seeing in the Knight Errant report that Vale was killed in a gang incident, right?"

I nodded without looking back at her, so she continued. "Garnoff's got some local gang working for him. Maybe there's a connection there."

I shook my head. "Couldn't be the same gang."

"Are you sure?" she asked. "Why not?"

The lights of the sprawl glittered below, so serene and beautiful, but I had seen first-hand the kind of ugliness that hid in the shadows of those clean, bright lights. I turned back to Trouble. "Because I killed them."

The awkward silence hung in the air until the intercom beeped and the captain announced that we would be landing at Logan Airport in about fifteen minutes. Trouble busied herself with her portable data-reader, scanning a couple of chips holding all the data Jane had managed to dig up. I went back to staring out the window, rubbing a narrow white scar on my hand and remembering.

I recalled the day Jase died like it had happened yesterday. It was so stupid, not like the dramatic and heroic deaths of the tragic characters in the sims or on the trideo. He used a public telecom to make a call on the street while we were at the local Stuffer Shack, and a group of gangers called the Asphalt Rats felt like inflicting a little random violence that night. Hitting the streets and messing up anyone who got in their way. At the first sound of the gunfire I ran outside, but I was too late. All I could do was watch the Rats roar off on their bikes and hold Jase while he died, his blood all over the sidewalk and the wall and my clothes.

The next couple of hours were a blur, but I remember being surprised at how many people in the area were willing to help. I had no idea Jase had so many friends and people he'd helped, folks who he'd done a little healing magic for, or a simple banishment or some such. Sister Margaret from St. Patrick's kept leading me around like a zombie. I couldn't seem to get over the shock. Jase died like an extra in a bad sim, only he wasn't a faceless actor, he had a life . . . he was important to people, to me.

We had to cremate him. It seemed right somehow to do it that way. Jase was SINless, so Knight Errant wasn't interested in wasting any time dealing with the whole mess beyond getting names and dates for their files. They weren't going to look into it. The forensic division didn't have time for blanks. I never realized how little open ground there was in the plex until I had to think about finding a place to bury someone. I remember staring into the funeral pyre in the open lot in the Rox for a long time and it was then, standing there looking into the flames, that I knew what I was going to do.

I made my way back to the apartment I'd shared with Jase for almost a year since he had taken me in. I went through all the old books, printouts, and chips he'd been using to teach me magic, looking for something I'd seen once in passing, an old formula Jase had tucked away, all but forgotten. I hadn't paid it much attention before, but now I studied the wrinkled fanfold sheets with a burning purpose. I worked on it all night and into most of the next day. A couple of people stopped by, then politely left me alone when I yelled at them to frag off.

Pushing what little furniture there was in the main room of the apartment out of the way and rolling up the colorful throw rug, I took chalk and paint and started to draw on the worn wooden floor. I worked for hours, I'm still not sure how long exactly. Time didn't seem to have any meaning. When I was done, the floor was covered in a complex diagram. There was a large circle and a smaller triangle, edged with mystical runes and sigils.

Placing candles around the outside of the circle and braziers at the four quarters, I took a small silver knife from Jase's collection of magical tools. Soon, the flames were flickering and fragrant incense smoke rose from the braziers. A larger brass bowl filled with coals simmered in the center of the triangle. With the sharp edge of the gleaming dagger, I placed a shallow cut along the palm of my hand. Three drops of blood fell onto the glowing coals in the brazier, hissing droplets that covered the incense with the coppery smell of burning blood. Three more drops fell, followed by three more. A silken cloth stopped the flow of blood, and I bound it into a simple bandage.

From the center of the circle I gathered my anger. I hadn't slept in a couple of days at least. The sweet smoke of burning incense and burning blood filled the room, making my eyes water. The outlines of things seemed to blur. I thought about Jase's funeral pyre, staring into the flames of the candles, the smoke. I called on the fire, the fire of my anger and hatred. I stoked it slowly, lovingly, building it hotter and hotter. Flames crackled from the braziers, highest in the bowl where my blood fell.

I shouted arcane words, I wept, I ranted. At the height of my passion, I loosed the flames of my heart, felt them drawn to the flames where my blood burned. The flames flared with a roar that echoed my cry of anger, and a cloud of flames shot up and seemed to fill the room.

I found the Asphalt Rats partying later that night in a dead-end alleyway deep in their turf. From the amount of booze and discarded chip cases scattered around, it looked like they had recently come into some nuyen. I looked into the alley and saw those bastards partying and laughing after they had killed the best person I had ever known. I literally saw red, a rage that totally obscured everything else in a blood red haze. One of the gangers looked up from his debauchery and saw me standing there.

I raised my arms and screamed my grief to the heavens, a roar of rage that shot into the alley and erupted into a raging inferno of flames. It was as if Hell itself opened onto the street. Some of the gangers tried to run, a couple reaching for weapons, but most didn't even look up before being engulfed in a blast that charred their skin and set their hair aflame. A few moments later, the gas tanks of the bikes went off like a succession of bombs, and a black and orange fireball boiled out of the alley to the sky, blackening the sides of the nearby buildings with soot and ash.

I stood at the end of the alley and watched it all happen. I didn't care how horrible it was, my only thought was to see the ones responsible for my pain dead. The inferno in the alley was cool compared to the anger I felt as I watched the gangers burn, writhe, and die.

Then it was all over. The husks of the bikes burned and

a stream of acrid smoke billowed up from the alley. The gangers' blackened and twisted corpses lay where they had fallen. Most of them never even knew what hit them, or why. I turned and walked away from the alley without looking back. The cut on my hand throbbed and ached. I felt drained, empty.

I'd never killed anyone before that day. Even growing up in the violence of the Rox, I'd never even seriously hurt anyone, even in a fight. Then in the space of a day I killed fourteen people I didn't even know. The sims would have you believe that I'd have been wracked with guilt ever since, but to be honest, I'm not. They'd want me to say that roasting those gangers didn't bring Jase back and it didn't make my grief go away. It didn't, but to be honest, I don't care.

Nobody cried any tears for the Asphalt Rats when they heard about the weird incident in the alley, and another gang took over their turf and their niche in the Barrens ecology soon thereafter. I'm not bothered by the fact that I killed those bastards, then or now. What bothered me is the fact that I *enjoyed* it. The feeling of power when the Rats burned was an unbelievable high, better than drugs, better than anything. I liked that feeling, and the idea that I might be willing to kill again just to feel it scared the drek out of me.

I closed my fingers over the scar on my palm and looked out the window of the plane as we descended. Somewhere out in the dark, sprawling starscape that rushed up to greet us was a blasted and burned alley that no one went near anymore, and I was afraid of seeing it again.

# 6

The sun was coming up as we landed at Logan International Airport. Even this early in the morning, the airport was abuzz with activity from corporate commuter flights coming and going from New York, DeeCee, Atlanta, Seattle, and international flights from around the world. Corp types in suits made their way to and from the terminal as we left the plane. There was a fair security presence, mostly Knight Errant guards in their sleek black uniforms with the "KE" logo on the breast and shoulder, sidearms discreetly placed to provide a formidable image. The airport was busier and security was definitely tighter than I remembered it being on the day I left Boston, ten years ago. It was now a place where things were happening.

Since we had no luggage to pick up, we breezed past the baggage claim. Both of us traveled light, strictly carry-on stuff. Trouble did have to stop at the security checkpoint at the end of the terminal to have her deck and chips run through a standard scan. I didn't worry. She'd managed to get the deck through security in DeeCee without any trouble, and the check was routine. Her ID claimed Trouble was a corporate research consultant, someone who needed the compact, portable computing power of a cyberdeck. She spoke briefly with the bored-looking clerk.

"And you certify that these chips contain no illegal or contraband data?" the clerk asked in a droning voice. I watched the small trideo screens running reports from NewsNet. The rolling strip at the bottom of the image presented the local time and weather in Boston. It predicted a light rain for tonight by around 6:05. An announcer, pleasantly bland-looking, was reporting on breaking news in the metroplex.

"Knight Errant authorities are still investigating a series of brutal murders in the Boston area. Another victim of the 'Boston Slasher,' Ms. Elaine Dumont of Cambridge, was found near a red-line T-station early yesterday morning. The victim died from a single stab-wound, according to a representative of Knight Errant Security Services. Although the investigation is ongoing, authorities will say only that they are pursuing several leads." Hypertext links lit up the bottom of the screen saying "To download previous reports on this story, touch here," and "To report information on this crime to Knight Errant Security Services, touch here."

The news report went on to compare the murders to a series of killings years ago. I vaguely recalled hearing about them when I was in my first year at MIT&T. A representative of the pagan community of Salem was interviewed, denying any connection between the murders and any kind of "pagan rites," followed by a few other talking heads to explain the psychology of serial-killers and how copycats often sprang up, following the patterns of killers from years, even generations, before.

"All set," Trouble said, and I turned back to her as she slung the cyberdeck carrying case back over her shoulder. The clerk was already talking with another passenger, reciting the same bored speech. Obviously the "customized" (and illegal) modifications on Trouble's deck passed muster without notice.

"Just one more thing," I said, and Trouble led the way through the terminal and down to the customs area.

The customs clerk, a young woman whose features looked like they were sculpted from pink plastic, gave me a raised eyebrow as she slid a carefully wrapped package across the counter to me. I slipped the fake ID back into my pocket with silent thanks to Jane for coming through again and tore open the padded plastic wrapping to make sure the airport goons hadn't done any damage. I hated to leave it up to them, but there was no other reasonable way to get my prized possession through security in the kind of time frame I had in mind. The ID was sufficient to check it through airport customs, but not to carry it onto the plane.

Grasping the chain-wrapped hilt, I drew Talonclaw partway out of its black leather sheath. Everything looked fine, from the rune-carved blade to the polished fire opal that served as the pommel stone. The magic of the enchanted dagger tingled against my palm, alive and waiting to be called upon. I slid the blade home with a click that seemed to startle the young woman behind the counter out of her trance-like fixation on the gleaming dagger.

"Is everything in order, Mr. Nolan?"

"No problems, but I can't be too careful with the tools of my trade, you understand."

She smiled and nodded, despite the fact that I was sure she had no more clue about mageblades than what the tridshows portrayed on *Magus, P.I.* and *To Kill The Dead.* Sliding the sheath into my belt, I let my jacket fall back in place to conceal it, hefted my bag, and headed over to where Trouble waited.

As we made our way out of the terminal into Logan's protected parking area, Trouble took the lead. She slotted her credstick into the terminal at the entrance gate of the garage. It beeped, and a computerized voice spoke from the tiny grille. "Welcome back to Boston, Ms. Spenser."

Three floors up was Trouble's car, a dark green Honda ZX Turbo, a sleek, aerodynamic machine with silvery-tinted windows. It looked fast even while standing still. The car alarm chirped twice as we approached, and I made my way around to the passenger side.

I gave a low whistle of appreciation. "Nice ride," I said.

Trouble flashed me a smile of pleasure at the compliment. "Thanks, I'm rather proud of it. I sank some nuyen into it after a big job a while back. Hasn't let me down yet."

She slid easily into the driver's side, stowing the bag with her cyberdeck in the back seat, as did I. She took a slim optical cord from a pocket in the dash and snapped it into the jack behind her ear, synching with the car's auto-pilot computer and entering the ignition code. A second later the engine roared to life and the lighted panels on the dash illuminated.

"So, where to?" she asked.

"Landsdown Street. There's an old friend I want to look up."

Trouble navigated through the streets of downtown Boston like a pro. I'd forgotten just how harrowing Boston traffic could be. The common joke said all the streets in the Hub were paved-over cowpaths. They weren't. Boston was originally based on the layout of European cities like London, whose streets *were* paved-over cowpaths. The big quake brought about a lot of urban renovations, but the complex maze of one-way streets and multi-level roads remained as confusing and congested as ever.

It was still quite early, so traffic was light. It wouldn't get really bad for another hour or so. After we passed through the Williams/O'Neil Tunnel to get to the downtown area, I spotted several posters advertising the upcoming Samhain celebration on the Common. It was less than a week away.

"Samhain," I mused out loud.

"What's that?" Trouble asked as she dodged left around a slow-moving truck.

"Samhain. The Celtic New Year. Halloween. It's coming up soon. I'd forgotten all about it. It's a big pagan holiday. The biggest, for some pagans. I used to celebrate it with Jase. In fact, it was the first holiday we celebrated together."

"Are you pagan?" Trouble asked.

"I suppose so. Kind of lapsed. I haven't really celebrated any of the holidays for a long time, or called on the gods for anything except magical work. Just . . . didn't seem important, you know?"

Trouble nodded. The weather was unusually warm for the end of October, so she rolled down her window a bit. Her long, dark hair blew in the wind as she slipped on a pair of tinted glasses against the bright sunlight spilling over the buildings.

"I hear you," she said. "I was raised Catholic myself, Irish Catholic. My Dad was pretty devout and insisted on going to church every Sunday. I think it was his connection to the Old Country. He got forced out by the Danaan Families when they came to power. I don't know what they thought was so damn revolutionary about a university history professor."

I made a noise of agreement and shrugged. Who knew with elves? When the elves of Ireland claimed to be the legendary Sidhe, returned to claim their ancestral homeland, they backed up their claim with powerful magic. So many Irish folk, after facing years of struggle to gain independence from Britain, followed by years of political scandal and abuse, were completely taken in by the Sidhe's promises of a magical, revitalized Ireland. It wasn't even Ireland any more, it was Tír na nÓg, "the Land of the Ever Young," a bright new land of promise.

Only some of the Irish nationalists who'd fought so hard for independence from British rule didn't take too well to a bunch of elves coming in and taking over. Most of them were bought out, blackmailed, or forced out of the country as "subversive elements." People were too taken with the glorious image of the Danaan Families to worry much about anyone trampling on the rights of a few dissidents. A lot of the refugees ended up in the Boston area, which already had a big Irish population. South Boston was full of first- and second-generation Irish immigrants, not unlike what I'd read about the early twentieth century.

"I was raised Catholic, too," I said. "St. Brendan's, a mission in the Rox, took me in when I was just a kid and took care of me until I was fourteen. Then I hit the streets on my own. They did their best by me, but I got tired of the Father, the Son, and the Holy Spirit every morning with breakfast and every night before bed, to say nothing of sharing the place with about a hundred other kids the nuns took in. Wasn't too long after that I discovered my Talent. Good thing I got out when I did, or I probably would have ended up a priest-mage or something like that."

Trouble glanced at me over the top of her shades and broke out laughing.

"No way can I picture you as a priest, Talon. That really would be a sin."

"Yeah, I'm way too fond of having my Sundays off."

Trouble laughed again and took the corner with enough speed to make me grab for the handhold above the door.

"My family never bought into the whole 'new age of promise' drek dished out by the elves and all their political allies," she said. "Ireland had a lot of political trouble, but we were unified for the first time in a long time and a lot of people fought and died to make it a single country again. The elves promised unity, hope, and prosperity in the midst of troubled times, and most everyone was willing to go along with anything they said. They didn't even object when the elves changed the name of the country. It was all like something out of a fairy tale, or a legend.

"But some people didn't think so, including my parents. They were political dissidents. Not dangerous, just people with ideas and opinions who were willing to express them. I guess in the eyes of the Sidhe that made them the most dangerous of all. At first, the new government was willing to 'tolerate' other ideas, but when they got more control they started cracking down on all 'threats to public safety,' which included pretty much anyone who didn't approve of the government or their plans for the future. They started putting pressure on people to keep quiet. My parents lost their university jobs because of it. When that didn't shut people up, the government started arresting people, rounding them up in the middle of the night. People just disappeared and were never heard from again.

"I was only a little girl when the soldiers came for my parents. They'd gotten a warning from some friends and we ran. I was terrified, and my mother kept trying to keep me quiet so nobody would hear us when we slipped out of our house and into the night. My father was very angry, I remember."

Her voice took on a faraway tone as she recalled those times. "We managed to get out of the country and come to the UCAS. My father had friends in Boston, and we ended up in Southie. It wasn't a very nice neighborhood, and my parents had to take menial jobs to support us. Both of them were educated professionals, teachers back home, but my father drove a delivery truck and my mother waited tables for years because there were no other jobs.

"I was a wild kid. I grew up with the trid and the telecom for friends and baby-sitters. The good thing about it was I was playing in the Matrix from the time I was old enough to reach a keyboard. We didn't have a back yard or a playground, but in virtual reality, there was all the space you could ever want to play in. My dad thought it was good for me to know about the Matrix, and he worked extra hard to make sure we'd have at least some basic Matrix-access at home, so I could learn things. I suspect some of the things I learned my dad wouldn't exactly approve of." She smiled wickedly.

"A few years after we got to Boston, the troubles started here, too. Do you remember the Bloody Tuesday riots?" she asked.

I nodded. "Yeah. I was nine and living at St. Brendan's. Southie was like hell for days, with all the fires, the rioting and the looting. It was one of the few times I was glad to be near the church, although I heard even some of the churches were damaged."

Trouble nodded, resting her arm against the door and looking out the window. "I remember them, too. My mother was killed in one of the riots, trampled to death. My dad was never the same after that. He started drinking all the time and he pretty much left running the house up to me. Eventually, he lost his job and I started working the Matrix to get money to support us. Just small-time jobs at first, but I pulled in enough nuyen to help keep us going."

I looked at Trouble, imagining the burden placed on a young girl trying to support what was left of her family and risking death in the Matrix to do it.

"Eventually I got political myself," she went on. "I blamed everything that happened on the Sidhe and their damned fascist fantasy land. *Alfheim, alfheim uber alles.* They were the ones who forced my family out of Ireland, forced us to live in Southie, forced my parents into the jobs they worked. If it weren't for them, there wouldn't have been a Bloody Tuesday, and my mother wouldn't have died. I was just a kid.

"To me, people like the Knights of the Red Branch were freedom fighters, trying to free our homeland from the evil elven overlords who took it from us. Even though they were the ones who touched off the riots. You believe stupid drek like that when you're a kid and you're looking for something, anything, to hold on to.

"So along with running the shadows, I started getting involved with the anti-Tír movement in the plex. At first, it was just an expression of my anger for what the fragging elves did to me and my family. I wore my anger on my sleeve and I hated elves as much as any policlubber you could find. There were a lot of gangs operating in Southie then around racial lines, mostly norms against metas, especially elves. Even the metas were split up, with the orks and trolls against everyone else.

"I did some work for a few gangs, but I didn't join up. I tried to keep myself above all the little conflicts going on in the neighborhood. It was pure survival instinct. I figured as long as I kept neutral and provided what people wanted, they would leave me and my dad alone. And it worked pretty well, for a while. Then I met Ian.

"He was younger then, of course, but still had a good fifteen years on me. To a teenaged girl who ran the shadows from the Matrix, he was like a fairy-tale knight. A downtrodden hero exiled from his homeland and fighting for its freedom."

I glanced over and smiled, and Trouble gave a sheepish grin, ducking her head and letting her dark hair hide her face for a moment. "I know, it sounds stupid, but like I said, I was just a kid. To me, Ian was perfect.

"I first met him when I helped score a shipping schedule for a local gang. Turns out they worked for Ian and he met with me personally to get the goods. Said he was impressed with my work and had more work for someone like me. I didn't know he was involved with the Knights then, but he had such an imposing presence . . ."

She trailed off for a moment, lost in the memory. "Anyway, I started doing a lot of work for Ian and the Knights. At first, it was strictly a business relationship—I needed the money and they were willing to pay. After a while, though, it became more than that. I really needed somebody at that point in my life, and Ian was there for me. He listened to my troubles and paid attention while I poured my heart out about my mom, my dad, and everything else that happened. I think I was really looking for a surrogate father or a big brother back then, a substitute for my real

dad. I fell in love with Ian because he was a protector and
a friend. I suspect I reminded him of someone back home,
too, someone he'd lost. It was no way to build a relationship, but it was all either of us had.

"So I threw myself into the cause and worked with the
Knights of the Red Branch for a few years, working to
free Eire from the elven overlords and running the shadows to pull in the money and the contacts we needed. It
was an impossible fight. We were an ocean away from
home with no support, few contacts, and very little hope,
but we didn't give up. Some of the people in the KRB
had never even *been* to Ireland, but they had family or
friends who lived there or who had died in the riots. Some
just wanted to dream of reclaiming some kind of land to
call home. I guess when it comes right down to it, that's
what the Sidhe wanted, too.

"Frag," Trouble said, glancing over at me. "Tell me to
shut up any time. I don't even know why I'm telling you
all this."

"I have such a saintly face," I said, eliciting a smile.
"So what made you leave the Knights?" I already suspected the answer.

"I grew up," she said. "When I first started out, everything was black and white, us versus them. The more
things I saw and the more things I did, the more gray
everything got. Some of the things we did were no better
than the things the Sidhe did to us. I started to think about
things like Bloody Tuesday. The Knights set the bomb
that touched it off. Was all the violence really worth it?

"I started to have doubts, and that led to a lot of fights
with Ian. He never wavered from the cause, never thought
that what we were doing wasn't the right thing. Eventually,
I walked away from it all and became a shadowrunner. In

the shadows, you know where things stand or, at least, you used to. It was always strictly business for me . . . up until now, that is."

I nodded. "Right. Now it's personal."

# 7

Landsdown Street, near the financial district of the city, held some of the biggest clubs in Boston, including the Avalon. The club dated back to before the 2005 quake, but it was smaller then. Before the quake, most of the major clubs in Boston were owned and operated by a single company. After the damage done to the city, the company decided to rebuild Landsdown Street bigger and better than ever. Most of the clubs were built up higher and grander than before, with all the latest tech and equipment to make them attractions. The new club space pumped up the city's underground music scene, and plenty of small studios and record labels operated out of Boston. Although the big recording action was still in Los Angeles, the Boston club scene rivaled that of Seattle, and plenty of hot, new acts came out of the Hub on a regular basis.

The evening's fun was long since over and most of the club-goers were off somewhere having an early-morning breakfast at one of the nearby restaurants. The clubs were being cleaned up and readied for another go-round tonight.

Trouble pulled into a space directly in front of the Avalon and killed the engine. "You friend is here?" she asked.

I nodded and smiled. "He owns the place."

"You mean your friend is Pembrenton? The fixer?"

I laughed a bit at the mention of Boom's real name. I got out of the car and Trouble followed.

"That's right. Of course, he wasn't always fixing. He used to be in a band called the Nuclear Elves back in Seattle, and before that he sometimes ran the shadows for a little nuyen on the side. There was a while when we worked some runs together and hung out together afterward. I haven't seen him in, gods, it must be almost five years now. Definitely not since he inherited all of this." I gestured to take in the whole front of the club. "Dunkelzahn left it to him in his will. I heard something about Boom hooking up with some high-class talent. I guess this is what it meant."

Trouble looked thoughtful. "I remember scanning some data about it on Shadowland," she said, referring to the premier pirate Matrix node for black information. "Didn't he belong to some kind of network run by the dragon?"

I shrugged. "Hell, if someone had told me back in our running days that old Boom would end up a high-class fixer and club-owner in Boston, I would have told them they were crazy, but Dunkelzahn's will put stranger twists into people lives."

*Just ask Mary Beth Tyre,* I thought. Or any of the people I'd met through Assets in the past couple years. The dragon's will had definitely changed a lot of lives. It just remained to be seen if those changes were for the better or not.

The front door wasn't locked, so we walked right in. Just inside was a medium-sized room all in black, with a coat-check area to one side, stairs leading to the second floor, a hallway out to the lower dance floor, and one of the biggest and meanest-looking ork bouncers I'd ever seen, and I'd seen quite a few.

"We're closed," the ork said in a voice like he was gargling gravel. I ignored him and headed toward the stairs. There was a time when I knew the Avalon very well, and it didn't look like the overall layout had changed much in the last ten years or so.

The ork bruiser stepped between me and the stairs and put a beefy hand against my chest.

"What, are you deaf, chummer? I said we're *closed*."

I looked down at the hand, large enough to grab my whole head probably, and slowly followed up the arm until my eyes met with the dark, beady eyes of the bouncer.

"I want to see Boom," I said quietly.

"Mista Pembrenton isn't seeing anyone right now. He's busy."

"I want to see him *now*," I said, keeping my tone calm and even.

The ork looked at me in frustration. "He's not seeing anybody."

"He'll see me. Just tell him Talon is here."

The ork shook his head and didn't budge. With my peripheral vision, I could see another figure coming in from the main room, but I didn't take my eyes off the ork.

"Look, chummer," the bounder said, "I don't care if you're fragging Dunkelzahn come back from the dead. The boss don't want to be disturbed, and I'm not gonna interrupt him. You're gonna have to leave, *so ka*?"

"Some friend," I heard Trouble mutter from behind me. I was definitely losing patience with the muscle-brained flunky in front of me.

"Chummer," I said in a low, cold tone, "I've had a really long night and very little sleep and it's making me very cranky. And when I get upset, I tend to lose my natural grace and charm, and when that happens people start getting hurt."

As I spoke, power flared behind my eyes and I allowed bouncer-boy to see what I was. His eyes widened and he took his hand off me like my chest had suddenly become white-hot.

"Now," I said, "if you don't get the frag out of my way, this place is going to have to go wading into the shallow end of the gene-pool again, looking for a new piece of meat to replace you after you've been cooked to a nice medium-well. *So ka?*"

The ork took a step back out of the way as an impression of flames seemed to shimmer in my eyes. I walked past him without a second look, Trouble following quickly behind.

"Nice play back there," she said as we hit the stairs.

"Nothing much," I said. "Just a little trick of the aura."

"Would you really have geeked him?"

I shook my head. "Not over something like that. There are plenty of easier ways to use magic to deal with dim-brains like that. I prefer not to use magic at all in these cases."

"You're a better man than I am, Talon. If I had the Talent, I'd be using it all the time."

"It's not that simple," I said.

We hit the top of the stairs and I turned right down the corridor, past some of the upper dance-halls and bars, where a few people worked, cleaning up the leavings from the previous night. "Magic requires some effort, often a lot of effort, and that can wear you out pretty fast. Despite what the trid and even other magicians might want you to believe, using the Talent doesn't come without a cost."

I went to the door at the end of the hall and tried the knob. It was unlocked, so I threw it open and stepped into the room. In an instant, I was engulfed in wads of Hawai'ian shirt and steel-like muscles, heavy with the smell of expensive cologne and equally expensive cigars.

"Talon!" Boom yelled in a thunderous voice as he hoisted me off the ground in a crushing bear-hug. "Bloody 'ell! I never expected to see you, term!"

"Good to see you, too," I gasped, "but easy on the ribs, chummer. It's been a long night."

Boom immediately set me down and noticed Trouble standing in the doorway for the first time. Suddenly, I might as well not have been in the room.

"Hel-loooo," the troll said with his mild Cockney accent. "Who 'ave we 'ere? Welcome to the Avalon, dear lady." He caught up Trouble's small hand in his own massive one and bent low to bring it to his lips. "I'm Smedley Pembrenton, but you can call me Boom."

Trouble's lips quirked into a smile.

"You can call me Trouble."

"Well," Boom said with a laugh, "I always said that Talon knew how to bring Trouble into my life. I've never been so happy about it before, though. Your reputation proceeds you, Lady Trouble. There are some who speak very highly of you in the sprawl."

Trouble demurred at the compliment. "Thank you. I'm flattered to know I've come to your attention."

"If you hadn't, I wouldn't have recruited you to work on that business involving Fuchi Pan-Europa," the troll said.

"That was *you*?" Trouble said. Boom nodded with a smile and a wink and Trouble merely shook her head.

He ushered us into the spacious office and offered us our choice of the leather upholstered chairs and couches scattered in front of a massive desk of dark wood and plastiglass. I gratefully accepted a steaming mug of coffee—the real thing, from the smell of it—that Boom poured from a small service sitting on the well-stocked sideboard. It was what Boom always called "kid's coffee," heavy on the milk and sugar, which was the only way I drank it. I was impressed he remembered, but then Boom always had an amazing memory for trivia and assorted facts. It was one of the things that made him a good shadowrunner and, apparently, a good fixer.

He settled behind his desk, and I could see the changes that had come over Boom since I saw him last. The boisterous, fun-loving nature and the rough-and-tumble troll shadowrunner were still there, but I also saw Mr. Pembrenton, the shrewd fixer who'd built up a substantial reputation for himself as one of the best shadow-brokers in Boston.

"Talon, you told me you wouldn't come back to the Hub unless your life depended on it, so I'm guessing from that look that you're not back 'ere just to catch up on old times. What's going on?'

"You got it in one, chummer. My life *may* depend on it, and Trouble's too. We've got a problem with an ex-Johnson of hers who may be trying to ice us both, somebody who may have some yak connections."

Boom's beetle brow furrowed. He didn't like anyone messing with his friends. "Who is it?" he asked.

"A wagemage for Manadyne named Garnoff."

"Doctor Anton Garnoff?"

"You know him?"

Boom smiled at me, showing a lot of tusk. At this point

I should have stopped being surprised by my old chummer's connections. "Talon, term, I know a *lot* of people. Yeah, I know Garnoff, big noise with Manadyne's research department. Didn't have him pinned for a Johnson, though. More like a target than an employer. What's he got against you two?"

I shrugged. "It's got something to do with digging around in my life before I left Boston, but that's all I know. I figured you might be able to tell us more, maybe what kind of runs were going down lately. But if you haven't heard about Garnoff doing any hiring, then it must be something pretty secret."

"Well," Boom said, "you could always just ask him."

"We can't exactly make an appointment at Manadyne and tell his secretary we want to see him about his shadow-business," Trouble said with an edge of sarcasm.

"Quite so," Boom replied with a tusky grin, "quite so. But you *can* meet him on neutral ground and maybe get a better idea of why he wants you geeked. Seeing the two of you in the flesh might shake his tree enough to get something loose."

"How are we going to do that?" I asked. "Can you arrange a meeting?"

"Well, it just so happens that Dr. Garnoff is going to be at a little party thrown by Manadyne, a meet-and-greet the corp is running to garner more business and make connections, particularly with Novatech and some of the other local corps. I was thinking about going just to yank the chains of the Japanese suits over having to be polite to a troll for an evening, but this will be even better."

Boom grinned slyly. "You can see Garnoff, and maybe ask him a few questions. He won't be in any position to try anything tricky and you can get some answers out of him."

He reached out and clapped me on the shoulder. "It'll be just like the old days."

"Yeah," I said with a grim smile. "That's what I'm afraid of."

# 8

"What do you think?"

"Boom, I've seen smaller *countries* in my time."

The troll's "place" in the Back Bay area turned out to be an entire brownstone that Boom had bought and renovated, giving him enough space to house about ten squatter families back in the Rox. The four-story building had two guests rooms, a fully outfitted media-suite, and all the modern amenities. Trouble was obviously impressed, particularly with the state-of-the-art electronics in nearly every room. For someone who didn't used to know which end of a jack to plug into, Boom was pretty techno-savvy.

"So, do you like it?" Boom asked. He was like a kid showing off a new toy.

I smiled and nodded. "It's a long way from some of the digs you had in Seattle. Most of those wouldn't even let you stretch without touching the walls." Buildings were rarely constructed with trolls and other large metahumans in mind, even these days. The cathedral ceilings and wide rooms of the brownstone seemed barely comfortable for someone Boom's size.

"I still have to duck under the doors," he said, "but otherwise, it's not bad."

"You've definitely come up in the world, chummer."

"Can't live on the streets forever," Boom returned.

*Ain't that the truth?* I thought. Seemed like most shadow-runners managed to move up and out of the streets or found a permanent residence in an unmarked grave somewhere, sooner or later. I wondered a bit about some of the other chummers Boom and I used to run with and what happened to them. Boom showed us the rest of his place, including the guest rooms, then excused himself to make a few calls and arrange things for later.

The third-floor bathroom was pure heaven, and I made sure to take a nice, long hot shower. I used my time in the shower to clear my mind and organize my thoughts. Whatever Garnoff wanted from me, it was just a matter of convincing him it was more expensive for him to get it than to forget about it. In the old days, I probably would have retaliated against Garnoff with less provocation than he'd already given me, but I knew there was no profit in revenge or retaliation. Manadyne wasn't a major-league corporation, even with their windfall from Dunkelzahn's will. I had connections with bigger players than them, so it shouldn't be that difficult to get them off my back. By the time I started drying myself with one of the thick, plush towels, I was pretty confident about handling the whole thing.

When Trouble came into the bathroom I think I let out something of a yelp before trying to cover myself with the towel. I managed to babble out something that sounded like "Wha . . . ?" while I tried to get my voice to work.

"We have to share a bathroom," she said, undoing the clip that held her hair back and allowing it to fall across her shoulders. "Hope you don't mind." She started taking off her shirt, apparently heedless of the situation.

"Uh, no," I said, when I found my voice again. "Of

course not. Why would I mind?" I wrapped the towel securely around my waist. "No problem. I was done anyway." Trouble started taking off her neo-spandex sports bra, and I beat a hasty retreat out of the bathroom, without even retrieving my old clothes. She didn't say a thing, but I could have sworn she was laughing at me.

The place where Boom took us that afternoon was a branch of Armanté of Dallas, a very posh establishment that catered to corporate execs and other high-rollers. Boom was greeted the moment we walked through the door by a dapper-looking elf in a subdued, but fine-cut suit, something that wouldn't distract from the place's own wares.

"Mr. Pembrenton!" the elf said with what looked like a genuine smile. "To what do we owe the pleasure? Something for the Manadyne party?"

Boom returned the smile and nodded. "Yes, Marcel. I need something suitable for my guests here, Thomas and Ariel." He gestured toward Trouble and me.

I don't know what shocked me more, the idea that Boom was known in a place like this or the fact that his Cockney accent had completely disappeared as he spoke to Marcel, replaced by something vaguely like an upper-class Boston Brahmin accent. Even his speech pattern was different, perfectly suited to the tony atmosphere.

Marcel looked Trouble and me up and down, carefully appraising us. "I think we should have no trouble accommodating you. I'll have Alexa assist the lady in choosing from our selection of gowns." He turned to me. "If you'll come this way, sir, I can show you something in appropriate evening wear."

Boom and I followed the elf into the depths of the

boutique, and I placed myself in his care for the transformation that was to come.

Marcel quickly took my measurements, although I suspected he could tell most of them simply by looking at me. He excused himself, and I turned to Boom.

"How did he know you were going to the Manadyne party?" I asked, "And what's the deal with the high-class corporate-speak?"

Boom almost blushed under his greenish skin tone and gave a sheepish smile. "Lingasofts," he said, pointing to a small jack nestled near the back of his neck, with a few small optical chips slotted into it. "They contain all the right etiquette so I don't hose up in the wrong situation. I've learned most of it over the years, but the 'softs provide a lot of subtle cues you tend to forget about, and they modify my accent and my language as needed for the situation. I've got a Japanese language and corporate-culture 'soft for the party, too. I can probably get you one, if you want."

He glanced at my datajack, and I was suddenly very conscious of the cool metal of the jack against my skin.

"No, thanks," I said. "I think I can manage." If he took any notice of my discomfort at the idea of giving control of my behavior over to computer subroutines on a chip, Boom didn't mention it.

"As for the party," he said, "it's Marcel's job to know about all the soirées going on in the plex at any given time. He has to be ready for whatever his customers want, and there's a big business in passing guest lists for parties around to the different caterers and boutiques, so they know what to expect. In addition to being a great tailor and social engineer, Marcel is one of my better contacts. You can learn a lot from what people wear and what parties they go to. To say nothing of their spending habits, their measurements, and who they buy gifts for."

In a matter of minutes, Marcel returned, laden with articles of clothing for me to try on. He did a very good job with my measurements; everything fit almost perfectly. I picked out a charcoal Armanté suit in a modern style, high-vent, split cuff, with understated lapels and a collarless shirt. The fabric was woven with Kevlar II fibers to provide some light protection, enough to stop the penetration of a small-caliber round. Marcel seemed to approve and began carefully marking the suit to get an exact fit.

As he checked the waist, Marcel looked up at me. "Will you be wearing any . . . special accessories with this suit, sir?"

I pondered for a moment. There might be ways for me to get a gun into the Manadyne party, but I didn't much see the point. A mage is never really unarmed, and a gun could cause trouble and arouse suspicion.

I shook my head. "The only accessory is this," I said, holding up the belt with my sheathed dagger on it.

"Hmmm," Marcel said, looking it over. He reached out to take it from me. "May I?" he asked. I nodded and handed him the belt.

He held it up against the suit from a couple of angles. "I believe hiding in plain sight my be your best option, sir, unless a level of concealment is required."

Marcel arranged a belt sheath that would fit comfortably under the suit jacket, allowing me access to Talon-claw. The sheath would be covered by the jacket most of the time, not making the dagger too obvious. Looking at the whole image in the mirror, I nodded my approval. The fall of the jacket was perfect and hid the weapon from view.

"One final touch," Marcel said. He draped a black evening cloak over my shoulders, lined in deep burgundy, and closed it with a silver clasp with a Celtic knotwork design, then handed me a charcoal fedora with a deep burgundy hat band.

The overall effect was quite impressive, even I had to admit that. I looked at my image in the mirror and hardly recognized the slick, well-dressed mage looking back at me.

"Very nice, Marcel," Boom said.

The tailor smiled in pleasure. "The cloak-lining is Kevlar II as well," he said, "so it should provide an extra measure of protection. One can't be too careful."

I nodded. That much was certain.

Marcel made some final marks and checked the fit of everything, then took the suit for alternations.

"We'll deliver this to you for tonight," he said.

"Good. Have it sent to my place," Boom said. Then we went to meet Trouble in the foyer, and she seemed quite pleased with the whole process as a stately human woman finished covering a dress with an opaque plastic cover.

"I feel like Cinderella getting ready for the ball," she said with a grin.

"Just as long as we're not the ugly stepsisters," Boom joked, then reached into a pocket of his jacket to remove his credstick.

I held up a hand. "It's okay, chummer. I've got it," I said. Boom shrugged and put the stick away. He'd already done a lot by offering to help us out. Working with Assets paid quite well, so I had a very healthy cred-balance. I slotted my credstick into the reader on the counter and tried not to quail at the figures that flashed by. I could afford it, but the amount was still sinful.

"Have a good evening," Marcel said as we left.

"I'm sure we will," Boom told him.

I made sure to lock the bathroom door that night, and Trouble didn't try to burst in on me. True to his word, Marcel had our clothes dropped off at Boom's place a few hours after we left Armanté. Examining myself in the mirror I looked even more corporate than I did in my car mirror the previous day. That seemed so far away now.

Boom was looking very posh in a dark suit with a collarless shirt and no tie. The bulk of the jacket concealed a slim pistol in a shoulder harness, and the jacket itself could stop medium-caliber rounds, from what Boom told me about a time when it saved his life. We chatted as we waited for Trouble to come downstairs.

"Things sure have changed, eh, Tom?" Boom said with a wide grin, showing his prominent tusks.

"Chummer, if someone had told me even five years ago that this is where I'd be today, I'd have told him he was crazy. It seems like, since Dunkelzahn got killed, nothing has really been the same."

"Dunkelzahn's death was a turning point in many ways," Boom said, lost in thought. He turned his eyes back toward me. "You know, you never asked me how I ended up in his will."

"Did you know him?" I asked.

"Somewhat. After I got out of the band, I discovered I had a real knack for organizing things. Remember how I used to take care of a lot of the details of the runs we were on? I started doing that for other runners, handling the details, working the numbers. I'm good at it. Dunkelzahn noticed and started sending work my way. Of course, I didn't know it was him at first. Those jobs helped me build a reputation in Boston. For the first couple years, it was strictly small-time, but when Fuchi started to break up, there was business to spare. By that time Dunkelzahn was already dead, but he left me the club and enough nuyen to jump-start the business."

Boom grinned again. "I remember how I used to think fixers were some of the worst money-grubbing leeches in the world, but now I see it from the other side. Took a long time to find something I really wanted to do when I grew up." He cocked his head at me. "How about you?"

"I think I'm still growing up," I said. "After you left Seattle, I kept running, working the shadows. I'd built a rep, got some good jobs, then kind of fell into this whole business with Assets. It was the wildest run I've ever been involved in. Real end-of-the-world apocalypse stuff, chummer. It still gives me sweats just thinking about it. When it was all over, they asked me to become a member of Assets. How could I say no? They're the best. I've seen and learned drek working with them I never thought I'd see in my time on the streets. I thought I'd hit the big-time. Now this business has brought me back here, and I'm thinking about things I haven't thought of in a real long time."

"So, are you guys ready or not?" came a voice from the hall, and Trouble entered the room. We both turned toward her, and Boom let out a low, long whistle.

She was wearing an Armanté "starlight" gown in forest green, shot through with silvery threads of neo-diamond filament, making the whole dress sparkle as she moved and providing no small amount of protection. The gown was backless and featured a plunging neckline that showed off her white shoulders and arms, along with a fair expanse of cleavage. Over her shoulders was a black, fringed shawl of a filmy material spangled with tiny silver stars and, no doubt, additional protective material.

Her dark hair was caught up in an elaborate French braid secured with a silver comb decorated with Celtic knotwork. Similar Celtic-knot designs decorated her silver necklace and earrings, which had small green stones that matched the dress. The jewelry complemented the silver of the datajack port behind her ear, the only real technological touch on her person. She held a slim, dark purse, large enough to accommodate a holdout gun, but not the Predator she leveled at me when we'd first met. The overall effect was breathtaking.

"You look . . . great!" I said. "Amazing."

"My dear," Boom said rising from his chair, "as usual, my friend and associate Talon has a gift for understatement. You are a true vision of grace and beauty."

He caught up one of Trouble's hands in his own massive grip and gently lifted it to kiss it. Man, those skillsofts must have been working overtime. I'd never seen Boom so smooth, and his accent shifted to become a very slight, upper-class Bostonian, like someone who'd lived his whole live on Beacon Hill.

Trouble smiled at the compliment and almost curtsied. Maybe there was something to having those 'softs, after all.

"You should definitely make an impression," I told her, shooting Boom a look, which he ignored.

"Yes, we should," Boom said. "Hopefully enough of an impression to make your friend Garnoff think twice about who he's messing with. Shall we?"

"I'm ready," Trouble said with a smile. "Let's party."

# 9

The party was in full swing when we arrived at the upper floor of the Colonial Hotel, overlooking Boston Common. Some of the sprawl's wealthiest and most influential people were gathered together to celebrate, talk, and play their games of power and control. The private ballroom was two stories tall, with floor-to-ceiling windows affording a spectacular view of the Common and the glittering lights of the metroplex beyond, matching the bright stars in the clear night sky over Boston. From a balcony above, some of the guests appreciated the view, while others leaned against the rail to watch the activity on the ballroom floor below them.

Light classical music filled the air from hidden speakers throughout the room, providing a soothing, pleasant atmosphere and ably masking any conversation taking place more than a few meters away, allowing guests to congregate in small groups and hold private discussions with little fear of being overheard. It wasn't the most hi-tech protection against eavesdropping available, but anyone discussing anything truly sensitive in a place like this was already taking a chance.

The edges of the room were lined with catering tables laden with fine delicacies, artfully arranged, along with beautifully carved ice-sculptures in the form of fantastic beasts like unicorns and mermaids (no dragons, I noticed). Liveried waiters carried trays of drinks and hors d'oeuvres through the crowd, whisking away empties and keeping the room tidy and always active. Others tended bar or saw to various needs of the guests. A uniformed hotel employee appeared at the door to take my hat and cloak, Trouble's jacket, and Boom's topcoat. Waiters offered us champagne and tiny crab puffs from trays as we entered the room. I took a drink, just to have something in my hand.

Boom munched on several of the snacks, but declined anything to drink. "Mmmm," he said. "Not bad. Carolyn has good taste in catering."

"Carolyn?" I asked.

"Carolyn Winters, CEO of Manadyne and our hostess for the evening." Boom's etiquette skillsoft was already doing overtime, and I could just imagine them feeding him subtle cues and information he wasn't even consciously aware of. The effect was somewhat unnerving.

"Of course, she probably didn't handle the catering herself," Boom went on. "She has an expert staff and a lot of public relations people."

"So what's this party for?" Trouble asked, idly sipping from a champagne flute while looking around the room. High-class corporate soireés were obviously as rare for her as they were for me, although I'd attended my share while working with Assets over the past couple years.

"Up until a few years ago," Boom said, "Boston was a quiet town when it came to corporate action. There was plenty of business going on up around Route 128, but it was mostly little hi-tech corps, nothing to really interest the big boys. The stock exchange is still a big deal, but the megacorps all agreed to play nice around it. Manadyne was one of the larger outfits to operate in Boston, a big fish in a little pond.

"Since the Fuchi breakup, Boston's become a much bigger pond. With Richard Villiers setting up Novatech here, there's a lot more going on, and more corps want in on the action. Manadyne wants to take advantage of it and ride the wave into megacorporate status. They've got money from Dunkelzahn's will backing them up, and they're building more corporate contacts through little get-togethers like this. So far, Manadyne is a neutral party in the Boston scene, so they can pull off gatherings like this, where Novatech or Renraku would be too factional to get everyone together . . ."

"I can see that, but why Manadyne, what have they got to offer that's so important to everyone?" I asked, then it hit me. ". . . Ah, of course, magic."

Boom nodded, looking around the room as he spoke. "Got it in one. Magic. Manadyne is the biggest independent corporation concentrating on magical research and services. They're probably equal to the megacorporate magical departments of Mitsuhama or maybe even Aztechnology. Manadyne is hoping to get a lot of sub-contracting work for the megas that aren't heavily invested in magic, maybe even for the corps that *are,* giving them a leg up on the competition. A lot of corporations don't want to sink resources into building up their own magical R&D departments, especially when good wagemages are still hard to find."

"Tell me about it," I said with a grimace. "I nearly ended up a Mitsuhama wage-mage myself."

"You're in good company," Boom returned. "I see several Mitsuhama people here, along with some from the other top-tier corps and plenty of the local ones. Most of them are either courting Manadyne for magical research projects or trying to get the jump on what their competition is up to."

"That still doesn't tell us what Garnoff wants with information about me," I said.

Trouble broke in with a gentle touch on my elbow. "No, but you may get a chance to find out. There he is."

She nodded slightly off to the right, and I turned to look at the man who was after me.

He was standing by one of the catering tables, sipping bubbly and studying the room. He wore a dark suit of a decent cut and conservative style, with a silver lapel pin in the shape of a small magical diagram, covered with arcane symbols. I estimated his age at late forties or early fifties, although modern bodysculpting always made it difficult to be sure. His hair was dark, graying at the temples, and his neatly trimmed beard and mustache were streaked with gray as well. No doubt he considered the look distinguished enough that he didn't bother covering the gray with cosmetic treatments or spells. He wore spotless white gloves, an odd affectation, I thought. Occasionally, he would smile and nod or exchange a word or two with a passing guest, but otherwise he slowly scanned the crowd like he was waiting for someone.

He glanced over in my direction and our eyes met. I didn't look away too fast, tried not to give him any reason to believe my glance was anything other than idle curiosity. For a moment, Garnoff returned my gaze with an intense look. I saw a flicker of recognition in his eyes and a kind of electricity passed between us.

Then all heads in the room turned to stare as Richard Villiers, CEO of Novatech, entered the ballroom with a ravishing female companion on his arm. Garnoff turned to look too, and I took the opportunity to guide Boom and Trouble a bit deeper into the crowd.

"I'm not sure if he recognized me or not," I said. "I got the feeling he knew who I was."

"Well, I never managed to get him any holopics of you," Trouble said. "So he couldn't have recognized you from the jacket I compiled. Hell, I wasn't even sure it was you in your apartment until you said you knew Jason Vale."

"I'm still pretty sure he had some idea. There was something there. The weird thing is, I don't really think he was looking for me."

"He couldn't have any way of knowing you'd be here, could he?" Trouble asked.

"If you mean magic, probably not. Precognition and divination are pretty vague, to say the least. But Garnoff might have a lot more contacts in Boston. Someone could have told him we were coming here."

Richard Villiers was working the crowd like a political candidate on the campaign trail, offering friendly greetings and shaking hands, moving through the room and leaving a collection of dazzled guests in his wake. Even though he was only just another guest at the party, Villiers acted like he owned the place. Now that he had acquired many of Boston's major hi-tech companies, Novatech was the largest corporation based in the city. He acted like a king holding court, and most of the people treated him as one.

"Who's the woman?" Trouble asked.

Boom smiled. "I know her. She's a bodyguard. Under that Zoé designer gown is enough cyberware to stop a truck, and she's really sharp. Villiers isn't taking any chances. Neither is anyone else. I'd guess at least a third of the people here are hired protection of one kind or another."

"I didn't see any hovering around Garnoff," I said.

"Doesn't mean there isn't any," Boom replied softly, snagging a drink from a passing waiter. "Of course, Garnoff might not be important enough to rate his own bodyguard. Manadyne must have security keeping an eye on the whole place to make sure there aren't any problems. Besides, Garnoff is supposed to be a mage, which means he could have *other* protection."

That was quite true. Mundanes needed bodyguards and weapons, but magicians had spirits and spells for protection. Garnoff might have an elemental bodyguard and some protective spells on his person. In fact, the lapel pin he wore might even be a focus for such a spell. I resolved to examine him more closely when circumstances permitted.

"Looks like Garnoff found who he was looking for," I said.

Across the ballroom, two men approached Garnoff and bowed. Both were Japanese and, from the way they walked, one was clearly a subordinate or bodyguard to the other. Garnoff returned the bow and began speaking with them.

"Recognize them?" I asked Boom and Trouble.

"You could say that," the troll said in a low voice. "That's Tomo Isogi, kobun to Hiramatsu-*sama,* oyabun of the Hiramatsu-*gumi* of the East Coast yakuza. It's the biggest yak clan in Boston."

"The yakuza," Trouble said grimly. "I wonder just what exactly is their connection with Garnoff?"

I watched as Garnoff politely waved the two men

toward one of the side-exits from the ballroom, and they quietly left the room.

"That's what we need to find out," I said

I made my way over to one of the food tables and pretended to examine the selection. Trouble hovered nearby, playing the part of my companion for the evening perfectly.

"I'm going to do some magic to find out what Garnoff and Isogi have to talk about," I said. "Just keep an eye out and nudge me if someone says something to me, because I won't be able to hear what's going on around me, okay? I might set off some magical security, in which case we may have to cover things."

Trouble nodded and smiled like I had just told her a clever joke.

"I'll work the room a bit and give you some breathing space," Boom said. "I might be able to pick up a little more about Garnoff while I'm at it." The big troll strolled off and began greeting guests like old friends.

I cleared my mind and focused, feeling the mana flow all around me. The intention of the spell came to mind, and I poured my will and energy into it to make it a reality, sending it out. I was right, there was some magical security. The wards around the ballroom weren't strong enough to keep out any determined astral intruder, only enough to provide an alert if an astral form tried to get into the place without permission. They made the spell a bit more difficult, but I'd worked my way around tougher wards before.

My hearing passed through the ballroom, picking up snatches of conversation, then passed through the wall following the faint sound of conversation coming down what sounded like a long hallway.

I closed my eyes for a moment to focus on the sound and moved my awareness toward it, hearing the hushed voices get louder and more distinct. Clairaudience was not my best spell, by any means, but Garnoff and Isogi weren't very far away, and projecting my hearing was far easier than sending out my astral body, leaving my physical form lying in a senseless heap on the floor. That would have been a great deal more difficult to explain. My astral form also wouldn't be able to get past the wards without alerting security six ways to Sunday.

I opened my eyes and glanced around the ballroom a bit, but the music and drone of conversation were silent. I kept my hearing focused on the conversation in the room a short distance away.

". . . is not acceptable," someone, probably Isogi, was saying.

"Hiramatsu-*sama* must be patient," Garnoff replied in an even tone. "All is going as planned. The benefits of his support of Manadyne's research . . ."

"Are barely enough to justify the risks," Isogi interrupted. "And they will not continue to justify them for long. There are those who do not favor the support of magical research and experimentation, no matter how potentially profitable."

"That is because, Isogi-*san,* other factions are not as visionary as the New Way. Following the wisdom of Honjowara-*sama* in New Jersey, you understand that the Awakening has changed the old ways. Magic is part of our future. It is a power that must be harnessed, or else others will harness it and use it against you. If it can be mastered, it can be a weapon to use against your enemies. Look at the success you and your people have gained so far from such vision."

"We understand the value of your work, Garnoff-*san*, but we must see progress for the amount of money being put into this venture," Isogi replied. "Hiramatsu-*sama* requests you turn your research information thus far over to us for study, so we may determine how we will proceed."

There was a moment of silence before Garnoff spoke again. "It will take some time to gather my notes and present them to you. May I at least have a few more days?"

In the pause that followed I could almost hear Isogi mulling over the idea. "Very well. You have a week in which to show progress to us. Otherwise, the oyabun will decide if we can continue to support you."

"I assure you, Isogi-*san*, a week is all I will need to prove the value of my work to you. You will see just how much of an advantage it will bring us all."

At the sound of a door opening, I dropped my spell. The noise of the ballroom resumed, and I waited a moment for my senses to reorient themselves before turning toward Trouble.

"So?" she asked, leaning on my arm.

"I'll tell you later," I said, "but I heard a few interesting things. Now I think it's time to take a closer look at Garnoff."

When Garnoff and the yakuza re-entered the ballroom, they quickly parted company. Garnoff moved along the outside of the ballroom, and I made my way toward him. I focused on my breathing and willed my awareness to expand, to take in the unseen astral plane mundanes were entirely unaware of, but that magicians like me could perceive.

The music and conversation of the party seemed to fade into the background a bit as the astral opened up to my awareness. I could see the glowing auras surrounding all the guests. They showed their emotions, their feelings, and the power of their individual life force. Dark patches and bands revealed the presence of cyberware, places where living flesh had been replaced with metal and plastic. The astral space in the room was a sea of emotions, mostly greed, self-interest, fear, and pleasure, all mixing in a heady current. The wards, faintly glowing walls that followed the contours of the room's physical walls, seemed to contain and amplify the energy in the room.

Garnoff's aura was smooth and bland, showing only mild interest and simple contentment. There was a distinctive glow of magic to it, showing his magic nature. I was fairly certain he was masking his true aura. The words I heard from the other room suggested that Garnoff was either hiding his true feelings now or he had ice-water for blood. He didn't bother to hide his magical nature, since so many people here knew he was a mage, but I couldn't be certain if the power I saw reflected in his aura was any true measure of his ability.

A shimmering aura around his lapel pin confirmed my suspicions regarding its magical nature. It was clearly some kind of focus, but it lay dormant at the moment, waiting for its owner's will to bring it to life and draw on its power. I wanted to examine it a bit closer, but something else caught my attention first.

Above Garnoff's right shoulder hovered a disembodied eye about the size of a fist. It was a watcher spirit, invisible in the physical world, but present on the astral plane. Before I could do anything to hide my astral presence or slip back into the physical world, it spotted me.

Garnoff lifted his head like he was listening to a voice I couldn't hear and then he gave a tight-lipped smile. The pale image of his physical self, as seen from the astral, began to take on more color and substance as his own astral form appeared and looked at me. He studied me for a second or two, and I was fairly sure my own masking held against his scrutiny. He would learn from my aura only what I let him learn. Point one to me, I hoped.

"Talon, I presume." Garnoff's mouth never moved, but his spirit lips shaped the words. Although his voice was low and quiet, the sound carried clearly to me over the faint background noise of the material world.

"You presume a great deal, Dr. Garnoff," I responded in kind. I kept my anger and my true feelings from showing in my aura, but the tone of my voice left little mistaking my intent.

If he noticed, Garnoff didn't show it. "I hadn't expected to meet you in quite this way," he said, idly plucking a ripe strawberry from the nearby table and biting into it.

"I'm sure you didn't. Exactly how were you planning on meeting me?"

"Let's just say under other circumstances, for now," Garnoff said as he chewed and swallowed. "You're more resourceful than I thought."

"I'm just full of surprises, all right."

"Indeed. Your Talent has developed a great deal over the years."

I was taken aback for a moment. Was Garnoff bluffing? How did he know anything about my magical development? His aura betrayed no hint. It was an impenetrable facade, but my own masking wavered a bit.

"I'm sure Jason Vale did a good job of showing you the ropes," Garnoff continued.

I very nearly surged out of my body to seize his astral form and throttle it. I wanted nothing more than to wipe the arrogant expression from his face and his aura, but I held myself back. It was stupid to go up against an opponent I knew nothing about in a setting like this. Even if I could take Garnoff, which was by no means certain, I'd never get out of the ballroom before Manadyne's own magical security came down on me like a ton of bricks.

"I'll tell you this just once, Garnoff," I said in a flat and controlled voice. "You made a mistake coming after me, and you made a mistake bringing Jason Vale into this. By my count, you've got one more mistake coming to you. Three strikes and you're out. After that, I'm taking you down."

I turned and walked slowly away, allowing my astral awareness to fade. Just as the astral plane slipped from my sight, I could hear Garnoff's spirit-voice, speaking as if from very far away.

"Let the game begin."

I walked back to Trouble and we found Boom chatting in Japanese with some local Renraku suits eager to build bridges and garner allies after all the trouble their company had been through recently. I snagged Boom's attention and pulled him aside.

"What is it?" he asked.

"Let's blow this pop-stand, chummer. We've got a shadowrun to plan."

# 10

I let Trouble arrange the meeting at the Avalon for the following afternoon. We took one of the tables tucked into a corner with a view of the dance floor. The club wasn't open yet, and the place was quiet. A few employees went about their business, pointedly ignoring our little gathering as Boom, Trouble, and I sat and waited.

"They'll be here," Trouble said. "Don't worry."

I realized I was drumming my fingers on the table and stopped. "I'm not worried. It's just odd, being on this side of the table."

Boom chuckled. "You don't know the half of it, term. It's like being a kid playing dress-up sometimes."

"Yeah. Makes me wonder what was going on in everyone else's head during all of those meets I went to as a shadowrunner."

Just then, muffled footsteps sounded and I looked up to see two men approaching the table; a burly ork and a tall, well-muscled human with close-cropped blond hair. Both of them walked with the moves I'd come to associate with street samurai: barely restrained energy, ready to burst into action at any moment. Both also wore street clothes and carried no obvious weapons, but I was sure they had them nonetheless, just the same as I did. It was expected.

"Hoi, Trouble," the burly ork said with a grim smile and a nod. Then he turned to me. "Mr. Johnson." His voice was low and gravelly. "It's a pleasure to meet you."

For a moment, I almost looked around to see who he was walking to. Then I realized it was me. All of a sudden, I was Mr. Johnson, the anonymous face-man hiring shadowrunners. Like playing grown-up, indeed.

"Likewise, Mr. Hammarand," I said, returning his slight nod.

"You can call me Hammer. Everyone else does."

"You can call me Talon." I gestured toward the empty seats on the other side of the table. Hammer took one while his companion stood behind his chair like a bodyguard. When the second guy made no move to sit, I figured Hammer was in charge of the negotiations, just as Trouble had said he would be.

"Trouble told you about the run?" I asked.

Hammer glanced over at Trouble. "She told me you could be trusted, which is why I'm here. I'll be honest. I don't know you, Talon, but I do know Mr. Pembrenton, and I've known and worked with Trouble for years. I trust both of them not to frag around with me or my team. I just want you to know where I stand."

"I appreciate your honesty," I said. "Let me be equally blunt. I need some runners for a job and I'm willing to pay well for it. But this isn't a run where the Johnson hires you and you report back when it's all done. I'll be going along and you'll have to work with me directly. I know what I'm doing, and Trouble assures me you and your team are professionals. Can you handle those terms?"

Hammer regarded me with his dark eyes, taking my

measure. It wasn't astral perception, but something almost as magical, that sixth sense shadowrunners develop about who is and isn't worthy of their trust. It's a necessary survival instinct in the shadows.

"Okay, Talon," he said. "We're in. What's the job?"

"A run on Manadyne for information on a research project headed by one Anton Garnoff, along with any useful personnel files and personal data we can turn up. I can handle anything Manadyne's got in the way of magical security, but I need some backup, logistics, and transportation people. That's where you come in."

"Hmmm," the big ork rumbled. "Manadyne security isn't the best, but it's no cakewalk. They've got a contract with Knight Errant." The Ares subsidiary was one of the best private security providers in the world.

"The trick is going to be getting access to the databanks," Trouble said, speaking for the first time. Now that we had an agreement, she became part of the team rather than a go-between for me and Hammer. "Like a lot of corps, Manadyne keeps its sensitive R&D stuff in an isolated system. It's going to be near-impossible to access from the outside. That means I should probably go in with you."

I shook my head. "Not necessarily. We might be able to get the isolated system on-line so you can access it from the Matrix, and we'll probably need you on the outside taking care of some of the electronics."

"It'll be easier to get at the data from a jackpoint inside their defenses," Trouble said.

"Shouldn't make any difference," I returned. "The ice inside the datastore is going to be the same one way or another, and there's no way you're going to be able to shut down the other security systems except from the outside."

Trouble opened her mouth to offer another protest when Hammer's deep bass cut through the conversation.

"I agree with Talon," he said. "You're going to be the most use to us on the outside, kiddo."

Trouble flashed a dangerous glance at Hammer and something passed between them for a second, then she backed down a bit and directed her gaze down at the table. "I suppose you're right."

"We've got some intel on the R&D facility," I said, changing the subject. "It should give us a good idea on how to approach the place."

Trouble obliged by rolling out the flatscreen on her cyberdeck and punching up the information she'd acquired. A three-dimensional model of the fenced-in Manadyne research lab appeared on the screen and rotated to show each of the sides. Trouble turned the screen so Hammer could see it.

"Won't be easy," he said. "The fence definitely has monowire strung along the top, and I'll bet there's some pretty heavy electronics to go with it."

I nodded agreement. "That's why we need more detailed information on the security setup and the best ways to get around it. I want this run to go down as soon as possible."

"I've been doing some more checking on Manadyne," Trouble said. "The weakest point of any security system is always the people running it. I think there may be a way to get the codes we need to get inside, provided"— she gave a wicked grin—"Talon is willing to use his talents to get them."

She tapped a couple of keys, and the schematics of the

facility vanished, replaced by another file. She turned the roll-out display screen of her cyberdeck toward me so I could read the information on it. I felt a smile tug at the corners of my mouth as I caught the gist of Trouble's idea. I glanced up to see her grinning, and Boom giving me a quizzical look.

"Perfect," I said.

Saturday night, Arthur Waylan came into the Avalon nightclub as he often did. It was something of which his wife never would have approved, if she'd known about it, that is. It was also something that would look bad to Arthur's hard-working corporate superiors, should they ever find out. But no one knew about Arthur Waylan's secret little habits, except for Trouble, and Boom, and now me. Arthur worked for Manadyne, and he had a fondness for the hottest nightclub in Boston, where he found plenty of boys and girls to his taste there. Once we knew that, the plan was simple.

Waylan showed up fairly late, just after midnight. He was dressed in the latest street-wear, but he still looked frumpy and corporate compared to most of the clubbers. The Avalon was dark, lit by a complex of flashing strobes in a variety of colors sufficient to send almost anyone into fits. They certainly seemed to have that effect on the people writhing and moving on the dance floor. The colored lights cast beams through a haze of smoke that hung overhead.

The sound system blasted "Puta" by Maria Mercurial. The music was raw and primal as Maria's angelic voice sang about dirty people doing dirty things to themselves and each other. The crowd was really getting into it.

After Waylan made his way into the club and had a

chance to adjust his senses to the light, the haze, and the noise, I made sure he saw me. He looked across the dance floor and saw his fantasy come to life. I glanced up and there was a moment when our eyes met and he was mine.

I was wearing neo-spandex shorts that fit like a second skin and left very little to the imagination, along with a half-shirt, short leather jacket, and a spiked collar (a nice touch, I thought). I was dancing up a storm, too. All other concerns aside, I've always loved Maria Mercurial and I was seriously getting into the music even before Waylan decided to finally wander in the door. Once I spotted him, though, play time was over. It was time to get down to business.

I pointedly ignored him for a few minutes, giving him a chance to wander over to the bar and get himself some courage. I had no lack of willing dance partners, after all, and the music was nova-hot. It would take some time before he was going to make a move, and everything needed to seem as normal as possible.

After downing his first drink and ordering another, Waylan spent some time at the bar nursing it and staring quite openly at me. I looked back in his direction a couple of times and offered a smile of encouragement, enough to keep him interested and keep him wondering. I danced through a club re-mix of a Speed Coma song, then made my way over to the bar when it ended, my skin gleaming with sweat. I remembered all the nights I used to spend in places like the Avalon and Underworld 93 in Seattle, dancing the night away out of the simple pleasure of having survived another day in the shadows. It had been a long time since I'd done that, but I wasn't too out of shape, as Waylan's appreciative leer suggested.

"What are you having?" he said as I leaned on the bar.

Already the drink and the atmosphere were making him bolder than he would ever have been outside the club.

I turned toward him with what I hoped was a devastating smile and said, "Laser beam."

He turned toward the elf bartender, nodded and said, "And another one of these," raising his glass and downing the contents. The bartender started mixing Jim Beam and peppermint schnapps for my drink. It wasn't my personal favorite, but it was what Waylan expected of me, and I didn't want to disappoint him.

"I don't think I've ever seen you in here before," Waylan said, leaning heavily on the bar.

"Oh, I've been here a few times. Maybe you just missed me."

"I definitely couldn't have missed someone like you."

I could feel his gaze caress my feminine wiles up and down. "I'm Chance," I said. "What's your name?"

"John," Waylan said, after a momentary pause. Gods, could he have picked a lamer pseudonym?

"So what about you?" I asked. "Do you come here a lot?" It was an equally lame gambit, but Waylan didn't even seem to notice. He was too busy trying not to stare.

"Yeah," he said, "I come by pretty often. I'm a security specialist with Novatech." It was a lie, but not much of one. Novatech was the biggest and brightest corp in Boston. Obviously, Waylan didn't want anyone to know who he really worked for and figured he could impress people by pretending it was Novatech.

I pretended to be dazzled. "Really?" I said, as the bartender delivered my drink. I started to reach into my jacket pocket when Waylan took his credstick from a wrist sheath.

"Here, let me." He paid for both drinks, then slid the stick back into its holder with a flourish.

"Thanks," I said.

Waylan raised his glass in a toast. "Here's to a great night," he said.

I gave him a big smile and said, "I'll drink to that." He had no idea how great a night it was going to be.

By the time Arthur Waylan invited me back to his hotel room (which he'd booked earlier that evening, according to Trouble) he was seriously buzzed from all the drinks. It occurred to me that the whole plan could come to a very unhappy ending if he simply drove his car into a wall or something, or if we got stopped by a Knight Errant patrol cruiser, but Waylan managed to drive the short distance to the hotel without any problems. Having someone keeping a covert eye on the traffic computers and police bands from the Matrix helped.

He discreetly guided me into the elevator and upstairs to his room, occasionally glancing around to make sure nobody he knew saw us or was following us. He had to fumble a bit with his credstick to get the door open. He leered suggestively as he slotted the stick into the lock and the green light flashed on.

Inside the room, I pushed the door closed. If the intel Trouble and Boom had scanned was right, now was the time to take charge of things.

"You're a very bad boy, aren't you, John?" I said, and Waylan turned toward me with a slack-jawed expression and pure lust in his eyes.

"Yes," I said slowly, "a very bad boy. I think you need to be punished."

"I . . ." he began, but I pressed my fingers to his lips.

"Shhhh, no talking," I said. "I have this fantasy, and

only you can help me make it come true. Do you think you can take Chance?" He nodded vigorously. "Take off your clothes."

Waylan wasted no time in shedding his shoes, socks, pants, and shirt. When he was down to his boxer shorts, I reached into my jacket pocket and took out a folded-up set of latex strips.

"Lie down," I commanded, and Waylan obeyed like an eager puppy. Trouble had his psyche profile nailed dead on. It short order I had his arms and legs tied firmly to the four corners of the bed and Waylan was practically panting in anticipation. Using my astral sight, I could see the desire and lust in his aura, nearly all other thoughts and feelings smothered beneath his need. I climbed on top of him and straddled his body, dropping my jacket on the floor.

"So," I said in a deep and sexy feminine tone. "Are you ready to fulfill my fantasy?" Waylan whimpered slightly and nodded.

That's when I dropped the mask spell. Waylan's eyes bugged out as the willowy, blond, elven bombshell with the breasts and thighs of his wildest dreams became a dark-haired man with a very similar smile and disturbing similarities in voice. I could feel him recoil under me as he struggled against the bonds that held him tight. I leaned in close and looked deep into his eyes, but all he saw in mine was cold, steely control.

"Then you can start by telling me everything you know about Manadyne's security protocols, Artie . . . darling."

He didn't resist for long, and soon had babbled out a very clear and detailed picture of what we would have to deal with to get into Manadyne. He also provided all his personal security codes and a few additional details when

I pointed out the vidcam concealed in the room and described the pictures it contained of him with me, in both forms. Once I got everything I needed from him, I pressed a tranq patch against his neck. His eyes glazed over and he was out almost immediately.

"Typical man," I muttered to myself. "Fell asleep right afterward."

I keyed Channel 1 on my headlink. "So," I subvocalized over the headware, "was it good for you?"

Trouble's laugh carried loud and clear over the microspeakers linked to my hearing center.

"The best, baby, the best."

# 11

Arthur Waylan "called in sick" the next morning, thanks to some well-placed email from Trouble. After discreetly slipping him out of the hotel, we moved him to a nondescript coffin hotel Boom had arranged for on the outskirts of the Rox. It was a place where no one asked any questions and it was well off the beaten path. We kept him doped up enough to be happy and quiet while we made preparations to get into Manadyne.

"It's a research and development facility located in the Route 128 area on the edge of the sprawl," I said. My audience consisted of Boom, Trouble, Hammer, and two other members of the Hammermen. One of the latter was Sloane, the big, blond bruiser who'd stood in as Hammer's bodyguard at the meet. He was as stone-faced as ever, listening intently to every word. The other was Val, a woman with short-cropped black hair and a datajack behind her ear linked to a headware system and the hardware for a vehicle control rig. She wore dark clothes under a bulky black leather jacket. Trouble and Hammer both said she was one of the best riggers in the Boston sprawl. She would be the one to get us in and out of the place smoothly and easily.

I gestured to the modified trideo unit in the room,

which showed a holographic model we'd constructed of the facility.

"The main building is surrounded by a ferrocrete parking lot, with a narrow strip of landscaping between the building and the lot. A wider swath of grass and trees encircles the lot itself, and the whole thing is enclosed in a three-meter-tall chain-link fence topped with three strands of monowire. One false move climbing the fence and you can lose a limb, at worst, a hand or finger, at best. The fence is also equipped with pressure sensors set to detect and alert the main security system if anyone tries to climb the thing.

"Fortunately," I said with a smile, "we don't have to go over the fence. Thanks to the cooperation of Mr. Arthur Waylan, we've got the security codes we need to clear the automated systems running the perimeter gate, so we can just drive right on in. After that, things get a little trickier. There are some guards in place, and we'll have to deal with them without raising an alarm or twigging anyone to the fact we're there. The codes will get us past most of the electronic security and Trouble can handle the rest, but dealing with Knight Errant is up to us."

"I still say I should go with you," Trouble interjected. "The data will be isolated from the main system."

"Which is why we're going in," I returned, "so we can link it to the main system and you can access it from the outside."

"It would be easier if I did it from the inside," she said.

"We've been over this before, and we agreed," I told her, trying to keep the tension from my voice. "You handle the Matrix and the electronics and leave the physical stuff to us."

Hammer cracked his knuckles and gave a tusky grin. "Sounds like fun. You got a plan in mind for that, too?"

"As a matter of fact, I do," I said, and proceeded to outline the rest of it to the team.

That night, Boom, Hammer, Sloane, and I sat in a dark van as it cruised up to the entrance of the Manadyne research facility. The three of them sat in the back, while I took the passenger seat. Val was in the driver's seat, jacked into the van's controls and driving the van like an extension of her own body. We cruised down the road at a leisurely pace. It was late, so traffic was very light.

A voice spoke in my head as the gates came into view.

"Comeback Two to Comeback One, I'm in place," Trouble said. There was no note of our earlier disagreement in her voice. Everything was cool and professional.

"Copy that," I replied. "We're ready to roll. Keep watch, Comeback Two."

The van came to a stop in front of the gates, and an automated camera atop one gate-tower panned slowly across the van. Val sat up a bit, then turned her head and lowered her window. She reached out and entered the security codes Waylan had provided into the small keypad beside the gate. They told the security system we were a maintenance crew, replacing a crew Trouble had canceled earlier in the day. There was a pause as the system juggled the numbers and began cross-checking facts. If the information we got from Waylan wasn't good for some reason, or security suspected something, we would find out in a matter of seconds.

No alarm sounded, no lights flooded the area round us. Instead, the gate hummed quietly and slid open to admit us. Val drove the van into the parking lot and parked near the side entrance. Then Hammer opened the side door of the van and we piled out, wearing pale gray coveralls lifted from the maintenance company. Hammer held his Ingram smartgun somewhat uneasily and looked around the empty lot like a trapped creature. "Are you sure this is going to work?" he asked in a low voice. "What about the weapons?"

I took Arthur Waylan's security card from a pocket of my coveralls. "It'll work. The illusion spell includes the guns. They look just like maintenance equipment— buckets and mops and things like that. As long as we're careful, nobody will notice anything strange about them."

"If you can do that," he said, "why bother with the monkey suits?" He plucked distastefully at the gray coverall he wore over his armored jacket.

"The less the spell has to work to create the image, the more convincing it'll be," I said as I swiped the card through the door's maglock and punched in a code. The locked clicked and the light over the keypad switched from red to green.

I pulled the door open. "After you," I said to Hammer. He took the point, followed by me, with Boom and Sloane taking up the rear. Val stayed behind in the van to keep watch on the lot and be ready to get us out in a hurry, if need be.

The corridor beyond was starkly white, lit by overhead fluorescent panels. We moved down the hall at a brisk pace, but no more than a walk. If we encountered anyone in the hall, it wouldn't do to be running around. There was no one in sight.

Stepping into the corridor, I willed the shift in my perceptions. The images of the astral plane opened up to me, and I became aware of the shimmering aura surrounding my own body as well as the auras of the rest of the team.

I could see a nearly opaque wall of pearly light glowing across the door we entered, a ward protecting the facility from astral intrusion. I would also be able to see any astral security present inside the building, giving us a little warning and a chance to deal with it. There was nothing in our immediate area; no spirits on guard or other magical defenses likely to detect the presence of my spell.

We made our way toward the cold-storage area where the isolated data-storage systems were, following the layout provided by Waylan. After we took a turn into another corridor, Trouble's voice sounded in my head again.

"Comeback One, you're going to have to pass a pair of Knight Errant guards on your way to the vault."

"Any way around them?" I subvocalized. There was a momentary pause.

"Negative," was the reply.

"Understood." I nodded to Hammer and turned to look back at the others. Everyone heard Trouble's message. They readied their weapons and we continued down the hall. Coming around a corner, I saw the two Knight Errant guards, their black uniforms distinct against the white walls. There was a man and a woman, both human. They carried submachine guns on shoulder slings and their hands automatically rested on them as they saw us. Their auras showed caution, but some confusion. My illusion spell was working, giving them pause.

I took a step forward, careful to keep my empty hands in plain sight. The guards relaxed only slightly.

"Hoi," I said slowly. "We're here to check out a maintenance problem with the air system." I took a few steps closer. A look of suspicion came across their faces at the same time that concern colored their auras.

"I haven't heard anything about that," the woman said,

shifting her hand toward the butt of her weapon. Her aura shifted toward suspicion and threat-response.

"C'mon," I said, "we got the call in about an hour ago . . ." I narrowed my eyes and focused the power of my will against the woman, since she seemed to be in charge. For an instant, her eyes widened in surprise and she tried to struggle against me, then the power of my sleep spell overcame her and she began to crumple to the floor, the colors of her aura fading toward unconsciousness.

The other KE guard reacted instantly. But even instantly wasn't fast enough, as Sloane covered the distance between them like a blur and delivered a powerful strike to the man's neck. Then he too crumpled to the floor in a heap.

"Comeback Two, are we still clear?" I said over the link.

"Confirmed," Trouble said. "Cameras and other monitors are in the clear. No one has noticed anything yet."

We moved the unconscious bodies of the two guards into a maintenance closet and locked it, after relieving them of their weapons and commlinks. Then we headed for the storage vault.

The vault room was sealed off with a heavy security door and another maglock. I used Arthur Waylan's keycard on the lock, and it opened. Inside was a row of data-storage systems, the "cold storage" where the lab kept its sensitive data. Closing the door behind him, Boom made his way over to the databanks and looked them over.

"Should be no problem to get these linked up to the main system," he said. Boom had apparently picked up a lot of knowhow about computers in the past few years, so I deferred to him.

"Comeback Two," I said, "stand by for link-up."

"Confirmed."

Boom took a coil of optical cable from his belt pouch, terminated with standard jack connectors, and plugged one end into the databank system and the other into the wall outlet connecting to the main computer net for the building. He powered up the data drives for active access.

"Window's open," Trouble reported over the commlink. "There's some ice protecting access to the data. I'm going to try to—"

Suddenly, a burst of hard static washed over her voice, cutting off the comm signal. At the same moment, the door of the room burst open and a voice shouted, "Freeze!"

Time seemed to speed up as Boom, Sloane, and Hammer reacted in a blur of motion. Weapons roared and Sloane went stumbling back into a bank of equipment as I dived for cover behind one of the heavy lab benches. Boom and Hammer took similar protective positions as loud cracks sounded all around us.

Boom slid down near me, his broad back against the side of the bench.

"What the hell . . . ?" I started to whisper.

"They're not Knight Errant," Boom said in a low voice. "I'm not even sure they're any kind of private security."

"Then who?"

"I dunno, term."

The gunfire ceased and there was a long moment of silence. Behind the bench across from us, Hammer popped the clip on his weapon and slammed another one home. His aura shimmered with tightly controlled emotion, focused entirely on the situation at hand. There was no malice, only a cool, professional need to survive, whatever the cost.

Then a shimmering blue-gray mist began to creep across the floor between and through the benches themselves.

"Oh, frag," I said.

"What is it?" Boom said.

"They've unleashed a spirit on us," I said.

Hammer began gasping and coughing, followed by Boom as a terrible, choking odor reached my nostrils. The air elemental materialized all around us as a choking, noxious stench, forcing the air from our lungs as it tried to suffocate us.

Placing my hands on the cool tile floor to ground myself, I reached out to the elemental with the power of my will.

"Begone," I gasped. "I banish you from this place. Depart, never to return." A surge of magical force pushed back, as the spirit fought against me. I focused my intent and pushed harder, feeling the elemental yield slightly.

"Begone," I repeated. "I banish you from this place. Depart, never to return." The elemental began to fight more forcefully, but I kept the pressure of my will on it. My vision was starting to swim and I could hear footsteps cautiously approaching our position. The spirit started to diminish, and the terrible stench with it.

*Begone!* I shouted in my mind, striking the spirit with the full force of my power. The air elemental shrank into little more than a hovering cloud that seemed to collapse in on itself until it contracted to a tiny, glowing pinpoint. Then it suddenly winked out like a candle extinguished by a strong wind. The air cleared and I could breathe again.

Boom and Hammer seemed to be recovering as well. I glanced over at Boom and up toward the top of the bench behind which we huddled. The troll raised his gun and nodded. I gathered mana and began shaping it into a spell. When I was ready, I surged up over the top of the bench along with Boom. Hammer followed our example.

Five Japanese men stood on the other side of the lab

benches, armed with submachine guns. They wore dark street clothes and looks of surprise on their faces. Clearly, they'd expected the elemental to finish us off and were closing in to see if it had done the job.

I thrust my hands toward them, fingers spread, and flung my sleep spell. For an instant, I felt their wills struggle against mine. Then they began to drop to the floor, unconscious. One man shook his head and managed to keep his feet. He began to bring up his weapon, but Hammer shot him in the shoulder, sending him spinning to the floor, clutching the wound. His weapon hit the floor with a clatter.

As I sagged against the edge of the counter, I noticed the alarms going off for the first time.

"Trouble," I said into the commlink, forgetting the code we'd established for the moment. "Trouble, are you there? Respond!" Nothing but static came back.

"We're clearing out of here," I said. Hammer was already helping Sloane to his feet. The big man's armor must have absorbed the impact of the bullets, since he didn't look too seriously hurt, mostly shaken up.

We left the computer vault at a run, all pretense of stealth abandoned. As we headed for the side exit, I expected a squad of Knight Errant security to appear at any moment.

"Comeback Three to Comeback One," Val's voice spoke in my head. "We've got company, boss."

"We're clearing out," I said over the link. "Get ready to run."

"Roger," she said.

A few seconds later, we burst out the side door and climbed quickly into the open van. Val peeled away just as a dark car with tinted windows came squealing around the corner. Gunfire chattered from a side window, sparking off the ferrocrete just behind us. The van accelerated rapidly toward the front gate.

"Hang on," Val said. The van hit the gate going at more than eighty kph. The chain-link and metal struts parted with a shrieking sound, and the gate bent around the front of the van. Tire spikes sprang from the pavement beneath us, but the solid tires of the van rolled right over them. The gate flew to one side as Val hit a hard right and I was nearly thrown out the open side door. I held on to one of the roll-bars for dear life as the black car came out of the open gate behind us.

The car fishtailed before accelerating to give chase. More gunfire chattered off the pavement and sparked along the back of the van. The armored panels kept it from penetrating, and the rear windows cracked in spider-web patterns from bullet impacts, but did not shatter.

"If they're trying to kill us, they're not doing a very good job," Hammer yelled. "Those sound like pretty low-caliber rounds."

"Maybe you'd prefer they used assault rifles!" Boom shouted back.

Hammer gave a tusky grin. "If they won't, I will." He pulled an AK-97 from underneath one of the bench seats and popped open one of the back doors of the van. Another volley of gunfire sounded, pattering off the back panels. Hammer waited for a pause in the fire, then threw the door open and responded with a long burst of his own, the muzzle-flash lighting up his face.

"Eat this, fraggers!" There followed a squealing of tires and the pursuing car swerved wildly. Hammer tracked his fire up along the hood, and bullets smashed into the tinted windshield, leaving silver spider-web patterns across it.

The car spun into a turn and crashed into a lamp post, which bent over the wreck, spitting sparks over the crumpled front of the car. The van continued down the road, leaving the scene behind.

"Nice work," I said to Hammer, who gave a grunt of satisfaction at the sight of the wreck and pulled the van door closed.

"What the hell happened?" Val asked from the front seat as she negotiated quickly through the darkened streets.

"Beats the hell out of me," I said, slumping down onto one of the bench seats. The after-effects of the effort from banishing the air elemental and putting the gunmen to sleep was catching up on me and my limbs were starting to tremble a bit. "Those guys sure as hell weren't Manadyne security, or Knight Errant, either. Who were they, and how the hell did they know we were going to be there?"

"Rival shadowrunners?" Hammer asked. It happened sometimes. Shadow teams got hired for the same job and ran into each other, but it was rare.

"But why try to kill us?" Boom said.

"They weren't runners," Sloane put in, speaking for the first time since the start of the run. "And they weren't trying to kill us, at least, not at first."

"What do you mean?" I said.

Sloane pushed himself up to a sitting position in the back of the van. "The ones who jumped us in the computer vault were using gel rounds," he said, gesturing to the dark stains on his armored jacket that I had taken to be blood. Some of the rounds had burst on impact, leaving their mark. "They didn't want to hurt us too bad, from the looks of it."

And the air elemental could have just rendered us unconscious, I thought. I originally figured an air elemental would do less damage to the computer equipment than, say, a fire or water elemental, but it was also the least lethal spirit to send to incapacitate a group you wanted taken alive.

"That still doesn't explain who they are," Hammer said, and an idea sprang to mind.

"Garnoff was talking to someone at the party," I said. "A kobun from the Hiramatsu-*gumi*."

"Yakuza?" Hammer said. "Those slags did look Japanese . . ."

"Makes sense," Boom chimed in. "From what you said, Talon, it sounds like the yakuza have an interest in whatever Garnoff is doing. It might be something they don't want Manadyne to know about, either. That's why they sent their own people rather than trust Knight Errant to take care of things."

"Frag, for all we know Garnoff *let* me overhear that conversation between him and Isogi. It was all a trap. But even if he did, how the frag did he know we would hit Manadyne *tonight*?"

Suddenly another thought came to mind. "Trouble. She said something about encountering some ice in the system."

I keyed my headcom. "Comeback Two," I said. "Comeback Two, come in. Are you there? Talk to me." Static crackled over the line.

"Val, we need to get back to the safe house, right now. Trouble's still not responding. She may be hurt, or . . ."

Val shook her head. "Talon, the first thing we need to do is stow this hunk of junk and find some alternate transportation."

"But . . ."

"Listen, Trouble is my friend and I've known her longer

than you have. She can take care of herself. There's nothing we can do for her if Knight Errant picks us up. They may not have stopped us from leaving Manadyne, but you can be sure they've got this thing's description and ID numbers out there already. I know a place where we can stash the van, then we can get back to the safe house. Either Trouble will be chill for a little longer, or else there's nothing we can do for her."

She was right. I nodded and let Val do her job. Feeling exhausted, I slumped back into my seat. I was tired of being jerked around by Garnoff, always being one step behind him. It was time to start fighting fire with fire.

# 12

Despite her sensible advice, I was sure Val was as worried about Trouble as I was, maybe more. We made good time from Route 128 toward the Rox. We stashed the damaged van in a garage Val knew near the highway, then took Val's heavily modified Ford-Canada Bison truck to the safe house. Sloane and Hammer parted company with us at the garage. Hammer wanted to find out more about the team that attacked us at Manadyne and get a feel for how the corp and the authorities were reacting to the intrusion. I wished him luck.

"Take good care of Trouble," he said, leaving unsaid the possibility that she was beyond anyone's care.

Val drove quickly through the streets of Roxbury to get to the safe house, and other traffic quickly cleared the way for the heavy off-road truck. I headed up the stairs and deactivated the security system to get inside.

I found Trouble slumped over her cyberdeck. There was no blood, no outward sign of injury. I turned my vision inward, probing her aura with my astral senses. She was alive, but unconscious, the power of the intrusion countermeasures hidden in the Manadyne system too powerful for the defensive filters programmed into her cyberdeck. Her aura was strong, and I let out a sigh of relief. She was in no physical danger, but what might the ice have done to her mind?

Boom and Val came into the safe house as I prepared to move Trouble from the chair where she was slumped.

"Give me a hand," I said and Boom picked Trouble up in his arms as if she weighed almost nothing. He carried her over to the ratty couch and set her there gently, with a look of concern on his face. Val stood by silently, watching.

"Sorry about this," I said softly to Trouble as I knelt by the couch. I gently touched my fingertips to her forehead and whispered the words of a spell.

I entered Trouble's mind and found a chaotic jumble of images: the electronic vista of the Matrix, seen through her eyes as she waited for the connection to the isolated Manadyne system to open up. A neon tunnel through the blackness of cyberspace as she flew down the connection to the cold-storage system. Surprise and shock at the heavy layers of ice protecting the system, highly sophisticated programs, but not deadly ones. A struggle. Trouble being overwhelmed by a horde of ice, dragging her down, down into blackness.

I reached out and tried to still the storm of images, bringing a sense of peace and calm to her mind. I looked carefully for any damage and found none. Her thoughts indicated nothing more than a deep sleep. There was something else, but it didn't look like damage from ice. I brushed along the edges of it, not wanting to invade Trouble's privacy any more than I already had. I looked around carefully and noted some things for future reference.

After what seemed like an eternity, I withdrew from Trouble's mind and opened my eyes. My muscles felt cramped and my hands shook a bit from the strain of the spell. Boom was immediately at my side, helping me to my feet. Val pressed a cup of something warm into my hands, and I sipped the sweet soykaf gratefully.

"How long?" I asked Boom.

"About twenty minutes or so," the troll said.

It seemed like days. I collapsed into the chair Trouble had vacated by the table and sipped the soykaf some more. "She's fine," I said. "The ice didn't do any damage, just knocked her for a loop. All she needs is to sleep it off."

"I'd recommend the same thing for you," Val said. She brought out a blanket and laid it carefully over Trouble, making sure she was covered. "Gel rounds. Non-lethal ice. No response by Knight Errant yet. It sure seems like someone is trying to make things easy on us."

"Yeah," I said, "that's what's worrying me." I pushed myself out of the chair with some effort. "I think I'm going to take your advice and crash for a little while. Boom, there's something I need you to do."

I explained what I had in mind to the troll, and he said he'd do what he could, but made no promises. With that, I crawled onto a cot in the corner of the safehouse, without even removing my boots or my armored jacket. The last thing I remembered was someone draping a blanket over me before sleep claimed me.

I woke feeling considerably better and heard someone coming into the safehouse. I was totally awake in an instant, but I relaxed when I saw Boom closing the door behind him, carrying several paper sacks that gave off a smell that made my mouth water and my stomach rumble. I had no idea how long it had been since I'd last eaten. Hammer and Sloane came in behind him, looking pretty tired. I felt a bit guilty for sleeping while everyone else kept working.

"Rise and shine," the troll said, spreading the contents

of the sacks on the card table in the middle of the room. "Breakfast is served."

I called up a time-display on my headware, and a cool blue number appeared, glowing at the corner of my vision. It was 11:14:03 A.M.

Over a late breakfast of hotcakes, soy sausages, and coffee we talked about the aftermath of the Manadyne business. Trouble was awake and feeling no ill-effects from her Matrix run the previous night.

"Even my deck looks clean," she said. "But I still want to run some more diagnostics to make sure there aren't any nasty surprises hidden there."

"That's the thing I don't get," I said, spearing another soy link with my fork. "Everything that happened says that Garnoff, or somebody, *knew* we were going to hit Manadyne last night. Yakuza or not, the people who jumped us weren't regular security or Knight Errant. They must have known we were coming. Yet they only used gel rounds. They must have wanted to take us alive."

"Dead men tell no tales," Sloane said. "They probably wanted some bodies to interrogate."

"Maybe," I said, "but who were they, and why did they want to capture us?"

"Don't know about the why," Hammer said. He and Boom were each putting away as much food as the rest of us combined. "But I've got some more scan on the who. Word on the street is that the op was set up by the Hiramatsu-*gumi,* just like you suspected, Talon. Seems the oyabun is none too pleased with how things turned out. I'll bet some yak fingers are coming off over this one."

"Then it's definitely yakuza," I said slowly. "And that means Garnoff. The question is: what's the yakuza's real interest in all of this? They've got some kind of deal going with Garnoff, obviously. Do the Boston yaks have any other ties to Manadyne?"

"They don't, as far as I know," Trouble said, "but I found somebody who does: MCT." Mitsuhama Computer Technologies was one of the top megacorporations in the world. They were best known for their computer hardware and software products, but MCT was also one of the major corporations in the field of magical research and development. There were also persistent rumors linking MCT with the yakuza.

"Mitsuhama and Manadyne are working together on a top-secret research project involving exploration and mapping of the astral plane," Trouble continued. "And guess who's the head of that project? None other than Dr. Anton Garnoff. It seems Mitsuhama has a fair amount of money invested in the whole thing."

"And Garnoff was talking to a Hiramatsu kobun at the Manadyne party the other night about his project," I thought aloud. "MCT is running some scam behind Manadyne's back, and Garnoff is in on it. That explains why he'd call in the yakuza rather than turn to corporate security. He doesn't want Manadyne to know what he's up to."

"Talon, didn't you go to MIT&T on an MCT scholarship?" Trouble asked. "Maybe that's the connection. Maybe it's Mitsuhama that's pulling Garnoff's strings."

I shrugged. "Still doesn't explain why MCT would be interested in me, or what it has to do with Garnoff's pet project."

"Wait a second," Val interrupted as she came in from the kitchen, carrying another pot of soykaf. "If MCT paid for you to go to school, why aren't you working for them right now? Most of those corporate education deals usually involve some kind of lifetime contract, don't they?"

"Yeah, they do," I said. "But I managed to get out of it. I arranged to get caught cheating on a major exam and the Institute expelled me. I had to pay back all the money the corp sank into my education up to that point as part of the contract's default clause, but I'd already been doing some shadowrunning on the side and had enough nuyen stashed away. I handed it over to MCT and we were quits, although I'm sure they weren't happy about it. It was all legal . . . technically."

"Why did you do it?" Trouble asked.

Boom glanced over at me sympathetically, and I turned to Trouble. "You found out that Jason Vale died because of gang violence," I said. "That's true, as far as it goes. While I was in school I was doing some shadowrunning on the side, strictly small-time stuff back then. A run on an MCT subsidiary netted me more than just the data we went in after. I also found out that Mitsuhama paid to have Jase killed so they could recruit another wagemage off the streets: me. Jase was my teacher, he . . . meant a lot to me. After he died, there was nothing tying me to Southie, so I took MCT's scholarship offer. When I found out the truth, I had to get out. I couldn't work for the corp that killed Jase. I never found out who was involved, but I never worked for MCT after that."

"You never went after them?" Hammer asked.

"Why?" I said. "What good would it do? Mitsuhama buried their tracks too well. It was pure chance that I found the records of the black-ops nuyen paid to the gangers. Taking on a whole megacorp would have been pure suicide, and I was pretty sick of revenge already."

I thought of the Asphalt Rats on fire, the smell of burning hair and burning flesh. I remembered standing at the end of the alley and watching them burn. My appetite was suddenly gone. I set down my fork.

"Well," Boom spoke up, breaking the moment of silence. "We do know the Hiramatsu-*gumi* and Mitsuhama are involved, and that, along with some social wizardry on the part of yours truly, gives us the in we need to call in some extra help."

# 13

Kelly's was an old-fashioned Irish pub in South Boston, the kind of place where I would have hung out as a street kid fifteen or so years ago. Just walking in the door brought back memories of my old turf and all of the people I used to know. The interior was dimly lit and smelled strongly of smoke, scotch whiskey, and sweat. It was an honest place, with no pretense of being anything other than what it was.

Even in the late afternoon, many of the tables were occupied. The regulars looked at us with no small amount of suspicion and distrust, but they carefully minded their own business. I'm sure the presence of the big troll watching my back had a lot to do with it.

I walked over to the bar and ordered a couple of beers, slapping some scrip on the countertop to cover them, along with a generous tip. The bartender took the bills without comment and waved us toward a table in the back of the room. I sat where I could see the length of the pub and keep an eye on the door. Boom sat watching the rear area. The beer was good, and made me realize how much I missed some parts of my old life in Boston.

"You should probably let me do the talking at first, term," Boom said. His Cockney accent was back in evidence, although I suspected it would disappear again when there was a need. "The man's interested, but he doesn't know you from a hole in the wall. I think I can get on his good side."

"Okay," I said. "I'll leave it to your courtly charms. I'm still impressed you managed to set up this meeting."

"We've got something he's interested in," the troll said. "And I've done him a few favors in the last couple of years. He owes me at least this much." It was still so hard to think of Boom as a fixer, dealing in favors, services, and information, rather than as the down and dirty shadow-runner I used to know.

The door of the pub opened and a dark figure appeared, silhouetted for a moment against the brightness outside. He scanned the room before allowing the door to swing closed. Even in the dimness, he wore a pair of dark shades that I was sure covered cybereyes capable of adjusting to any level of gloom. His suit was dark and conservative, neatly pressed, with creases sharp enough to shave with. The cut of the jacket almost completely concealed the slight bulge of the holster under his arm. I wondered for a moment if he and Boom frequented the same tailor.

He walked up to the table with purpose in his stride. I felt Boom tense slightly beside me and I did the same, ready for the possibility of a double-cross, but none came. The razorboy looked us over from behind his shades.

He said simply, "My boss is waiting."

Boom and I exchanged a look, then rose and followed the razorboy out of the pub. Parked in front was a dark Rolls Royce Phaeton limousine, its engine running. The back door opened silently and Boom gestured toward it.

"After you," he said. The Cockney accent was gone,

replaced by one that was more an amalgam of the faint Irish and Italian accents found in South Boston. I climbed into the car, followed by the troll. It was a bit of a tight fit for Boom, even in the spacious interior of a Phaeton. A smoked glass barrier separated the back of the limo from the front. The door closed behind Boom and, a moment later, the car pulled smoothly away from the curb.

Seated in the back of the limousine was an elf with dark hair neatly slicked back from a high forehead, falling just short of the white collar of his shirt. He wore a dark suit and a green and gold silk tie worked with Celtic knot patterns. As with many elves, it was nearly impossible to guess his age. He hovered in that ageless elven range between twenty and who knows how old. His green eyes, however, were mature and his gaze steady. He took us in carefully, sizing us up.

"Gentlemen," said Conor O'Rilley, the don of the Boston Mafia, "I understand you have some information for me." His accent was faintly Irish, giving a slight lilt to his vowels.

"That's right," Boom said. The troll's presence seemed to fill the small space as much as his bulk. I suddenly realized that I wouldn't want to find myself having to negotiate with him in a confined space like this. "It's about the Hiramatsu-*gumi*'s involvement with Manadyne."

"I've heard," O'Rilley replied. "Hiramatsu has ties to Mitsuhama here in Boston, and MCT is working with Manadyne on a project."

"Yes, but it looks like there may be some kind of private deal going on between the yaks and Manadyne," Boom said. "Whatever it is, you can be sure Hiramatsu is planning to use the leverage to expand yakuza operations in town. That is the New Way, after all."

O'Rilley's face darkened. He clearly wasn't pleased by the idea. Boston was a Mafia stronghold in northeastern UCAS, but the influence of the yakuza was growing just about everywhere, and plenty of Mafia bosses were feeling the pressure.

The New Way was a yakuza movement that had begun along the East Coast, down in New Jersey, with the Honjowara-*gumi*. Honjowara—and their corporate interests, the Nagato Combine—had broken with yakuza tradition by allowing women and metahumans into their ranks. The Honjowara oyabun's own honor guard was made up of a group of elven adepts specially trained to protect him. The New Way also included embracing magic, something the yakuza had traditionally shunned or treated as an afterthought.

Since the Mafia was often superstitious, they too tended to shun magic and metahumans. Conor O'Rilley was the only metahuman don in the Cosa Nostra, and he knew firsthand the advantages of magic and metahumans in a mob operation. The fact that the Hiramatsu yakuza were catching on to the same idea had to be a concern for him.

"What do you want from me?" he asked.

I took the opportunity to speak up. "I have a personal matter to settle. In return for some information, we will pass on whatever we learn about the yakuza and their operation. They, or their allies, have decided to target me for some reason, and I aim to find out why. If the yaks get in the way of the truth, then I'll have to deal with them."

"Are you asking me to go to war with the yakuza?" O'Rilley said in a tightly controlled voice.

"No. I may be helping you to *avoid* a war with the yaks, at least for now. If Hiramatsu is in with Mitsuhama and they're working on a deal, it can only hurt your position. I want to put a stop to that. In return, I need what you know about the Hiramatsu-*gumi* and their allies."

O'Rilley considered for a few seconds, his green elven eyes intent on me. "Well, then," he said with a pleasant smile. "I'm always willing to help out someone who wants to hurt Hiramatsu. I'll give you what I have on the yakuza operations in the plex, but if you tangle with the Hiramatsu-*gumi* and they hand you your head, then I never heard of you."

"Fair enough," I said.

A few moments later, the limo pulled over. The Don reached into the inside pocket of his jacket and handed me an optical chip. The door of the car opened and Boom climbed out, followed by me.

"A pleasure doing business with you," I said.

"One more thing," O'Rilley said with a hint of steel in his tone. "If I find out that my information has gone wandering, you and I will have another . . . talk."

The Mafia razorboy gave me a wolfish smile as he got into the limo alongside his boss, pulling the door shut. Then the Phaeton pulled away.


"So, how'd it go?" Trouble asked. I had the visual-feed on my headphone turned off so I could concentrate on driving while I talked. The East Coast quake of 2005 may have sparked a lot of urban renewal and renovation in Boston, but the streets were still as tangled and congested as ever, probably more so.

"It went," I said. "O'Rilley gave us what the Mafia has on the local yakuza, including the Hiramatsu-*gumi*. It's not a whole lot, but it looks like Hiramatsu is the big fish in the small yakuza pond in Boston. They also have some definite ties to Mitsuhama."

Rumors about MCT's ties to the powerful Japanese yakuza clans abounded in the shadows, but Mitsuhama kept a tight lid on such things. No one was able to *prove* that the major backers of the corp were actually mobsters, using Mitsuhama as a legitimate business front to launder some of their ill-gotten gains, a "front" that had grown far beyond any of its founders' expectations.

"Isogi, the slag who was talking to Garnoff at the party, is Hiramatsu-*sama*'s right-hand man," I said. "Whatever is going on, the yakuza are in deep on it. How's it going on your end?"

"Still doing some fishing in the corporate databases. Mitsuhama has seriously upgraded their ice in the past couple of years. Hell, everybody has since Renraku's network was compromised. It's made all of the corps ultra-paranoid about Matrix security. So far, if MCT knows about any top-secret operations involving Manadyne, they've managed to hide the connections pretty well. I'll keep looking, and hopefully I'll have something by the time you guys get back."

"Wizard," I said. "See you soon."

"So?" Boom asked when I disconnected the cellular link.

"She's still looking."

"She's good. If there's anything to find, she'll find it. In the meantime, why don't you drop me off at the club? I'll do some more asking around and there's some other business that's kind of been piling up." I realized that, as a fixer, Boom probably had a lot of irons in the fire, not just my problems to worry about.

"Sorry about taking up all your time, chummer," I said.

"Talon, this is me you're talking to, okay? We've put

our lives on the line for each other before. There's nothing else going on that I can't handle. There aren't enough people in the shadow-business these days who understand what loyalty means, term. Don't worry about it."

"Okay," I said.

"So," Boom said, changing the subject as he idly looked out the window of the car. "Are you going to tell me what's bothering you about Trouble?"

I nearly swerved into the wrong lane.

"What are you talking about?" I said.

"Oh, c'mon, Talon! I'm a bloody troll, not an idiot. I've made a profitable career out of reading people, you know. I can tell there's some tension where she's concerned. I can also tell that she likes you . . . a lot. What is it about her that bothers you so much?"

I thought about it some before answering.

"Honestly? I just don't know, chummer. I like her too. She's a good runner and a good person. There aren't nearly enough in this line of work. But there's something else. Something I noticed."

"What?" Boom asked.

"I'd rather not say until I'm sure," I said. "It might be nothing. It's always hard to tell with magic whether you're seeing something that's really there or it's just your imagination getting away with you."

I glanced over at the concerned expression on my friend's face. "Don't worry. If I figure it out, you'll be the first to know."

"You should probably have a talk with her anyway," Boom said.

"Why?"

"Because she's interested in you, term. Don't you see it?"

I shrugged. "I dunno what you're talking about. She's a lot more charmed by your smooth-talking."

Boom shook his head. "I don't think so, Talon. Charming as I may be, I don't think Trouble is the type who goes for trolls. She's got her eye on you, mark my words. You haven't told her yet, have you?"

"No," I said. "It never came up. It's not important. This is a professional relationship."

"I think you might want to mention it," Boom said. "Before things go any further."

"Okay, okay, I'll think about it," I said. That seemed to satisfy him for the time being.

I dropped Boom off and he promised to come by the safe house later. When I got back there, Trouble was sitting on the couch, jacked into her deck. I hoped she was making more progress that I had and went to the little tabletop fridge to get something to drink. You don't disturb a decker while she's working any more than you mess around with a mage while he's doing magic. It was best to leave the experts alone to do their thing.

A gasp from Trouble almost made me drop my can of Tribal Tropics. I saw her muscles tense up for a second as her fingers flew faster across the deck's keyboard. Frag. Was it ice? Was it dangerous? For a split second I thought of jacking her out, but decided that would probably do more harm than good. Trouble was a grown-up and she knew what she was doing.

So fraggin' much of shadowrunning involved watching over a chummer's meatbody while he was off doing something in cyberspace, astral space, or remote-land without you having a clue of what to do if something went wrong. I shifted to my astral senses, hoping they might tell me something if she was in danger from lethal ice or the like.

Her aura looked strong and stable. There was a high level of tension and euphoria that I've learned to associate with deckers in the 'trix. I watched for a moment, studying her aura. I hadn't really had much of a chance to up until now. A few seconds later there was a burst of smug satisfaction as she tapped several more keys and jacked out.

I let my astral sight drop away and went over to her. "Any luck?"

"Maybe." She slid the deck's roll-out viewscreen into place and tapped a couple of keys. A long series of notes, symbols, and diagrams scrolled past.

"What do you make of it?" she asked.

I shook my head and reached out to pull the deck a bit closer where I could see the display. "I'm not sure. It looks like some notes on astral modeling, using a multidimensional structure. I'll need some time to look it over. Where did you get it?"

"From Garnoff's files."

"In Manadyne? How did you access the isolated system from here?"

She shook her head. "Not Manadyne, Mitsuhama. Garnoff has been filing regular reports with them. It looks like he actually works for them."

"Mitsuhama? Doesn't he work for Manadyne?"

"Might look that way on paper, but from what I pried out of the MCT system, Garnoff has worked for them for years. He's just on loan to Manadyne for this joint project, although I don't know if Manadyne knows that the arrangement is strictly temporary."

"You got this out of the MCT system? No wonder it looked like rough sailing for a while there."

"I told you, Talon. I can take care of myself."

"I know, I know, I was just . . ."

"It's sweet that you worry," she said with a smile.

"I just think you should be careful."

Trouble smiled and her eyes sparkled wickedly. "Sometimes taking risks is more fun. Don't you think?"

The kiss was totally unexpected. When her lips pressed against mine, I froze and tensed up a bit. Trouble broke the kiss and backed away, a hint of concern in her green eyes.

"What is it?" she asked.

I got up off the couch and moved over to stand behind a nearby chair, resting my hands on the back. "Nothing, that was just kind of . . . unexpected."

"Don't you like surprises?" Trouble asked playfully, a note of concern coming into her voice.

"It's not that. I just don't think it's a good idea."

"Don't tell me, let me guess," she said. "You never get involved with a teammate."

"Not exactly, I . . ."

Just then the doorknob turned. I thanked the gods for the interruption, but as soon as I got a look at Boom's stone-cold-sober features, I knew there was a problem. As I reached for the Ares Viper under my coat, two big orks pushed into the room behind Boom and leveled the big handguns they were carrying at us.

Boom cleared his throat. "Um, Talon. There's some guys here who want to talk to you . . ."

# 14

The tunnels the orks guided us through were in a part of
the T-system that was closed down a long time ago, maybe
even before the Awakening. The only light came from
the faintly glowing lichens and mosses that grew on the
cracked, damp concrete, so Trouble and I stayed close together and moved carefully. Boom and the orks, with their
natural thermographic vision, had no difficulty negotiat-
ing the tunnels.

For a moment I almost regretted not getting cybereyes
along with the rest of my 'ware. I'd thought about it, but
the idea of having my natural eyes cut out and replaced
with cameras was just too much for me. I knew a lot of
people who had cybereyes and there was something disquieting about them, like they'd shuttered over the windows to their spirit.

I still wasn't sure where we were going or why, but I
knew we were safe for the moment. The orks who guided
us were members of a gang with the rather incongruous
name of Mama's Boys. It was a well known fact, even
when I was last in Boston, that the Boys worked for a
mysterious shadow-fixer known only as "Mama." Almost
nothing else was known about her, except the fact that
she was top-class, a virtual legend in the shadows. Now it

seemed this mysterious power-broker had taken an interest in us, or in me, at least.

With a grunt that passed for intelligible speech, Jambone ordered us to stop. The ork leader had to be the ugliest thing on two legs I'd ever seen, and that was saying a hell of a lot. His greasy dark skin was covered with warts and lumpy nodules that looked like dermal bone deposits. His muscles were thick, ropy, and heavily veined. What hair he had stood up in stiff, bristled clumps like a brush and his flared ears sported several earrings each. A nosering and a matching silver cap on one tusk completed the whole ensemble. He was one scary-looking fragger, like a creature out of a fairy tale made into a ganger.

The big ork made his way around a pile of brick and concrete from a collapsed part of the tunnel wall. A moment later, he reappeared and gestured for us to follow. Set in the tunnel wall was a heavy steel door with a hand-turned wheel in the middle of it, like an old fashioned airlock. Jambone barked a command in guttertalk, and the other two ork gangers grabbed the wheel and turned it with a squeak that echoed in the tunnel. With a dull "clunk" the door opened.

Jambone made an exaggerated bow and waved his hand toward the entrance. "Mama Iaga is waiting for you."

The creature on the other side of the door blew away Jambone's position as the ugliest thing on two legs I'd ever seen in a heartbeat. He—I'm fairly sure it was male—was probably a troll, nearly three meters tall, with bulging muscles. Where Boom's appearance, and that of most trolls, was something I'd gotten used to, this thing was something else altogether. His skin was fish-belly white, covered with thick, dermal bone deposits like the shell of some subterranean insect, making him look almost like he was carved out of rough, white limestone. Three curling horns sprouted from his domed head, and tiny pink eyes glared out from under beetled brows. He wore nothing but a simple loincloth of ragged black fabric. Silently sizing us up, he took a single step back from the door to allow us to enter. A brick-lined tunnel went off to the right-hand side. We walked down it, with the pale troll following behind.

The tunnel was lit by lamps glowing with a pale yellow light. It ended in a thick velvet curtain. I reached out and moved it aside.

"Bloody hell . . ." Boom whispered as we entered.

The chamber beyond the curtain was like stepping into another time. The large room was filled with graceful, Victorian-style furniture, all dark wood and plush burgundy upholstery. Heavy velvet drapes covered the walls, with gold brocade edging and cords. A fire burning in a gray marble hearth chased away the chill of the dark tunnels and cast a warm glow on the various small objects of brass and crystal scattered about on shelves and tables.

The steel door closed behind us with a clang that made me jump. With the door shut, the only sound in the room came from an antique phonograph that played soft classical music filled with haunting flutes and violins. It was easy to imagine that we were in the private estate of some wealthy eccentric on Beacon Hill rather than deep below the streets of the metroplex. The place had an odd feeling to it, like a museum rather than a place where someone lived.

The pale man-mountain followed us into the room and stood by the entrance like a silent statue, watching us.

The draperies rustled off to the left and a figure entered, as silent as a shadow. She wore a black velvet gown whose folds covered her from neck to ankles. Around her slender waist was a belt of knotted cord holding a number of small pouches and trinkets, dark feathers, and carved bones that dangled and clicked quietly as she moved. A jewel-toned shawl was draped over her bony shoulders and head like a kerchief.

The hands that clutched the ends of the shawl were skeletal thin, like the rest of her figure, the bony claws covered with scabrous gray skin. Faint traceries of lines formed the shapes of strange runes across them.

Her face was like that of all the classic fairy-tale witches molded into one. Thin and gaunt, with a hooked nose and dark, deep-set eyes that glittered like black stones, a pointed chin, and thin lips that pulled back in a smile to reveal sharp, yellow teeth. Wisps of brittle white hair escaped the confining kerchief in places. When she spoke it was a high, thin voice that sounded like it might break into a maniacal cackle any moment. She had a strange accent I couldn't place. It sounded vaguely European or Slavic, but I couldn't be sure.

"I am Mama. Welcome to my parlor, dear children. Please, please, make yourselves comfortable," she said. I threw a glance at Boom and Trouble, then chose a straight-backed chair near the hearth. Trouble sat in its mate on the other side of the small table between them while Boom gently lowered himself onto the wide sofa. Our hostess ensconced herself in a wing-backed leather chair on the opposite side of the fireplace whose flickering flames cast her features in strange dancing shadows.

"Would you care for any . . . refreshment?" she asked.

Boom cleared his throat, but I shook my head. "No thanks." All I could think of was stories of people eating or drinking in the Otherworld and never being able to leave. In the Sixth World, myths had a disturbing way of coming true, so it was best to err on the side of caution.

Our hostess showed her toothy smile again and laughed, a high, thin sound. "Are you certain? I do have some things that you might like, which are not suited to my taste."

"Thank you, but I would rather get to the reason you asked us here, ma'am."

"Please call me 'Mama,' my dear, as my darling boys do. As to why I wanted to see your handsome face in my humble home, I think that we have a common interest."

"Garnoff?" Trouble asked, and the old woman favored her with a shark-like grin.

"Yes, the little mage . . . and the one he serves."

"You mean Mitsuhama?" I said.

The old woman spat into the fire with a hiss. "Pah! Moneygrubbers and bean-counters! They know nothing of the old ways or of the paths of the Otherworlds. No, Garnoff's master is even less an inhabitant of the sunlit world than I, and has even less claim on the title of living creature."

"Then Garnoff isn't doing this for the corp?" I said. That put a whole different spin on things. Whatever Garnoff's scam was, I'd assumed it was some kind of corporate operation, perhaps a deal with the yakuza on the side.

"Oh, no, my sweetling. If anything, it is he who is manipulating his corporate masters where you are concerned. Just as he manipulated events to bring you into his company's service all those years ago."

"What?" I said. I felt the blood drain away from my face and I sank back into the chair, stunned.

"Didn't you know?" Mama said casually. "No, I suppose not. Garnoff recognized your Talent and wanted you for MCT, but you had already come under Jason's protection by then."

"You knew Jase?"

"I know everyone of importance, boychik, and your teacher was known in parts of the Catacombs."

"Mitsuhama offered me a scholarship," I said, thinking aloud. "A chance to get out of the Rox. But after all Jase did, after we . . . I couldn't leave. So they killed him. And Garnoff was the one?" I asked. Mama nodded.

"Half a mo 'ere, Talon. What the bloody 'ell are you talkin' about?" Boom asked. His accent grew particularly strong when he was nervous. Apparently, the setting was unnerving him as much as it was me. I figured I might as well fill everyone in on the whole story.

"While I was with Jase, this recruiter from Mitsuhama offered me a scholarship to MIT&T, with the usual corporate indenture to follow. I told him to go frag. I wanted to stay in the Rox with Jase, to use my Talent to do something other than provide magical security and research for a megacorp.

"A couple of weeks later, Jase got killed in an incident of 'random' gang violence. I was so fragged up by it, I never even considered a connection. It was the Rox, people got cacked by gangs every day.

"I dug up the card the MCT guy gave me and told him I'd take his offer. There was no reason for me to say in the Rox after Jase died, and I wanted to put the whole thing behind me."

I took a deep breath and turned back toward Mama Iaga, who sat perched on the edge of her chair like a vulture, digesting the choice morsels of information I had just fed her.

"You're saying Garnoff was behind all of this? He's the one who arranged it?"

Mama gave a tight-lipped smile and nodded.

I slowly shook my head. "Why?"

The old crone settled back into the embrace of her chair, almost vanishing into its shadowy recesses. She folded her hands in her lap and licked her dry lips as she pondered a moment before replying.

"Garnoff acts for the best reason of all, my dear: power. He desires power over others. That is why he works to improve his lot with his corporate masters and why he sought to recruit you to serve him. His thirst for power led him to explore the dark paths, made him open to the call. Garnoff discovered something here in the depths of the Catacombs, a kindred spirit that spoke to him of a common cause. All Garnoff's efforts have been turned toward supporting his new patron, providing it with what it needs to grow strong and in turn provide him with greater and greater power."

"The killings," I said, recalling the news report. "The murders, down in the subway."

Mama nodded and her grotesque smile grew wider. "Blood calls to blood as power calls to power."

"Garnoff is using blood magic," I said, and Mama nodded again. "Oh, gods."

Every magician knew about blood magic. It was one of the first things they warned you about when you began learning to use the Talent. Magic and life were strongly connected. With the right rituals, it was possible to draw magical power from the life force of living things, killing them in the process. The rituals were dangerous because they nearly always corrupted the user. So much of magic was a matter of mindset, and the mindset required to murder in cold blood simply to gather power was pure madness.

I thought about some of the things I'd seen when I first joined Assets for the Dragon Heart run—the Aztechnology magicians with their blood-soaked altars, the terrible rituals they used to gather the power they craved—and shuddered.

"But why *me*?" I said. "I haven't been back to Boston for years. Why did Garnoff come after me after all this time? Revenge?"

"He needs you, *it* needs you," Mama said, her voice falling to a hoarse whisper. "Without you, the circle cannot be closed, and all his efforts will be for nothing. He wants you alive, for now."

"For what?" I asked.

Mama glanced into the depths of the fireplace, the orange and yellow flames reflecting in her dark eyes. "There are some things you must discover for yourself, Talon." It was the first time she'd used my name, and it sent a shiver down my spine. "Do you understand the power of true names?"

"I know a true name grants power over the thing it names," I said. "Especially powerful spirits, who hide their true names. They can be used to enslave them. Every magician learns that."

"Then you must seek the true name of the mystery at the heart of this," Mama said. "Garnoff found his power while exploring the depths of the Otherworld."

"You mean the metaplanes?" I asked.

Mama waved one bony hand in a dismissive gesture. "The metaplanes—such a foolish name. The Otherworld, the Second Road, the Twilight Realm, the Nether World,

Heaven, Hell, call it what you will, that is where the secret lies. You can find it. All you need is a map to guide
your way."

"Do you have it?" I asked.

"No," she said, "but I know who does."

"Wait a nanosec," Trouble interrupted, turning toward
Mama. "What do you get out of this? What's this paydata
going to cost us?"

The old woman made a face that was a mocking parody
of girlish embarrassment. "Let us simply say there is
limited room in the jungle of the Catacombs. Too many
predators can strip away all the prey and lead to starva-
tion for all. When one predator enters another's hunting
ground unbidden, a struggle to the death ensues and only
the strongest survives. I offer you the chance go from being sheep to wolves, from hunted to hunters."

"A chance to do your dirty work for you?" Trouble said.

Mama Iaga's predatory grin grew wider until I thought
it would split her face in two. "Of course, my dear. Isn't
that what shadowrunners are for?"

A plan suddenly came to mind. It was risky, but it was
the only way I could see to get to the bottom of all this.
Mama Iaga provided the inspiration and Garnoff had in-
advertently supplied the means. I glanced over at Trouble and gave what I hoped was a reassuring look, then
turned back to Mama.

"Tell me where I can get the map," I told Mama. "If
I'm going into hell, I should at least know how to get
there."

# 15

"Well, *that* was interesting," Boom said once we made it back to the safe house. He was always a master of understatement. "Now what?"

"The first thing we need is a new place to hang," I said. "Mama may keep our location to herself because she wants something from us, but I don't trust her for a second. I'd rather we were someplace she didn't know about."

"Gotcha," Boom said. "I can make a couple of calls and have another place inside of an hour."

"Good," I said. "Tell Hammer and Sloane to meet us there and I'll fill everybody in on my plan."

True to his word, Boom had a new safe house arranged within the hour. This one was a bit farther from the Rox, in South Boston, near the old neighborhood where I grew up. I decided to take it as a good sign. Driving through the area certainly brought back memories, not all of them unpleasant.

On the drive, I thought about what Mama Iaga had said about Jase and why Garnoff was interested in me, specifically. If it was true, the man was a rogue, running his own scheme behind the scenes using the resources of both Manadyne and Mitsuhama, not to mention the yakuza, to cover it all up. That made things both easier and harder for us. Easier because Garnoff would be even more cautious than we were about getting caught. If the big boys in the corps found out what he was up to, they would probably shut him down and Garnoff would be "reassigned" to where his employers could keep a watchful eye on him. Assuming, of course, that they didn't just kill him outright. On the other hand, if Garnoff was running his own shadow operation, it must be very well-hidden to avoid the notice of the corps so far. Which was going to make it that much harder to ferret out if what I had in mind didn't work.

Val pulled the van up in front of the address Boom gave her, and the troll rolled the door open with a theatrical flourish.

"Here you go, terms," he said. "One new hideout, as requested."

"You have *got* to be kidding," Trouble said, looking out the open door at our new safe house.

The building had once been a church, and most of it was still standing. The walls were heavy stonework, blackened in places and covered in graffiti and gang symbols. There was a narrow steeple that may have once housed a belfry, which stood like a ragged stump on top of the structure. The door and the windows were boarded up with heavy sheets of gray construction plastic and plastered with "CONDEMNED" signs.

Around the building stood a small yard heavily overgrown with weeds that were encroaching on the cracked concrete path leading up to the front steps. Around the yard was a rusting wrought-iron fence topped with sharp spikes. A heavy padlock and chain held the front gate closed, and another "CONDEMNED" sign hung across the gate.

"A church?" Trouble said, echoing her earlier disbelief.

"A *former* church," Boom corrected. "It was seriously damaged during the quake and condemned by the city. Rather than spend the money to rebuild it, the church de-consecrated it and built a new one a few kilometers away. It's been slated to be torn down forever, but it's so far down on the municipal reconstruction and reclamation projects list that they won't get to it for another twenty years at least. A contact of mine in the Department of Public Works passed me a list of potential sites. This looked like the best one.

"A real-estate development company is supposed to be looking at it as a possible building site over the next few weeks, which should cover us with any city officials who might wonder why there's activity around here. The best news is that the power and water in the place still work and I've got them turned on, for a while, at least."

A church. I decided to take that as a good omen as well, with only a momentary flinch of concern over blasphemy or desecration. Boom said it was de-consecrated, after all, and I wasn't Catholic—not by a long shot—but being raised by Catholics as a kid still leaves a strong impression. Old habits die hard.

"Good job, Boom," I said, shouldering my gear. "Let's check it out and get to work."

The interior of the church building was nearly bare of any furnishings, but we tossed down temprafoam pads from the van and set up our gear in the vestry. The van was concealed in the alley behind the building, where it wouldn't be easily visible from the street. Hammer and Sloane arrived in short order and brought Chinese food

with them (more of Boom's good planning, I suspected).
Soon we were sitting on the floor of the vestry, chowing
down on noodles and kung pao chicken as I told everyone my plan. As I suspected, some people didn't like it.

"It's crazy, Talon!" Trouble said for about the fifth
time. "It'll never work."

"I think it will," I said, trying to stay calm and reasonable. "It's our best chance to get at Garnoff."

"Do you really trust that old hag?" she asked.

I shook my head. "No, but I do trust her greed and her
desire to get rid of Garnoff without having to dirty her
own hands. She was honest enough about that."

"She might just want you both out of the way! Did that
ever occur to you?" Trouble said. Actually it *had* occurred to me, but I wasn't going to mention it right then.

"Mama is a lot of things," Hammer said, "but she's got
a reputation for doing business fairly. You don't get the
kind of shadow rep she's got by slotting over everyone
you meet. If Talon thinks she's on the level, then I'm willing to go along with the rest of the plan."

Sloane sort of nodded and shrugged. "You're the boss,
Talon. We'll do whatever you say. Your call."

I glanced over at Boom. The troll looked me square in
the eyes. "It sounds risky," he said.

"It is."

"Do you really think it'll work?"

"I still think it's our best shot." It obviously wasn't
quite the answer he wanted to hear.

"All right," he said. "Let's do it."

Lastly, I turned back to Trouble.

"You don't make things easy, do you?" she said.

"I need everybody for this," I said. "Especially you.
Are you in?"

She bit her lip and stared at me for a second. I wondered what was going through her head. We'd never had a chance to finish the conversation we started back at the other safe house, before the Mama's Boys interrupted. I wondered if it had any effect on her decision.

"Okay, I'm in."

"Good," I said. "Here's what we need to do."

Dr. Alan Gordon was a brilliant man once. He had been a celebrated member of the staff at MIT&T when I was a student there, a Professor of Thaumaturgy specializing in astral theory and the study of the complex, multidimensional structure of astral space. I remembered sitting in his class entranced at the way his mind worked. He seemed able to understand the most intricate interrelationships between the different layers and levels of the astral planes with ease, opening up literal new worlds to his students and colleagues. It wasn't just his intelligence and insight that made him a popular teacher, but his charm and his infectious enthusiasm for his work.

A year or two after I left the Institute, not long after I left Boston altogether, I heard that Gordon had been committed to a mental institution, after having some kind of fit. The Institute press release claimed it was due to stress from overwork and the pressures of academic life. I hadn't really given my old teacher a second thought in years, so I was understandably surprised when Mama gave me his name as the man who could provide the map I needed. I was even more surprised when she provided an address in the Rox, the worst area in the sprawl.

"Are you sure this is the place?" Boom asked as we entered the foyer of the building. He insisted on coming with me and I was glad for the company. The air stank of

decay and human refuse, and the only light in the stair-
well came from a bare bulb hanging from a cord near the
very top, casting long shadows behind us.

"This is where Mama said he was." The place was eerily
quiet. There was no sound of other tenants, screaming children, arguing adults, none of the noises I generally associated with a place where people lived. I kept my hand
close to the gun concealed under my long coat, just in case.

"Explain to me again why you need a map to go somewhere in a dream that doesn't even really exist in the first
place," Boom said as we climbed the rickety steps of the
tenement building.

"The metaplanes exist, chummer," I said. "They're just
on a completely different level of reality. They're vast,
maybe even infinite. Nobody really knows. If I'm going
to find what we need, I've got to have an idea of where to
start looking for it. That's where the map comes in. It's
not exactly a map, per se, more like a kind of ritual guide."

Boom just shook his head and muttered something under his breath about "fragging magicians."

At the third floor, we turned down the hall toward
apartment 23. The "2" hung upside down by only a single
nail, while the "3" was only in evidence from the lighter
shade of wood where the number had once been.

With a look of caution at Boom I knocked lightly on
the door. We both tensed and waited, but there was nothing. I rapped again.

"Dr. Gordon?" I said, then knocked a third time.

"Go away!" a voice shouted through the door. "I'm
not bothering anyone!"

"Dr. Gordon," I said again. "We need to talk to you."

"I don't talk to anyone. Now go away or I'll place a
curse on you!"

Boom looked at me in alarm. "Can he do that?" he asked in a whisper.

I shook my head. "I doubt it."

"Hope you're right . . . fragging magicians," Boom muttered again as I turned back to the door. I was tempted to simply break it down but I needed Gordon's cooperation and I preferred not to get it by force. Also, as much as I tried to reassure Boom, I had no idea what the man's magical abilities might be these days. Gordon used to be an accomplished mage and, while I doubted the likelihood of him cursing us, I didn't dismiss the possibility of something equally nasty getting thrown in our direction.

Once more I rapped on the door. "Dr. Gordon, Mama sent us to talk to you. It's very important." Only silence came from the other side of the door. Suddenly the hairs at the base of my neck stood on end and I had the intense feeling of being watched. I fought down all my defensive instincts and tried to stay calm, and the sensation washed over me, then passed. A series of clicks and clatters sounded from the other side of the door, and it swung open to show a face hidden in shadow.

"Come in," he said, stepping back from the door and pulling it open wider. "Enter freely, and of your own will, heh, heh."

The tiny apartment on the other side of the door was dim, lit by a collection of thick candles sitting on metal stands and scattered over nearly every flat surface available. The windows were covered by heavy curtains that sealed out what little daylight could fight its way into the room, as well as the moonlight and the neon glow of the plex. The furniture and nearly everything else in the room was lost under a flood of books and loose papers that were stacked everywhere. I could barely make out a couch, a coffee table, and a desk, all covered with paper. The walls were lined with stacks of plastic crates and with shelves made from loose planks stacked with bricks, all sagging under the weight of old books and stacks and stacks of paper.

"Bloody 'ell," Boom said quietly, "I've never seen so much real paper in my life. Musta killed a whole forest to get this much."

Gordon closed the door behind us and carefully re-engaged at least four different locks before turning to look at us.

"Not easy to get," he said quietly, still standing near the door.

"What?" I asked.

"Paper! Paper!" He suddenly became animated, rushing over to the coffee table to scoop up a handful of the stuff. "Real paper. I don't trust computers, oh no. Don't trust them at all. They have cold spirits, so very cold, and they whisper and say things behind your back. Gateways for ghosts, they are, ghosts in the machine. Paper is real, paper you can hold, touch, trust. Don't ever trust machines. They can turn on you."

As he stood, looking up at me, I got a good look at him for the first time. The transformation was shocking. The Dr. Alan Gordon I remembered was a distinguished, handsome man in his late thirties. The man who stood in front of me, clutching a wad of yellowed paper in his hands, had none of the vitality or poise of the man I knew. His skin hung in sallow, wrinkled folds from his face. Deep lines were etched around his eyes and his mouth, creating dark shadows in the flickering candlelight. His hair was entirely gray and chopped bristle-short on his head, receding from a high forehead that gleamed with sweat in the yellow light.

His clothes were unkempt and loose on his almost skeletal frame. They made him look like a kind of living scarecrow. Around his neck he wore a thin golden chain with a pendant, a five-pointed star within a circle. Seeing it made me think of Jase. I looked up from it and met Dr. Gordon's eyes.

They were strange to look at, his eyes. They were the same pale, icy blue I remembered, but the spark, the hint of genius, was replaced by something else, a wild look, like a cornered animal.

"Dr. Gordon," I said slowly, "I'm Talon . . . Tom . . . do you remember me?"

"Remember you?" he said, as if he'd seen me for the first time. He looked more closely, and I could feel those blue eyes boring into me. They widened for a moment, then he looked away, tightly closing his eyes and pressing his balled-up fists against them.

"No! Can't remember! Mustn't remember!" he cried. He backed away a few steps, throwing his head back like he was silently screaming or having some kind of seizure. I was about to try and reach out to him when Boom touched my arm. He silently shook his head. Gordon slowly lowered his hands and looked around the room like he didn't know where he was.

"Why are you here?" he said.

"Mama sent us," I said slowly.

The mention of the crone fixer's name seemed to make Gordon slightly more coherent. He glanced down at the floor and back up at us. "Mama, yes . . . what did she send you for?"

"A map," I said. "I need to go on a journey, and I need a map."

"A map. Oh, yes, I have maps." With the sweep on one hand, he took in all the piles of paper. "Many, many, many maps. Maps of the city, maps of the subway, even maps of the Catacombs."

"I need a specific map," I said slowly. "Not a map of this world. Mama said you would know which one."

"Ah," Gordon said in a hushed voice. "You want the *other* map. Come with me." Picking up a candle, he scurried into the other room.

I moved to follow, and Boom laid his hand on my arm again. "Talon, this bloke is a nutter," he said quietly. "And you're relying on him to provide what we need? I think I'm starting to hate this plan."

"He has what I need," I said. "Otherwise why would Mama send us to him?"

Boom snorted and left his opinion unsaid. I went into the other room, and he followed, shaking his head.

The room was probably Gordon's bedroom, or at least the room where he slept. There was a foam pad on the floor, barely visible beneath a pile of soiled clothing and more paper. The walls were covered with sheets of paper tacked together to form a strange kind of mural all around us. The pages were covered with arcane writing, symbols, and diagrams written in a firm, dark hand. I stood just inside the room and stared at the collection of pages, barely readable in the flickering glow of the single candle Gordon carried.

"Gods," I said in awe, "it's a map of the metaplanes. All of them."

"Yes, yes," Gordon said. "A map of the Otherworlds,

all the worlds beyond this one. All the ones I've found so far, anyway."

"It's amazing," I said. I'd heard that Dr. Gordon was working on a project to map out the metaplanes and the undiscovered depths of astral space, but I had no idea he had continued his work after leaving the Institute. I grasped only the barest concepts of the diagrams I was looking at, and I considered myself pretty good at understanding astral theory after my time with Assets, Inc. There were levels of complexity to the whole thing that made my head hurt just looking at them.

"Doesn't look like much of a map to me," Boom said.

"It's not like a physical map," I said without turning my head, raptly staring at the diagrams. "It's a symbolic representation of certain abstract astral states, entirely non-physical and outside of three-dimensional space."

"If you say so. It still looks like a lot of squiggles and arrows to me. How are you going to use a map this big?"

That was a bit of a problem. Fortunately, Gordon supplied the answer.

"You don't need the whole map," he said. "Only part. To get you where you need to go."

I was about to say something about the information I was looking for when Gordon went to one wall, carefully took down a few of the sheets covered in formulae and diagrams and brought them over to me.

"Do you know what lies in the Otherworlds?" he said, looking me in the eyes. He pressed the sheets of paper into my hand and said, "Everything. The question is: do you really want to look upon it?"

The blue eyes looked into me and I recalled being on the bridge in the depths of astral space, standing with Ryan and the others and facing the endless dark horde of the Enemy. I recalled the darkness, the hunger, the power, the sheer *evil* of the things that came from the distant depths of netherworlds humans were never meant to see, and I shuddered at the memory of it. Did I really want to see something like that? Where would this map take me?

I looked back into Dr. Gordon's sad, pale eyes. "It's something I have to do. I have no choice," I said.

"Neither did I," he replied, shaking his head sadly. He put his hand over mine, closing my fingers tightly over the pages. "Neither did I."

# 16

"There's no choice, no choice at all," Gordon said in a sad voice.

"I don't understand," I said. "What do you mean?"

He still held my eyes. "You know what's out there, don't you?" he said. "You've seen some of it. I can tell."

I felt like I'd been hit by an electrical shock. I recalled the bridge in the depths of the astral plane, places where I'd never been before. The battle with the Enemy, Thayla's voice, the blinding power of the Dragon Heart, and becoming lost in those places beyond comprehension, thinking I would never return. If not for Lucero, I might not have. How did Gordon know about it?

"Yes," I said. "I've seen."

"Then you know what is out there."

"But, Dr. Gordon," I said, "they're no longer a threat. The bridge is gone and the power of the Dragon Heart will keep the Enemy at bay. The world is safe. You're safe."

Gordon shook his head sadly. "No, no, no," he said softly. "You don't understand."

"I sure as 'ell don't," Boom said. "What are you talking about, Talon?"

I turned to the troll. "I was hired for a run a couple years ago. A team needed a mage who knew one end of a spell from another. The team was Assets, Inc., and they'd lost their mage on a tough run with some serious stakes. It all goes back to Dunkelzahn's death and some other complicated drek.

"To make a long story short, we all ended up in this weird astral place I'd never even heard of before. There was some kind of bridge there, being built by these . . . things, spirits of some kind, I guess, that wanted to cross over into our world from whatever weird metaplane they came from. They were using the increasing power of magic to try and get across. Some people set up a sort of stop-gap measure to hold them off, but it wasn't strong enough, and it started to break down. So we went there and used a powerful talisman called the Dragon Heart to stop them."

I turned away a bit. "I nearly didn't make it back," I said quietly. "In fact, I was pretty sure I was dead, my astral form lost in the depths of the metaplanes forever, but something happened, something, some*one*, guided me back to the world of the living."

"You were reborn," Dr. Gordon said. "But not all the affairs of your previous life are done."

"What do you mean? How do you know?"

"I know," the old man said. "I know far more than I should. More than anyone should. The Enemy is not the only thing out in the depths of the astral planes. They are only a drop of water in the vastness of the cosmic ocean. There are many things out there, more than can ever be counted. Some of them so vast the mortal mind cannot comprehend them. Some more cold and alien than we can imagine, others so beautiful and loving your heart weeps to behold them. What you've seen is only a tiny part of the greater whole. We're not ready for some of the things that are coming, we're not ready."

"But the Enemy . . ."

"You delayed the Enemy, yes," Gordon said, "but there are other things coming to our world. Some of them are already here, and others are coming soon. The signs and portents are in place. It's written in the stars, heralded by the night sky. I know, I've seen the signs."

"I don't believe in prophecy," I said.

"Believe what you wish. It doesn't change what is. A change is coming to the world. The Awakening is far from over. In fact, in many ways, it's only just beginning."

I started to ask Gordon for more information, but Boom interrupted.

"Talon . . ." he said quietly. "We've got what we need, right?" I glanced over at the troll, who nodded his head slightly toward the doorway, then down at the papers I held in my hand.

I turned back to Dr. Gordon. "We should go," I said.

The mage locked his icy blue eyes on mine and I saw a hint of his old, brilliant self in them. He smiled sadly.

"The real enemy is not out there," he said. Then he reached out and tapped my chest with a single, bony finger. "It's in here. Beware the demons in your own heart, magician."

"Talon . . ." Boom said again, a little louder this time.

"What?" I said, somewhat irritated at the interruption. I felt very close to understanding something.

"Is it getting hot in here?"

Now that Boom mentioned it, it *was* getting hotter in the room. The air in the cramped apartment was warm and oppressive from the moment we came in. Now it was becoming stifling. There was a dull, whooshing sound and a bright, flickering light came from the other room.

"I've got a bad feeling about this," Boom said, drawing his weapon from the shoulder holster concealed under his jacket.

We moved into the other room just in time to see one of the thick candles flare up again. As the flames shot up, the candle dissolved like water, showering the area around it with droplets of hot wax. The flame detached itself from the candle and hovered about a meter above the surface of the table where the candlestick rested. The flames swirled into a fist-sized sphere of fire, glowing with a white-hot core at its very center.

"Oh drek," Boom said. "Fire elemental!"

The elemental finished materializing. The sphere of flame grew rapidly to become a hideous reptilian creature, like a snake with stunted legs, hovering in the air. Its scales were iridescent red and black, marked in diamond-shaped patterns. Its eyes were like black coals and its entire body was surrounded by an aura of flames, heat coming off it in waves. The spirit glared at us and I saw no humanity or mercy reflected in those dead black eyes.

Sparks and tongues of fire shot from the spirit's halo of fire, touching the piles of paper and books all over the room. The dry paper caught instantly and, in the blink of an eye, the apartment turned into an inferno.

"Noooooo!" Gordon shouted. "My work! All my work!" The flames spread quickly across every surface, greedily licking at the papers, printouts, and books, the dry cloth and dry wood. I heard a low, hissing sound. Whether it came from the flames or the spirit, or both, I couldn't say.

Without hesitation, Boom barreled for the door of the

apartment, with me right behind, leading an incoherent Dr. Gordon as he continued to scream and moan. The big troll almost made it to the door before the spirit, all fire and shadow, moved like a leaping spark to intercept him. Boom howled in pain as he struck the spirit's burning body and stumbled back, nearly knocking the both of us over.

"We're not going out that way," Boom said, slowly backing away from the door. He clutched his hand to his chest, but I couldn't see how seriously he was hurt. The room was filling with thick smoke, and I knew a rickety place like this, on the edge of the Rox, had no fire alarms, no smoke detectors. The old wooden structure would burn like a house of matchsticks. Metroplex fire services wouldn't come out here except to contain the blaze and, perhaps, sift through the ashes for bodies or any valuables not destroyed in the fire. We had to get out on our own.

"Into the other room! I can try and get us out that way!" I shouted over the roaring of the fire. Boom was smart enough not to question me. He slipped past me and headed for the doorway. I backed away from the spirit, holding Dr. Gordon's wrist. He stood staring in horrid fascination as his life's work went up in flames around him, like an accident victim unable to tear his eyes away from a horrible crash.

The spirit began moving toward us, slowly. I had the distinct feeling it was playing with us, trying to corner us before moving in for the kill.

I pulled on the doctor's wrist. "We have to go!" I shouted.

Gordon jerked his wrist out of my grip. "No! My work . . ." he moaned.

"We can't save it," I said. "Damn it, we've got to get out of here!" I was starting to choke on the thick smoke and my eyes were tearing, my vision blurred. The spirit circled to the side. I thought it might try to break past us and get at Boom.

"You can save it," Gordon said. He didn't seem at all affected by the smoke or the heat. He turned to me, his face streaked with soot and ash, his bright eyes standing out in stark contrast. "You can carry on what I began."

"What? What are you talking about?"

"Tell me you'll do it, Talon. Tell me you'll continue my work to protect everyone from the things that are coming. Keep them safe."

All I could think of was that we had to get out of there, pronto. The smoke was making me dizzy. "Doctor . . ."

"Promise me. Please."

The spirit coiled to strike.

"All right, I promise. I'll do it," I said. I drew Talon-claw from the sheath at my hip.

"Then go!" Gordon cried and pushed me toward the other room with far more strength than I could have imagined from the looks of him. The spirit, about to be deprived of its prey, hissed and leapt through the air.

"Hold, spawn of fire!" Gordon shouted. "Hold, creature of the pit!"

The elemental stopped as if it had hit a brick wall. It roared and flames shot out of its open mouth. Gordon stood his ground and held his hands wide over his head, fingers crooked in a magical gesture. Flickering energy seemed to arc between them, leaping out to touch the spirit's flaming aura with a pale blue light.

"Avant, ye elemental!" Gordon intoned. "Avant, ye nature unbound! Begone from this place and trouble it no more!"

The spirit shrieked and thrashed against invisible bonds,

struggling to reach the frail mage. It inched closer and Gordon faltered back a step. I stopped in the doorway, watching them struggle. I held out a hand and prepared to call the power to me to strike the creature with a spell, but the words of invocation caught in my throat as I coughed.

"Talon!" Boom called from the other room, coughing and choking. The smoke was almost too thick to see through, and the flames were everywhere.

Gordon turned away from the spirit for a moment to look at me, his eyes fierce, his hair wild. "Go, damn you! Go!" he shouted.

The spirit seized the moment of his distraction to lash out with its serpentine tail. The blow sent the old man to his knees, but he held his hands high and shouted more words of power. The spirit recoiled, shrieking.

"Talon!"

I looked for an instant more as the dark smoke obscured the battle between the mage and the spirit, then turned and raced into the other room.

Boom had already torn down the heavy drapes and smashed the narrow window. Smoke poured out, but it was still difficult to breathe. The troll clutched his injured arm as the flames continued to spread into the room. The map of the metaplanes covering the wall blackened and shriveled as the fire crawled up the ceiling.

"No fire escape," Boom said with a nod toward the window, "and I don't exactly think they had trolls in mind when they designed the windows."

"Let me take care of that," I said. I stood in front of the window and sent out the call across the depths of the astral plane. When I felt a response, I gathered power to me, holding it with my will like a tightly coiled spring, drawing it tighter and tighter. I narrowed my eyes and brought my hands down, thrusting them out at the ancient brick wall.

"Shatter!" I yelled and released the power I held. It flowed through me like a lightning bolt, and an invisible wave of power struck the wall with the force of a speeding truck. The casement and brickwork exploded outward, raining in flaming shards down to the street below.

I gazed out into the night air as it filled with dark smoke and I spoke my command. "Carry us from this place and bring us safely to earth."

The wisps of smoke swirled and danced in the cool autumn air and took on a vaguely human-like shape that bowed and spread its arms wide.

"Jump," I said to Boom.

"What are you . . ."

"Jump!" I said, and I stepped out into empty air. With only a second's hesitation, Boom followed.

Instead of falling, we hovered for a moment, embraced by a cooling breeze. Slowly it lowered us to the street, where a small crowd of people gathered. They backed away from us as we touched down lightly on the cracked and broken sidewalk.

As soon as we touched the ground, I sent out the call again, feeling a different presence respond to it.

*What is your will, Master?* spoke a voice in my mind, like a rushing stream.

"Go into that dwelling," I said. "Destroy the fire spirit there and quench the flames." The invisible astral presence of the water elemental sent a flowing feeling of obedience and moved to obey. We stood and watched for a few minutes as the flames shooting from the windows and the hole in the wall above slowly flickered and died.

Smoke continued to pour from the blackened ruins of the apartment as my water elemental returned.

*The fire spirit is gone, Master,* it said, *and the flames are quenched.*

"What about the human inside?" I asked, already knowing the answer.

*He is dead, Master,* the spirit replied. *His spirit has gone.* Its words were without emotion or concern, simply relaying the facts.

I closed my hand tightly around the sheets of paper in the pocket of my long coat, and Dr. Gordon's words seemed to echo back to me.

*Protect everyone from the things that are coming. Keep them safe.* Then I remembered his other words, when he'd touched my chest.

"The real enemy is not out there," Gordon had said. "It's in here."

# 17

As the first light of dawn poked through the cracks around the covered windows of the old church, Trouble came over, holding a steaming mug, which she held out to me.

"No, thanks," I said.

"Talon, you should at least drink something."

I shook my head. "I'm fasting. It helps to clear the mind and spirit and I'm going to need it. Have you heard from the others?"

She nodded, setting the plastic mug down on the nearby windowsill. "They're making the arrangements."

"Good. Boom can handle it, especially with Hammer backing him up."

"You're also going to need to be rested," Trouble said. "You haven't slept since yesterday."

"Sleep deprivation can help create the right state of consciousness, too," I said. "I'm going to be in a trance for a while, and it'll help facilitate . . ."

"Bulldrek," she said. "You're just saying that, Talon. What good is it if you're exhausted?"

I looked up from where I crouched. "We don't have that kind of time. The elemental Garnoff sent after us means he's playing hardball. Before, Garnoff and his people only tried to capture us—gel rounds, stun weapons.

This last spirit wasn't trying to knock anybody out, it meant business. Garnoff is scared, and that means we don't have a lot of time.

"Besides," I said, standing up and brushing off my hands. "Today is Samhain, so it's the best time to do this. It's when the paths into the depths of the astral plane are the most open and accessible. If I'm going to do this, there's no better time."

Trouble looked down at my handiwork.

"Looks pretty elaborate," she said.

It was that. The old slate floor at the front of the church was just perfect for the kind of work I had in mind, once I pushed aside the remains of the old carpet. The pockets of my long coat were filled with the various tools I needed to do magic: chalk, bits of string, candle stubs, crystals, and fetishes like strands of my shorn hair woven into a cord.

I took chalk in several different colors and drew a double circle in red on the floor, three meters wide. Between the bands, I scribed magical runes and symbols of protection and travel. Outside the circle I drew eight red triangles, pointing outward like arrows toward the eight airts, the primal directions of the compass. In the center of each triangle was a different rune or symbol associated with that direction. At the point of each triangle was a small white candle, stuck to the floor with drops of hot wax.

"It's not perfect," I said, "but it's the best I could do with the space I have to work with in here."

"You've been working on it all night."

"Well, everything has to be just right, or else the circle won't be able to protect my body while I'm journeying astrally."

"I'll keep an eye on things," she said, with a hint of reproach in her voice.

I turned to look at her again. "I know you will. That's not what I meant. The circle doesn't offer any physical protection, really. It only creates an astral barrier to protect my body from spirits and magic. If Garnoff sends another magical attack, I want to be ready."

"Now that it's ready, when are you going to go?"

"Soon," I said.

"Look," Trouble said, toying with the rim of the cup, "I wanted to say I'm sorry about what happened before. I shouldn't have presumed . . ."

"It's okay," I said. "I just wasn't expecting it."

"I want you to know I'm not in the habit of throwing myself at every guy who comes into my life."

"I know, I know. It's all right. I'm very flattered."

"Just not interested," she concluded.

"No, but I want you to know it's not you. I don't . . . I'm not good with relationships."

"Okay," she said coolly. "I understand. We keep this strictly business."

"I don't know about that. I consider you a friend. This isn't business for me. It's personal."

"For me too," Trouble said. There was a long moment of silence before she spoke again. "Do you really think this plan is going to work?"

"It's the best shot we've got," I said.

Trouble swallowed hard and picked up the mug, her unbound hair hiding her face as she bowed her head to drink. "All right, then, you'd better get to it," she said. "I'll make sure everything else is taken care of."

I sat in the center of the circle in a lotus position, calming my mind with meditation, preparing myself for what was to come. I thought about what I'd told Trouble, that I wasn't interested in a relationship. It wasn't a lie exactly, but it wasn't the whole truth, either. I wasn't ready to explain all of it to her. Not until we took care of Garnoff and whatever he was involved in. We all had enough on our minds right now. I pushed those thoughts aside and focused, quietly chanting mantras to calm and center me, body, mind, and spirit. Breathing slowly, calmly, in and out, letting the breath flow, letting the energy flow.

I opened my senses to an awareness of the astral plane, to the complex play of energies and life force all around me. Although the church was no longer consecrated, it had been the focus of worship and caring for many years, leaving a pleasant warmth lingering in the astral atmosphere of it. I let the gentle touch of it comfort me.

When I was ready, I opened my eyes. The interior of the church was dim and silent. The pages I got from Dr. Gordon were spread out on the floor in front of me. I used the diagrams to help construct the hermetic circle, and I would use the imagery to help guide me along the journey to where I needed to go.

I stood and drew Talonclaw from its sheath, facing north. Holding the dagger in front of me, point upward, I began to activate the circle.

"Spirits of the North, Powers of Earth, I call you to be present in my circle. Fertile soil, unyielding rock, brilliant sand, and precious crystal, send forth your power, make my circle strong and let it stand against all things that might come to do me harm. Hail and welcome."

I lowered my mageblade to point at the northern candle, and a green flame sprang up from the wick, causing the rune in the triangle to shimmer with a faint greenish light. The scent of freshly turned soil and freshly cut grass seemed to fill the circle. I drew up the light with the power of my will and used it to draw a pentagram shimmering in the air on the edge of the circle.

Then I turned toward the east, where the morning light shone through the gaps covering the windows. The remains of some stained glass turned the light into a cascade of jewel-tones on the floor.

"Spirits of the East, Powers of Fire, I call you to be present in my circle. Light of knowledge, forge fire, heat of passion, spark of inspiration, send forth your power, make my circle blaze with light to fight back the darkness that may come to do me harm. Hail and welcome."

A wave of warmth washed over my face and hands as I lowered my blade, and the eastern candle burned with reddish fire that I drew up to make a pentagram of red flames in the east before turning to the south.

"Spirits of the South, Powers of Air, I call you to be present in my circle. Gentle breeze, roaring gale, breath of life, wind of reason, send forth your power, make my circle resilient and blow away the mists that obscure the truth. Hail and welcome." The southern candle flickered with a pure yellow flame that formed a pentacle in the southern quarter as a cooling breeze seemed to blow through the circle.

Lastly, I turned to the west. "Spirits of the West, Powers of Water, I call you to be present in my circle. Gray twilight, ocean depths, cauldron of transformation, send forth your power, make my circle flow and change to protect me from harm. Let me drink of your depths and find the knowledge I seek." The western candle held a watery blue fire that I used to put the final pentagram in place as I heard a sound like the roaring of waves against a rocky shore.

I turned again to the north and held Talonclaw overhead, pointing up to the heavens. The remaining four candles ignited at the cross-quarters, all burning with a warm golden light that seemed to spread out all around me.

"Earth, Fire, Air, and Water," I intoned, "bind this circle and keep me from all forces that may come to do me harm. Watch over me as I travel on my journey to find the truth. I create a place between the worlds, a space beyond space and a time beyond time, standing on the border of the Otherworld, where the deepest paths are open on Samhain. I will journey along those secret roads until I find what I seek. So be it."

The pentacles of light flared and the circle was enclosed in a dome of opalescent light, mixing the colors of all the candles into one. I sheathed my mageblade and stretched out on the floor, placing my rolled-up jacket beneath my head as a pillow. I looked up into the light of the circle's protection and began to slip into a trance. My spirit slipped the bonds of my body and I traveled into the depths of the astral plane.

On the threshold, the twilight border between the metaplanes and the outside world, lives the Dweller on the Threshold. The Dweller takes many forms, and always tries to dissuade travelers from entering the metaplanes. Some believe it is a manifestation of subconscious resistance, the ego or id speaking to you through images in a deep trance, a kind of subconscious defense mechanism. Others believe the Dweller is a powerful spirit, guardian of the gateway into the metaplanes, with its own mysterious reasons for testing those who try to enter the domains beyond. If you ask me, it's nothing more than a serious pain in the ass.

As I passed through a long tunnel, I could see a dark

figure ahead, silhouetted by a blood-red light coming from beyond.

"You come because you must," said the figure of Dr. Gordon. He was surrounded by the reddish glow from the wide tunnel behind him. The light made it impossible to see what lay beyond. Gordon was on my mind, so it was no surprise that the Dweller took on his form.

"You won't keep your promise," the image of Gordon said. "After all, what is a promise made in the heat of the moment? You won't keep it. You'll turn away, find some reason to go elsewhere, like you always do."

"What?" I said.

"You always leave. When things become too difficult, you find yourself an out and you're gone."

"That's not true!" The Dweller always tries to rattle your cage, tries to create self-doubt to keep travelers from going any further. In this particular case, it was doing a pretty good job.

"Of course it is," the doctor's image continued. He was considerably more calm and rational than when I saw him last, more like the old Dr. Gordon I knew from the Institute. "I gave you an opportunity to escape the attack of that fire elemental and you took it. You already had what you needed from me. Tell the old man whatever he wants to hear, eh? It doesn't really matter whether or not you mean it."

"I tried to *help* you . . ." I started to say.

"You just can't think of anyone other than yourself," said the image of Ryan Mercury, the leader of Assets, Inc. "You have to grab all the glory. You can't follow the plan because you don't happen to agree with it."

"I did what I had to do. There wasn't any time to go according to the plan," I said.

"So you take it on yourself to make life or death decisions for everyone else? Do you think that makes you worthy of being a part of our team? Are you the kind of person we can trust with our lives?"

"Dammit, Ryan," I said. "I nearly died for you and the team, to get the Dragon Heart into place!"

"Maybe you should have died," Ryan said, his words like cold razors. "Maybe it should have been you instead of all the other people who died. Maybe you should have died and Lucero should have been the one to get her life back. Do you really think you're worthy of a second chance at life?"

"And what have you done with it?" asked Jane-in-the-Box, a virtual vixen clad in tight red leather. "When things get tough and you decide you can't handle it, what do you do? You run away again. You don't turn to your friends for help, to people who care about you. You just leave."

"I don't want anyone else involved," I said. "This is my problem. It doesn't involve anyone else."

"Don't want anyone else involved?" Trouble asked me. "Who do you think I am? I came to you because this whole mess I'm in is your fault. I'm involved up to my neck, and you treat this like it's your own personal vendetta, like nobody else matters. I reached out to you, and you won't even tell me the truth. You'd rather let me think there's something wrong with me."

"I am going to tell you, just not right now. It's not the right time," I said weakly.

"Oh, really? When were you planning on getting to the truth? Waiting to see if I walk away from this run? If you're lucky, maybe one of us will get killed and save you the trouble of talking to another person at all."

"It's not like that . . ." I started to say.

"No?" Boom said, his deep voice echoing strangely. "Isn't it? How long did we run together, Talon? A few years? After I came back to Boston and took over the nightclub, did you try and get in touch with me? Did our friendship mean anything to you?"

"Of course it did, but I was involved in so many runs after Dunkelzahn's assassination, then Assets took me on and . . . there was never any time."

"But when you needed something from me, there was plenty of time, eh?"

"It's not like that!" I protested. "I've been away from Boston for too long. I didn't know the shadows here! I couldn't operate on unfamiliar ground without help."

"I thought this didn't involve anyone else," Boom said. "I thought it was personal."

"It is," I said.

"Maybe it's personal for more people than just you."

"I just don't want anyone else to get hurt," I said.

"Why? Because you're afraid of how it will hurt you?" said a familiar voice. The deep green eyes and freckled features were just as I remembered them. Damn the Dweller to hell.

"Jase?" I said in a small voice.

"That's why you're here, isn't it? So no one else is at risk, so you can do what needs to be done alone. Is that it?"

"Yes."

"But you couldn't have come this far without help."

"Yes."

"So, doesn't your friends risking themselves for you make this personal for them, too?" Jase's image said. "Don't you care about them?"

"Of course I do but . . ."

"But not too much," he said.

"I don't want anyone to get hurt," I said weakly.

"Like I did?" Jase said. "Like *you* did? Life is risk, Talon. Everyone gets hurt sooner or late. Everyone dies."

"Gods, Jase, I miss you so much." The image began to fade from sight until there was nothing except the opening into the metaplanes, glowing dull red, like blood.

"Go on, Tal," Jase's voice said from all around me. "Go and finish what you started."

# 18

I stepped into the blood red light and it surrounded me. I was drifting alone in a sea of blood. The light was hot around me and I couldn't see anything but red. Time seemed to slip away and I was floating, drifting. I felt a gentle tug pulling me upward and flowed along with it. It was like swimming through light, which grew brighter and brighter.

My head broke the surface and I found myself swimming in some kind of sea. The waters were red like blood, and warm. I stepped onto shore and came onto a beach of golden sand, looking up at the wonder before me.

The narrow strip of beach hugged the walls of a vast city, towering high above. The walls were cut from black volcanic stone, polished smooth as glass, soaring overhead. The towers of the city stretched taller than the high walls, made of gleaming copper, brass, and gold, all shining in the heat of a brilliant yellow sun. The sky was a deep pink, strewn with clouds in shades of pink, purple, and gold, like a sunset, even though the sun was high in the sky.

I looked down at myself and discovered I was completely dry. I wore a caftan-like robe of white, trimmed in gold thread. Talonclaw remained sheathed at my waist, but I carried no other ornaments or gear with me. I wore supple leather sandals that crunched slightly against the sand of the beach. Looking at my reflection in the mirror-like black wall in front of me, I saw my own familiar features looking back.

A tall gate stood nearby, each of the gleaming doors covered with a complex relief of a phoenix rising from the flames, with the image of the city behind it. People in clothes that looked like something out of an *Arabian Nights* trideo-production for the Ancient Wisdom channel went in and out of the gates, under the watchful eyes of guards who looked like massive trolls with ruddy skin carrying huge scimitars. Some of the people were recognizable as human or metahuman, while others were of no race I'd ever seen before. Some led or rode strange animals that looked like domesticated dinosaurs, while most were on foot. I strode toward the gates and joined the throng of people going inside.

Just as I reached the wall, two burly guards stood in my path, looking down on me. The dagger at my waist suddenly felt very small, compared to the giant curved swords they carried.

"Ho, traveler," the right one said. "Who are you and why do you seek to enter the City of Brass and Gold?"

"Speak truly," said the left one, "or we will cleave your head from your shoulders and send you from this place."

"I am called Talon," I said, "and I am here on a quest. I am looking for something."

"There are many things in the City," the right one said again. "Some are best left alone. Are you certain about what you seek?"

"Are you willing to pay the cost of the truth?" the left one said.

I nodded. "Yes. The truth is what I seek."

The two guards took a step backward and parted, allowing me room to pass. "Then enter, truth-seeker," said the one on the right.

"And may you find what you need," said the other. "Whether you seek it, or it seeks you."

I walked past the two guards and through the gate. Beyond it was a giant bazaar, booths and brightly colored tents forming a maze of narrow passages choked with people. The air was filled with the smell of exotic spices, tobacco, animals, and the scents of food. Merchants shouted the virtues of their wares over the noise of the crowd.

"Sir!" called a dark-skinned elven woman from a nearby tent. "Your heart's desire, sir, for only a few coins!" She gestured toward the shadowy interior of the tent with a bright smile.

"Thank you, no," I said, as politely as possible. There was a great deal of magical lore warning against accepting any gifts or bargains in the Otherworlds. They spoke of travelers taking offers of food or hospitality and never being allowed to leave. In the Awakened world, legends had a disturbing way of turning out true, so I declined politely and continued on.

I made my way through the crowd, ignoring other offers from the merchants along the way, politely refusing when pressed and looking around for some idea where to go once I got beyond the bounds of the marketplace. I looked up at the gleaming spires of the city and saw one standing taller than all the others. It was a great tower of gleaming gold, copper, and brass, topped with an onion dome that shone in the sunlight like a beacon.

"So, you seek the citadel," said a voice very close to

my ear. I spun to see who had spoken and a flurry of feathers brushed the side of my face. A raven sat perched on my shoulder. It cawed at my sudden movement and took flight, landing on a nearby hitching post.

"So," it said again, "you seek the citadel." Its voice wasn't like that of a mynah bird or other mimic. It was quite urban, actually. Its tiny, dark eyes were like chips of stone taken from the city wall. They gleamed a bit as they regarded me.

"Yes," I said, "I'm looking for the citadel."

"You need a guide," the raven said. It was not a question. "The streets of the city have many twists and turns and there are dark places where travelers become lost. It is best to have a guide."

I considered the idea for a moment. It wasn't unusual for spirits to guide travelers on an astral quest, but I'd never encountered this particular spirit before.

"What will your help cost me?" I asked.

"Nothing," the raven said. "My aid to you repays a debt."

"What debt?" I said.

"An old one," was all it said.

"Who are you?" I asked.

"Memory," the raven said. "Follow me." The black bird took wing and fluttered above the heads of the people milling on the edge of the bazaar. I followed as quickly as I could, keeping up with the raven as it seemed to skip across the top of the crowd, leading me out of the marketplace and deeper into the city. When the crowd thinned, I was able to keep up, even though the raven moved more quickly.

"Through here," it called, flying into an alleyway.

I turned the corner and found myself somewhere else entirely.

I stood in Jase's apartment. The air was hot and sweat rolled down my face, collecting in drops on my chin and the end of my nose. A thin haze of smoke filled the room from the brass brazier. It was set on a tripod in the middle of a red circle drawn on the floor and marked with arcane symbols. I raised my hands, palms downward, and the symbols of the circle seemed to glow with an inner fire.

I cupped my hands above the brazier. I was very angry, and bitter, salty tears mixed with my sweat. I poured that anger into the brazier, and the dark coals hissed and began to glow cherry-red. The heat came off them in waves, and tiny droplets of salt water fell from my face, sizzling on the coals.

I opened a pouch and cast powdered incense onto the coals, sending sweet, pungent clouds of smoke into the air. The smoke made my eyes water even more. My vision blurred, but I didn't falter. The room filled with a faint, bluish haze. The glow of the brazier and the candles around the circle provided the only light.

I plunged the blade of the dagger into the coals for a moment, sterilizing the knife with the searing heat. I swirled it through the smoke, watching the sharp edge part the mists. Then I held my left hand out over the brazier.

I made the cut as quick and clean as I could. The pain was shocking, like a bucket of ice water in my face. My sweat turned cold and my hands tingled as I watched the dark red blood well up from the narrow cut along my palm. It overflowed the edge and dropped onto the hot coals with a hiss. The air filled with the smell of burning blood, hot and metallic, and the coals burned brighter.

Three times I allowed my blood to drop onto the coals, intoning as I did.

"By the power of blood, I call thee, blood calling to blood. From the fires of my heart, I call thee, fire calling to fire." Tears were streaming freely down my face, but I kept my voice firm and strong. "From the heat of my anger, I call thee, anger calling out for justice. By the power of Earth, by the power of Air, by the power of Fire Eternal and the Waters of the Deep, I conjure and charge thee, arise, arise! Arise at my command, and truly do my will."

Flames roared up from the brazier, sending out thick clouds of dark smoke. The smoke and fire gathered, infused with my will and my anger and my sorrow, and looked back at me with burning eyes. I took a step back from what I saw there, driven back by the wave of menace that poured off it like searing heat. I threw up my hands and cried out . . .

And found myself standing at the end of an alleyway. The raven sat perched on a windowsill, regarding me with its dark eyes.

"Come," it said, "this way," and it took flight down the street.

I followed as quickly as I could, booted feet pounding the cobblestones. That's when I noticed I wasn't wearing the simple robe and sandals I'd arrived in. I was dressed in modern street clothes that were at least ten years out of date, if not more. The raven was a good distance ahead and I couldn't seem to keep up, no matter how fast I ran. It banked around the corner of a building and I followed, when the sound of raucous laughter stopped me in my tracks.

The alley I'd turned into held a party, a bunch of gangers in street leathers, their bikes parked against the walls of the alley. My raven guide was nowhere to be seen. There were at least a dozen of them, maybe two, and several looked over at me and smiled or offered calls of greeting.

"Hoi, chummer! Zappinin?" a voice called. A tough-looking human girl who couldn't have been older than sixteen offered me a can of beer. She wore black leathers and her hair was styled in short blue spikes.

"You're already a couple behind," she said, handing me the beer. She tipped back her own, downing the rest in a couple of swallows before breaking out another.

Something seemed to draw me into the crowd of gangers, and I slowly made my way toward the back of the alley. People clapped me on the shoulders and back, shouting over the sound of the music blasting from portable speakers set up around the alley. Some of the gangers were dancing drunkenly, while others hung out near the walls and talked or made out. I tried to find the raven, or to pick out something that could tell me what I needed to do in this place to continue on toward the citadel.

"Bastards!" a voice cried from the far end of the alley. It was barely audible above the noise and the music. I turned toward it in time to see a young man, hair disheveled, face streaked with soot and grime, clothes spattered with blood. It was me. Me from more than ten years ago.

"Die, you fraggers!" he yelled, and the world exploded into flames.

My clothes and hair were on fire. I screamed and tried to drop to the ground, to put out the flames, but they were all around me. All reason fled as I tried to do anything to get away from the fire. Everyone around me was screaming. The music died with a hideous squeal as the speakers and the player melted from the tremendous heat. I saw the girl with the blue hair drop to the ground, her flesh blistered and charred. I rolled along the ground, up against the wall, thrashing around, trying to put out the fire.

There was a dull boom, and one of the bikes exploded. Shards of hot metal pelted me and the heat seemed to suck away all the air. There was nothing but fire. I couldn't breathe. I couldn't see. There was nothing but terrible pain. I tried to move, but I couldn't. All I could do was lie there and listen to the cries of pain and the crackle of the flames as both slowly died away, replaced by a sobbing sound like someone's soul had been torn out. I barely noticed it and in a few moments it died away, too.

I felt cold and my skin was wet. I was dying. I knew that for sure. The cold hand of panic gripped my heart. I didn't want to die. A warmth washed over my face and exposed skin.

*Then live,* a voice said, like someone speaking over a radio channel full of hissing and crackling static.

*Help me,* I thought, and the warmth fell over me like a blanket, spreading out from my heart into my limbs and my face. My body felt numb and I flexed my hands. My eyes opened and I could see my clothes and my skin, charred and burned. My hands moved of their own accord, lifting up in front of my face and turning over. I looked at them like I'd never seen them before.

"I live." My lips formed the words. It was my voice, but it wasn't me who spoke. It was something else. Something living inside me.

"I live!" it said again, raising my hands toward the sky.

I looked up at the top of the alley and saw a raven sitting there, staring down at me. The world went black and silent.

"Please, don't . . ." a voice said. It seemed to come from very far away. I fought my way toward it, but at the same time I was reluctant to leave the cool and comforting darkness. Then suddenly I knew why.

There was a man lying in front of me. He looked fairly young, probably no more than twenty. His features were a mongrel mix of racial types, liberally sprinkled with the piercings so common on the streets. He wore synth-denims and a jacket with patches sewn onto it, covered with scrawls in dark ink. His face was bruised, and dried blood covered his mouth and chin. I noticed his hands and feet were bound with silvery-gray tape.

"Please," he moaned, looking up at me with terror in his dark eyes, "please don't kill me, man. Please . . ." His words trailed off into a sob as he began to cry. I looked down to see the gleaming knife in my hands. The skin was blackened and shriveled, drawn tight over muscle and bone. I turned back to look at the sobbing figure in front of me.

*Please don't,* I thought, echoing his cries for mercy. *No more.*

"I live," my own voice said softly, "I must live. I must kill to live."

"NO! Please!" I couldn't tell if it was my voice or the victim's.

The knife flashed out and the man cried out in terror as the blade stroked his neck. Blood fountained from a severed artery, but it was nothing compared to the rush of energy that poured out of the dying man, like an explosion of heat and light. My arms spread wide, and I could feel the heat, the power of the man's life, pour into me, into us, like water filling up a vessel. It felt good. Better than drugs, better than chips, better than sex, better than *everything*. I moaned, or it did, I couldn't tell any more.

Part of me sobbed, the pleasure was almost painful. *No more,* I said in my mind, *please, no more.*

My lips smiled as the last morsels of energy were consumed. The dead body was limp and cold, lying in a pool of blood.

"Good," was all it said.

I couldn't tell how much time passed, how many died. It was a lot. Different faces, different races, men and women, old and young. It didn't care who. It chose them solely on how bright they were, how filled with the fires of life it needed to survive. It learned quickly that fear and terror stoked those fires hotter before death, that it could make the most of a victim by prolonging his or her end, making each moment count, savoring it. It got better and better at using my body, too. It never repaired the damage, the burned skin and clothes. It had no interest in such things. Only a desire to live and to kill. It said it cared about me, but it didn't, it didn't care about anything except what it needed.

Sometimes, after it fed, I could feel my body for a little while. It hurt so much and there was nothing I could do about it. It didn't last for very long, just a few minutes alone in the dark with nothing but pain and cold. Then the warmth would start to spread through my limbs again and it would be back, moving my body like a puppet.

In those few cold and lonely minutes after each death I started to carry out my plan. It wasn't too difficult to find a strong piece of rope in the home of one of its victims, to tie it around my waist to hide it. I carried the rope back with it to where we lived, in the underground. Tying the knot was more difficult, it took time to get it right, and I had to hide the rope whenever it started to return, hiding any hint there was something wrong. I don't know what it would do if it found out what I was doing.

Fortunate that it collected some old furniture, bits of junk for the lair. It wanted to know more about people, and I could feel it picking through my thoughts and memories like old trash, looking for more. I tried to keep what I know hidden. It didn't think much of me. I'm just something it needed, even less than a dog or a horse. It didn't suspect.

When I was ready, I tied the rope to a sturdy-looking pipe, standing on an old chair. I dropped the noose around my neck and slid it closed, feeling the rough fibers of the rope against my burnt skin. I didn't know how it was keeping me alive. By all rights I should have been dead. I should have died in the alley. It shouldn't have been allowed to do this. To use me like it has. It has to stop. I started to feel the warmth spreading through my body and, suddenly, it knew what I was planning.

*NO!* it said, *Stop!* It tried to seize control, but I still had enough control over my body to kick the chair away.

The rope went tight and there was a snapping sound. I heard it scream one last time before it all went dark.

It was dark for a very long time, and cold, so very cold. I was very angry. More than angry, anger incarnate. That smoldering anger kept me warm, kept me going. I used my power to seize the body's fleeing life force and hold on to it tightly, like a man clutching a lifeline. I held those last moments of life and didn't let go. *I cannot die, I must live,* I thought.

The body dangled limply from the rope. I wanted to remove it, burn it, break it, but I could not. I didn't have the strength left. All I could do was hold on, cling to life with all my strength. The physical world was so full of new sensations, brimming over with hot, simmering life. I could sense it all going on above me. So close, so close. All I needed was to hold myself in this world forever. Then my power would have no limit. I could feed on the life of this world as much as needed.

I could not say how much time passed. I was timeless. The seconds were like years and the years passed in the blink of an eye. I had no companionship, no one. I was utterly alone. There was nothing for me to do except cling to life and make plans, what I would do when I regained my freedom. The idea of giving up never even occurred to me. I cannot die, I must live.

More time passed, then, one day, I had a visitor. I sensed a presence, questing, searching, exploring. I felt the burning core of ambition within it, a hunger for power to rival my own. And I sensed something else, a connection, very tenuous, to my purpose. It was the opportunity I waited for. With a tiny bit of my carefully nursed power, I called out to the presence, drawing it to me.

He was a human mage, quite confused at first by my summons. He adapted quickly, knowing an opportunity when he saw one. As I suspected, he desired power and knowledge. I offered them to him in exchange for his aid. From the moment he agreed, he intended to betray me. I knew this. All people are treacherous. I learned that lesson from the moment I came into being. It didn't matter. I knew he would never have the opportunity.

He was wise enough not to ask my name, as if I would have given it to him. Instead, he asked what he should call me. I pondered for only a moment before an appropriate name came to mind.

"Gallow," I told him, "you may call me Gallow."

"Welcome to the citadel," a voice said. I opened my

eyes to see the raven perched on my chest. It took wing
and fluttered away as I pushed myself to a sitting position.

The room I found myself in was circular, ringed with
spiraling columns of gleaming metal. A hole in the ceiling let golden light pour in, falling on something in the
center of the room, covered with a cloth of gold. The
raven settled on top of it.

"You've found your way along the path," it said. "Now
you can find what you seek."

I walked over to the object, about my height, covered
completely by the drape of the gleaming cloth.

The raven hopped from it, perched on my shoulder and
whispered in my ear. "Look and see the truth."

With a trembling hand I reached out and whipped aside
the cloth. Beneath it was a rectangular bronze frame, cut
with runes and symbols. Inside it, a sheet of polished silver. I looked into the mirror and my reflection stared
back at me. My skin was blackened, my clothes scorched,
and around my neck dangled a crudely woven noose. I
knew who Gallow was and I knew its true name, whispered in the darkest corners of my mind. I knew more
than its name. I knew what it was, where it came from,
and why it wanted me.

I came back to my normal consciousness slowly, listening for a moment to the hum of traffic and the other
sounds of the plex outside. With a deep, cleansing breath
I opened my eyes to the flickering light of the candles
around the circle. They were burned down to small nubs.
It was dark outside, but I had no idea if it was still the
same day or if several had passed while I was journeying. The metaplanes often played strange tricks with
time. A moment could seem like a year and the blink of
an eye could be hours in the physical world.

My body felt stiff and cold, and with a shudder I recalled the feeling of being a burnt corpse, glancing down to make sure my skin wasn't charred and blackened. I got my legs underneath me and leaned back on one hand. As I did, a loud click drew my attention.

I turned to the side to see Trouble standing there. The long barrel of her Ares Predator looked even more menacing in the flickering candlelight as she leveled it at me. Dark figures moved in the room behind her as she gestured with the barrel for me to stand.

"Let's go, mageboy," she said in a voice as devoid of emotion as her flat stare. "We don't want to keep my boss waiting."

# 19

"If you try any magic, I'll blow your fragging head off," Trouble said, the long barrel of the Predator gleaming in the candlelight. "Get up, slowly." She was quite good at intimidation. I certainly wasn't going to argue with her.

I moved to comply as several shadows detached themselves from the darkness outside my small pool of golden candlelight and came up behind Trouble.

"Well done," Tomo Isogi said, hands folded calmly in front of him. He was flanked by a matched pair of bodyguards wearing dark suits and sunglasses, despite the fact it was dark out. Their eyes were probably cyber implants, not affected by light or darkness.

"Thank you, Isogi-*san*," Trouble said, without taking her eyes off me.

"Are we ready to proceed?" he asked, eyeing the circle on the floor and the colored candlelight. Even if Isogi was part of the New Way that embraced (or at least tolerated) many aspects of the Awakened world, there was a certain superstitious fear all mundanes had where magic was concerned. He obviously wasn't quite sure how to proceed, but Trouble was.

"Step out of the circle," she said. "And keep your hands at your sides. No tricks."

I stepped carefully over the boundary of the circle, keeping my attention focused on Trouble and wondering if there were more yakuza soldiers in the church other than the ones I could see. In either event, I wasn't going to try anything foolish.

"My car is ready," Isogi said to Trouble, who nodded.

"Good. We just have to prepare Talon for the trip."

She reached into a pocket of her jacket with one hand, keeping the gun trained on me the whole time. Holding a small skin patch between her fingers, she said, "This stuff will keep him quiet and make it impossible for him to concentrate enough to do magic." She took a few steps toward me, holding out the patch.

When she was close enough I stepped forward, inside the arc of her gun, and gripped the outstretched arm. The drug patch fell to the floor and Trouble followed. I turned toward Isogi, but his bodyguards were on top of me like a pair of dark-suited blurs. They must have hit me a couple times each before I hit the floor. I heard the sound of weapons being drawn and readied.

"*IE!*" Isogi shouted in Japanese. "No. He must not be killed. Garnoff needs him alive."

I stayed right were I was for the moment, my jaw and ribs aching. Trouble got back to her feet, rubbing her arm, and quickly retrieved the drug patch. She stood over me, then bent down and pressed the patch firmly against my neck, smacking it once to make sure it was in place.

"You should learn to wise up and take your medicine," she said. I lay limply on the floor, offering no resistance.

"He won't be giving us any more trouble," Trouble said with a smile.

"Pick him up," Isogi told the bruisers, "and bring him.

Dr. Garnoff is eager to see this piece of street trash and I am eager to see this business done."

With my eyelids at half-mast, I wasn't really able to appreciate the vista of light, chrome, and macroglass that was downtown Boston at night. The corporate towers and glittering plazas of the Financial District rose up all around us. It must have been quite late, since there was very little traffic on the streets and most of the buildings were dark and silent. It had rained at some point during the night. The pavement was slick and gleaming in the pale light. The dark clouds were beginning to clear away, showing a black velvet sky sprinkled with stars and a glowing gibbous moon.

I lay slumped in the back seat of the dark Mitsubishi Nightsky, with Trouble on one side and one of Isogi's bodyguards sitting across from us, facing me. He watched carefully for any further signs of resistance, but I offered none. I simply lay still. Trouble kept her Ares Predator close at hand.

Isogi sat in the passenger seat, while the other bodyguard drove. The transpex panel separating the two compartments was up and dialed to full opacity, blocking the view of the front compartment. Isogi wasn't taking any chances of me being able to cause trouble, despite the drugs Trouble fed me to muddle my concentration and keep me passive. They didn't bother to blindfold me, but they did tie my hands in front of me using a plastic binder strip, the kind security companies used to restrain prisoners. They took my Viper from its shoulder holster and Trouble took the belt with my sheathed mageblade. None of the yakuza seemed willing to touch it, since everyone knew it was unwise to frag with a magician's tools uninvited. That was pretty smart of them. Obviously the New

Way had taught the yaks something about handling magic and magicians.

Tires hissed on the glistening pavement as the car took a smooth left into the underground garage of the Mitsuhama Tower, which rose a hundred stories above us, black on black into the starry sky. Like a fantasy construction to challenge the gods themselves. At the very top of the tower glowed the MCT logo in cool blue neon. A microwatt laser scanned the fenders as we entered, picking up the Mitsuhama-authorized barcode on them, and probably a coded signal from a transponder in the car as well. The garage's computer opened the barricades and retracted the tire spikes angled to keep unwanted vehicles out.

We pulled into a space in the garage, almost empty except for the solid, conservative vehicles of a few suits following the fine corporate tradition of overwork, impressing the company with their diligence, or simply preferring to sleep at the office rather than return to whatever they had for a homelife. Trouble took her Predator and popped her door open. She gripped my upper arm firmly, pulling me to my feet and gesturing with the gun.

"Ride's over, Talon. Let's go." Her voice held no trace of compassion or remorse, completely controlled and professional. The yakuza bodyguard helped push my limp body from the car and I stood slowly, wobbling and leaning on the car slightly for balance. With a push of her gun in my lower back, Trouble guided me toward a nearby bank of elevators. Unless someone was standing right next to us, they wouldn't even see the gun, but there was no one around to see. Isogi and his other bodyguard fell into step behind us, where they could keep an eye on me and Trouble, no doubt.

Moving past the set of doors used by the wageslaves and low-level suits, we stopped in front of a smaller executive elevator. A red LCD blinked above the security camera beside the door, and Trouble looked right into the dead eye of the lens. We waited as the seconds ticked by, then there was a quiet tone and the elevator door slid open. With a nudge of her gun, Trouble said, "After you."

I stepped into the car, followed by Trouble and the yakuza. The doors slid closed, and the elevator smoothly deposited us on the eighty-sixth floor of the tower. Trouble kept an eye on the car's internal security camera on the ride up, while I leaned against the wall heavily. The ride seemed to take forever and the silence inside the elevator car was deafening.

Garnoff's office was decorated with enough class to impress most anyone, but I hated the place from the moment I saw it. Perhaps it was the circumstances of my visit, but there was a feeling about it that made my skin crawl.

The whole place was larger than Dr. Gordon's entire cramped apartment in the Rox. The wall opposite the door was all variable-tint, one-way armored macroglass, currently set on transparent to show the sparkling night skyline of the sprawl. The floor was covered in deep blue carpet and the furniture was modern techno-Nippon style; all chrome, smoked glass, and black-lacquered panels, with occasional *kanji* characters and *mon* emblems to break up the monotony. It was cold, immaculate, and lifeless, much like its inhabitant.

Trouble guided me over to a black leather and chrome chair in front of the broad, glass-top desk. I dropped into it like I was poured there and looked across at the man sitting behind the desk.

He fit the image of the successful corporate wagemage
to a "T." Tall and thin, with urbane, aristocratic features.
His dark hair and beard neatly trimmed, with enough gray
to show his solid years of experience and wisdom without making him look old. His suit was a charcoal gray,
double-breasted number with tasteful silver lapel pin. A
pale blue shirt and navy-blue and silver power tie with a
pentagram stickpin topped off the ensemble. All very stylish, businesslike, and fast-track.

I looked into his dark eyes and suppressed a shudder. I
hadn't been close enough to Garnoff to really see into his
eyes at the Manadyne party, but I was now. They were as
flat and cold as the smoked glass desktop between us, reflecting no more human warmth or emotion than the building's security cameras. I wondered briefly if they might
even be cyber implants. Even though most of the Awakened didn't care for the idea of sticking machinery into
their living flesh, I was proof that modern convenience
often won out over squeamishness. I got the feeling Garnoff had no qualms about such things. Indeed, no qualms
about anything at all.

"Now this, this is how I imagined we would first meet,"
he said to me. His real voice was a calm and mellow tenor,
but it didn't quite conceal a gloating note of triumph. "The
great shadowrunner Talon, brought low by such . . . simple
means." I barely suppressed an angry twitch, which was
about all I could do at this point.

Garnoff's gaze flicked from me to Trouble. "Are you
sure he's under?" he asked. She nodded. I felt a chill run
through me, but suppressed it. Garnoff was the suspicious type.

"I dosed him with enough neuro-stun to keep him
groggy for hours. He's not capable of much more than

assisted movement and sitting and listening." She tapped
the grip of my Viper, tucked into her belt. "He was armed
with this—not that he'd even be able to aim it at this
point—and this." She held out my mageblade to Garnoff.
He smiled and gripped Talonclaw's hilt, drawing it from
the leather sheath Trouble held. The fine steel of the blade
gleamed dully in the dead fluorescent light of the office.

"A fine weapon," he said, turning the blade over in his
hands, inspecting the edge. He came around the front of
the desk and sat on a corner of it, a gesture that reminded
me strangely of the priest at the South Boston mission
where I grew up, sitting on his desk to offer fatherly advice or a stern reprimand to the wild street kid.

Garnoff held Talonclaw and toyed with the hilt as he
spoke. "I was quite surprised to see you at the party. It
showed unexpected resourcefulness. I fully expected you
to skulk in the shadows a while longer before you tried
to confront me. Still, I'm pleased you did it. It gave me
an opportunity to see you at your best, before this.

"I would have expected a street mage of your . . . 'rep'
as they say, to have noticed the little surprise I left with
Trouble."

He walked over to stand near Trouble and lightly caressed the side of her neck with one finger. Trouble flashed
him a winsome smile that could melt the coldest heart.
"Such an apt name," he mused.

"The spell is really quite simple." Garnoff sounded
like a professor lecturing a room full of students. "It implants a powerful suggestion deep in the psyche, trig-
gered by a specific set of circumstances later on. You see,
I could have hired shadowrunners to track you down and
bring you to me, but you street scum have a distressing
tendency to take care of your own. Your involvement

with Assets, Inc. and their ties to the Draco Foundation complicated matters. If agents went after you directly, you could simply go to ground and it would take a very long time to track you down again, and time is very important to me. You might have become suspicious, been put on the defensive.

"Instead, I placed this spell on Trouble without her knowledge, then arranged for her to believe she was in danger because of what she'd discovered for me thus far. It took no more than a gentle subconscious nudge to send her looking to you for help. I knew the mystery of someone looking into your past and the lure of a lady in distress would be too much for you to refuse. Everything I've learned about you so far says you like to handle such things personally. What else could you do but come to Boston to confront me? That brought you here, minus your friends from Assets.

"Once you arrived, it was only a matter of time before the opportunity to betray you presented itself and Trouble took it. Your intrusion into the Manadyne facility was one such opportunity. Unfortunately, you refused to allow Trouble to go along personally. She was able to send me a message about your intrusion, but I had to rely on less resourceful assistance."

He threw a glance toward Isogi, who stiffened at the off-handed way Garnoff dismissed the yakuza.

"Still, it was only a matter of time. All of your so-called investigation was never of any concern. I knew I had time on my side all along. All I needed to do was wait for you to make your mistake, and Trouble would deal with you. Now you have done that. How did you put it? You only get so many mistakes, Talon."

He shook his head with a mocking look of sadness.

"Magicians such as you who do not do their research deserve their fate. Evolution in action, my young alley runner: only the strong survive."

"Why?" I said slowly and with visible effort. "Why are you doing this?"

Garnoff smiled and returned to his perch on the edge of his desk.

"Why?" he echoed, mocking my question. "Why do tigers hunt? Why do corporations acquire? It is the way of life. The strong consume the weak and use them to grow stronger. You could have been on the winning side, Talon. In fact, I actually imagined our first meeting many years ago, when you would have graduated from MIT&T and come to work for me."

I kept my expression as neutral as possible, but Garnoff was obviously looking for a reaction. I just clenched my jaw and stared at him.

"Yes, I was the one who arranged for your recruitment," he said. "You had such potential. Your Talent was strong and you clearly possessed an aptitude too great to waste doing hedge magic and charms in the gutters. You could have been so much more.

"But you wouldn't leave. You knew no other life and you couldn't see the potential I saw in you. Your . . . teacher wanted to keep you in the gutter with him, mold you in his image. No different from what I wanted, I suppose, except I had the means to make things happen. I was sure once you were in the proper environment, you would come around."

"You killed him," I said thickly. I knew it was true, but I had to hear him say the words himself.

"No," Garnoff said. "I *had* him killed. A subtle, but important, difference."

"You son of a bitch," I said. My muscles tensed but I didn't move from the chair. I couldn't. Not yet. Triumph radiated off Garnoff in waves. He was really enjoying this, the sick frag.

"Enough," Tomo Isogi said from somewhere behind me. There was a touch of irritation and impatience in his voice. "We have brought him to you as you requested, Garnoff-*san*. Now get the information you need from him so we can conclude this business. The oyabun cannot be kept waiting. He still expects a full report on your progress."

"Of course," Garnoff said, "but I cannot interrogate him here. I have made other arrangements. I will get the information I need and then I will be able to provide Hiramatsu-*sama* with a complete report in a day or two."

"That is not acceptable," Isogi replied. "I am not leaving until I have more information to bring back to the oyabun."

"I cannot interrogate him here," Garnoff repeated. "I require tools I have elsewhere."

"Then I will go with you, Garnoff-*san*, to ensure that our interests are maintained."

Garnoff looked past me at Isogi for several long seconds before replying. "Very well," he said, "if that is your wish, so be it." He took a dark overcoat from a rack near the door and shrugged into it.

"Bring our prize, Isogi. I have someone who's very eager to see him again."

Trouble came over and helped one of the yakuza lift me from the chair. Her gaze flicked across mine for a second, then her face resumed a look of bland disinterest.

We made our way back down the elevator to the parking garage. Trouble took the wheel of the van while Garnoff sat in the passenger seat. With only a moment of hesitation, Isogi climbed into the back with me and one of his bodyguards, after giving instructions to the other, no doubt to carry a message to his oyabun. He clearly didn't trust Garnoff, and he kept a careful watch on him and me both.

We only went a short distance, to a public parking garage. The place was filling up with people going to various parties and festivities in the clubs and hotels of the city. Everyone wore different costumes, tending toward frightening images of ghouls, vampires, and other creatures of the night. It was still Halloween Night then, Samhain, the night when the walls between the physical world and the astral plane were the thinnest.

Amidst the crowd of party-goers, we attracted little attention. If anyone noticed Isogi and his bodyguard practically carrying me down the stairs of the subway station, they saw only some friends helping another who'd gotten an early start on the party. There were several other people around who'd clearly been drinking or slotting recreational chips. No one thought anything was wrong.

The subway car was filled with a crowd of strange figures. It was a mix of corporate "straight citizens," street-types, and people dressed in the most outlandish costumes. For one night, all standards were turned upside-down. Some of the street-types wore their leathers and chains uncomfortably, playing on the wild side for a little while. I wondered how many real ghouls, ghosts, and vampires were abroad tonight. I knew of only one for sure and he sat quietly, with a smug look on his face, enjoying the spectacle.

The softly glowing green time display on the edge of my field of vision read 23:41:08. I thought about how deep underground we were. I hoped a signal could carry to the surface well enough from here. If it didn't, the others couldn't find me. I was very likely a dead man.

"I demand to know where we are going," Isogi said quietly to Garnoff, barely audible over the shriek of the train as it rumbled and lurched through the tunnels.

"In good time, Isogi-*san,* in good time," the mage muttered. "We are nearly there."

We got off at the stop where Garnoff told us and made our way through the throngs of people on the platform to the tunnel itself. T-security had their hands full keeping an eye on everything going on in the trains and on the platform. No one noticed us slip away down the tunnel. I sensed a hint of magic in the ease of our movements. Garnoff was probably using illusions to conceal our movements. It would be easy in the Halloween crowd, where there were so many things to distract an onlooker's attention already.

The side tunnel was dark and dank, filled with a scent of rusting metal and damp decay. Over the rumbling and screeching of the trains, I could hear the sounds of small creatures squealing and scurrying past in the shadows. Isogi was looking quite uncomfortable as we made our way down the tunnel. His bodyguard and Trouble wore emotionless masks, and Garnoff seemed to almost shiver with barely controlled anticipation.

The tunnel ended in a brick wall, but Garnoff didn't miss a beat. He drew a slim white wand from his coat and began to trace symbols in the air in front of the wall, muttering quietly under his breath. As he did, I noticed the dull, creaking sound that provided a faint counterpoint to the chants. The passes of the wand left faintly glowing images in its wake that seemed to sink into the wall itself and disappear.

"The wall is nothing more than an illusion covering a protective barrier," Garnoff said. "Take him through."

Isogi and his bodyguard paused for a moment and looked at each other. Garnoff sighed and turned to Trouble.

"Demonstrate, won't you, my dear?" he said with exaggerated patience. Trouble looked at Garnoff for a moment, then nodded and walked carefully into the wall. She passed through it like smoke and vanished from sight. The yakuza carried me by the arms and led me stumbling through the illusion, into the room beyond.

Trouble stood near the entrance, looking rather pale. The room had likely been some kind of maintenance or storage room at one point, but its gray walls were bare of any furnishings or adornment. A ring of standing torches stood in a circle around the center of the room. Dark, hunched figures clustered in the shadows near the walls of the chamber.

In the center of the room dangled a burned and blackened corpse, hanging by its neck from a rope affixed to one of the heavy pipes that ran along the ceiling. The body swayed slightly and the rope creaked, the only sound in the room except for the occasional whisper or giggle from the shadows. The body did not move. It showed no outward signs of life, but the hanging corpse's burning blue eyes still held the fires of anger and hatred. They seemed to stare right at me and bore into my own eyes. I felt like a bird facing the paralyzing gaze of a cobra.

Memories of the metaplanes flooded back, and I saw my own twisted reflection staring at me from the mirror in the citadel. A dry and crackling voice whispered in my mind.

*Hello, father,* Gallow said. *It's been a very long time.*

# 20

"What is the meaning of this?" Tomo Isogi said, looking aghast as his eyes went from the hanging body to Garnoff and back again. "Is *this* what you have been using our money for? Explain yourself at once."

"Gladly, Isogi-*san*," Garnoff said with an oily smile. "My research discovered a spirit of unprecedented power and potential imprisoned here. With the aid of your oya-bun and the resources of my corporation, I have learned a great deal about this spirit and offered it a means of achieving its freedom. In return, it will grant us magical power enough to crush your enemies and establish the Hiramatsu-*gumi* as the ruling force of the Boston under-world. That will in turn grant Mitsuhama additional lever-age in the metroplex, enough to edge out Novatech and any other company that opposes us here."

"And what of you?" Isogi said, his eyes narrowing. "Do you remain a humble servant of the company and the oyabun?"

"Of course," Garnoff said. "Although I am sure my station will be greatly improved by my success. And, of course, I will hold the secrets that will allow me to influence further research and development on the part of Mitsuhama."

"What of them?" Isogi said, gesturing toward the figures lurking in the shadows. "Who are they?"

"Barukumin," Garnoff said, using the Japanese word
for outcasts, the "untouchable" caste of Japanese society.
In the Awakened world, the barukumin mostly consisted
of the most hideous of metahumans, their bodies and
minds twisted by the return of magic. "They live down
here in the Catacombs and know them well. I pay them to
serve as my eyes and ears and hands in this place. They
are also versed in certain rites I have taught them, allowing them to assist me with my rituals."

Isogi was clearly uncomfortable with the presence of
so many twisted metahumans. Most Japanese didn't care
for *kawaru,* the "changed," as they called them. Still, Garnoff's explanation made it clear the barukumin were servants, and that was a concept Isogi could deal with.

"And this . . . spirit," Isogi said with some distaste,
looking over at the hanging corpse. "You can control it?"

Garnoff held out his hands. "Not control, Isogi-*san,*"
he said carefully. "It is willing to become our ally, provided
we help it escape from the prison of flesh it is trapped in."

"Is that why you need him?" Isogi nodded toward me.

"Exactly. Talon is closely linked to the spirit. His death
will free it and allow it to turn its powers toward helping us."

"Then why haven't you killed him already?"

Garnoff shook his head like a schoolmaster speaking
to a small child. "It's not that simple. There are certain
rituals that must be followed for his death to have some
meaning. Otherwise, it won't work. I've already made
the necessary preparations, it was simply a matter of
waiting for my web to bring the street mage to me."

I didn't much care for the way the two of them were

talking about me like I wasn't even in the room, especially considering they were discussing my imminent demise, but for the moment there was nothing I could do about it, so I waited and listened.

"And why were we not told the truth about your research before now?" Isogi asked.

*Enough of this!* Gallow's voice roared in my mind. *We must begin the ritual! The night is waning.*

"Because I knew there would be doubt in your minds," Garnoff said calmly, although I was sure he heard the same impatient words I did. "Even now you are wondering if I am mad. But when you see the kind of power we can call upon to further our goals, Isogi-*san*, you will understand why I decided on caution in revealing the truth to anyone."

Isogi paused for a long moment. He glanced at me, looked at Gallow, then turned back to Garnoff, his face set like stone, completely emotionless. He was a man who knew how to pick his battles. "Very well, proceed."

Garnoff turned toward the barukumin and said, "Make ready for the ritual." Four of them emerged from the shadows and approached me. They were all hairless, shrunken metahumans, their skins fish-belly white and their eyes blind and staring. Ghouls. I fought back a shudder as I slumped against Isogi's bodyguard, who supported me with little or no effort. He slid me to the floor and backed away as the ghouls approached. They grabbed my arms and carried me toward the center of the room, where a complex hermetic circle was painted dark red and black on the gray concrete. I glanced back to where Trouble stood, all but forgotten by Garnoff and Isogi.

As they placed me in the center of the circle, I realized that only some of the lines and symbols were drawn in

paint. The rest were drawn in dried blood. The smell of it
was strong near the floor, dusty and metallic.

I lay on my back, my arms and legs splayed out, looking up at the corpse dangling above me, only an arm's
length away. The concrete was cold against my back, even
through my coat, but I could feel a strange warmth ema-
nating from the physical shell that housed the spirit called
Gallow. It radiated off it like waves, and I was chilled inside even as the warmth seemed to caress my face.

*The circle is complete,* Gallow's voice whispered. *Once,
I was nothing more than a slave, a tool of your anger and
vengeance. Now, I will draw power from your destruc-
tion, enslaving your spirit to me. Your blood will break
the binding that holds me and I will grow strong, stronger
than ever before. I will have many feasts like the one you
gave me that first night, father.*

I shuddered and wanted to look away, but I couldn't.
My gaze was held in horrified fascination by the hyp-
notic swaying of the body, the sound of Gallow's voice.
My astral senses opened up and I could see a ghostly
flicker of flames around the hanging body.

*I enjoyed killing them so much,* Gallow's astral voice
whispered to me. *Like you did. The sweet rush of power
and pleasure as they burned, as they screamed for mercy.
There is no greater thing in this world. Garnoff under-
stands that. In fact, if it were not for him, I would not exist. If he did not kill Jason Vale, you would never have
summoned me. If he did not hear my call, you would not
be here now. My two "parents," together at last. Now one
must kill the other for me to feed.* The phantom flames
burned brighter in anticipation.

Garnoff came and knelt beside me. He had exchanged

his overcoat for a black robe, the edges stitched with red runes and symbols. He held a small bronze bowl, which he set down beside me.

"I have you to thank," he said in a low voice, pitched so only I could hear. "If you hadn't been so defiant, if you had accepted my offer to free you from the sewer you lived in, you would never have created a spirit as magnificent as this, and I would never have found my destiny."

He raised Talonclaw in his right hand, the edge gleaming in the torch light, the whole of it shimmering with dormant magical power. The blade flashed as Garnoff used it to cut through my shirt.

He bared my chest and dipped two fingers into the bowl, stirring them around slightly. I shivered from the cold shock as Garnoff drew magical symbols on my skin in red ochre paint.

"The drugs you've been given will dull the pain somewhat," he said conversationally as he put the finishing touches on the design. "But not too much. A certain amount of pain is necessary for the ritual to be successful. I'm sure you understand."

*Life is pain,* Gallow echoed like a mantra. *Pain is life.*

Garnoff took the bowl away and wiped his hands clean on a cloth. The ghouls and other twisted metahumans of the barukumin spread out to form a ring around the circle, just outside the flickering torches. Trouble stood outside the circle and looked on the whole scene, coolly distant, detached, one hand sliding into her jacket.

I couldn't see Isogi or his bodyguard from where I lay. It seemed they were staying quietly out of the way. It was never a good idea to interrupt a magical ritual, and Isogi seemed to have a healthy respect for the power in the

room. I sensed he was not happy with this whole arrangement, but that he also wasn't going to interfere with Garnoff. I was on my own.

Garnoff stepped into the circle and held Talonclaw in
both hands, the blade pointing upward.

"Let the ritual begin," he said. "The time of power has
come. We gather here on Samhain Night, when the barri-
ers between this world and the others are at their thinnest,
when the spirits of the dead draw close to the land of the
living, to offer a sacrifice to the Otherworld and to break
the bonds of earthly flesh holding immortal spirit, to loose
the fire of power."

The barukumin began a low chant, soft, guttural, in no
language I knew, as Garnoff began to slowly walk around
the circle, counterclockwise.

"I cast this circle to guard us from all forces abroad on
this Samhain Night. I seal this circle against all forces
and powers that may seek to disrupt our rite. I empower
this circle with the power of Air and Earth, the Waters of
the Deep, and the power of Fire Eternal. I draw down the
power of the comet, the omen of power in the night sky,
the sign of the coming times. Let the circle remain un-
broken until the rite is done."

The torchlight took on a greenish cast as the hermetic
circle surrounded us with a magical barrier, visible only
to my astral sight, like a dome of translucent glass arcing
overhead, its apex just above the head of the swaying
corpse that housed Gallow.

I flinched as the cold edge of my mageblade touched
my neck. The chanting grew faster, and the barukumin began to shuffle slowly around the outer edge of the circle.

"Blood is life," Garnoff intoned. "By the power of
blood I create and give new life. By the power of blood, I

break the bonds of mortal flesh and liberate immortal spirit. I call on Gallow to take this offering and grow strong, to escape his prison of flesh and take up his true power and place in the world of the living."

*As all gods slay the generation before them, so will I grow strong on the life of my creator,* the spirit responded in its astral voice. The chanting grew louder. The dancing grew faster, more frantic and chaotic. It was nearing a peak. Garnoff raised Talonclaw in one hand. My eyes rolled back in my head a bit as I concentrated with all my willpower. This needed to be timed exactly right.

"With this blade, forged by his hand, I liberate this life. To the spirit, forged by his will, I offer this life."

He looked down at me with cold, dead eyes and shook his head. "Poor boy. Too bad you weren't a bit more clever."

The barukumin and Gallow seemed to cry out as one, and Garnoff brought the blade down toward my chest with both hands.

There was a blue spark as the mageblade struck an invisible wall only centimeters away from my bare skin. With a burst of speed I grabbed Garnoff's outstretched wrist, pulled him off balance and punched him square in the face.

"Funny," I said, "I was thinking the same thing about you." I keyed open a comm channel on my headware and subvocalized over it, praying they'd gotten the signal as planned.

"Now," was all I said.

The barukumin, who stood in shock as Garnoff reeled from the punch, recovered their wits and started to move toward me. That's when an explosion shook the room as a small, powerful charge blew out the protective barrier covering the entrance, sending clouds of concrete dust and fragments flying everywhere. A shotgun blast split the air, sending one of the twisted ghouls sliding down the wall, leaving a bloody trail behind.

"Talon, stay down!" Boom yelled as he, Hammer, and Sloane burst into the room, guns blazing. Along with them came a pair of Sikorsky skimmer-drones that hummed and buzzed through the air like giant mechanical insects, controlled remotely by Val. Weapons and sensors on swivel-mounts attached to their undersides started tracking the barukumin. Gunfire stitched along the walls in lines of fire and dust, sending Garnoff's helpers scattering or cutting them down where they stood, bright sprays of blood spattering the walls.

I started to get to my feet just as Garnoff was doing the same. Before he could rise, I tackled him, sending us both sprawling to the floor. I grabbed his wrist as he tried to bring the dagger around to stab me. He was stronger than he looked, and his face was a twisted mask of anger and rage. I tried to keep him pinned long enough to disable him, but he struggled like a trapped animal and managed to throw me to the side. I landed hard on the concrete floor, knocking the wind out of me as Garnoff scrambled to his feet.

"You, you, street garbage!" he shouted. "I'll kill you!" He raised Talonclaw in one hand to lunge at me when a gunshot caught him in the wrist.

"Wrong again, asshole," Trouble said, holding her smoking Predator. I threw her a grateful glance as she gave an incoming ghoul a sharp kick that sent it stumbling backward.

Garnoff howled in pain and dropped Talonclaw as

blood splashed over the front of his robe. He lashed out with his other hand, fingers curled like claws, and Trouble was sent flying, like she'd been swatted by a giant's fist. Her second shot went wide, ricocheting off the floor. He raised one hand, and the dome of light around the circle became visible in the physical world as a translucent barrier, blocking all other attacks from the outside, sealing the two of us in together.

I scrambled forward and grabbed Talonclaw, heedless of the gore spattering the hilt. The moment I touched it, I sent the power of my magic flowing into the blade, awakening its enchantment and feeling its power thrum in my hand. I focused my perceptions to take in the swirling magical forces that played about the chamber, centered on the darkly glowing form of Garnoff, shimmering with unrestrained power.

"Now," I said to Garnoff, "let's finish this."

"You arrogant pup, do you think you can match the power I possess? Have you any idea how powerful I am now?" The mage gestured tightly with one hand and hurled a blast of green flame at me. Holding Talonclaw in front of me like a shield, I focused on directing the energy of the magefire away from me. The inferno flowed and hissed all around me, but I remained untouched.

"I don't think I'm the one doing the underestimating here," I said. I took a step closer and Garnoff started to back away.

He gestured again and flung a powerbolt. It also spattered against my shields. I staggered slightly under the force of it, but continued to move closer and closer as Garnoff backed against the glowing energy shield. I backhanded him, sending him crumpling against the barrier.

"It's different with someone who can fight back, isn't it?" I said. "It's harder when you have to do your own dirty work, isn't it?" I punched him in the jaw, drawing blood from a split lip. Garnoff's form seemed to boil away like mist, transforming into a hideous black serpent, with a body nearly as thick as my waist. I narrowed my eyes and brought my knee up hard under the serpent's jaw and was rewarded with a dull cracking sound. The image of the serpent vanished as suddenly as it appeared, leaving Garnoff kneeling on the floor, trying to crawl away from me.

"No more tricks," I said. "No more games. You're finished playing with people's lives, you sick fragger. You're not killing anyone else to feed your need to feel powerful."

Tears flowed freely down my face as all of the emotions I'd kept tightly controlled while in Garnoff's presence poured out of me. Gunfire echoed and rattled outside the dome, along with muffled screams—from which side, I didn't know. At that moment, I didn't care. "You can't break my defenses, and you learn how to fight when you're 'street trash' like me."

"Please," Garnoff moaned. "I'll give you anything, anything. We could be partners, allies." The roar of gunfire dwindled.

"Anything?" I said. A momentary hope lit in Garnoff's black eyes.

"Anything," he said.

I grabbed the front of his robe and pulled his face close to mine. "Money?"

"Yes, as much as you want."

"Power?"

"Power like you've never dreamed of."

"Influence?"

"Yes, yes, whatever you want, just tell me," Garnoff babbled.

"I'll tell you what I want," I hissed, mere centimeters from his face. "I want Jase's life back." And I buried Talonclaw in his heart.

*YES!* cried a voice in my mind. *FREEEEE! FREE AT LAST!* I stumbled back as Garnoff's body burst into flames. The magical dome dissolved like ice on a hot skillet as the dry corpse hanging from the ceiling ignited as well, burning with a white-hot fire. I coughed and took a few more steps back from the searing heat.

"What the hell . . . ?" I heard Boom shout before there was a thunderous clap of noise, and the flames cleared.

Garnoff stood on the edge of the magical circle, taller and more forceful than I'd ever seen him before. A ragged hole stained with blood was torn in the front of his black robe, but the skin underneath it was unscarred, with no sign of the wound I'd just inflicted, and flushed with a pink blush of health. He drew himself up to his full height, threw back his head and laughed, a deep, booming laughter that echoed off the walls of the chamber. When he opened his eyes to look at me, the dull and lifeless blackness of Garnoff's gaze was replaced with a burning red-orange color, like an inferno raged inside the magician's skull just behind his eyes.

There was a sound from near where the mage stood as Trouble started to push herself away from the wall where she fell.

"Trouble!" I yelled. "Look . . ." but I was too late. With the speed of a leaping flame, Garnoff seized Trouble and dragged her to her feet, holding her in front of him like a living shield, one arm cocked around her neck. The other hand ignited, turning into a twisted black claw

wreathed in flames, which he held close to Trouble's face
as he glared at me.

"Well done, father," Gallow spoke through Garnoff's
lips. "You're as capable as ever. I knew I could count on
you if I needed a killing done."

# 21

"One false move, and she dies," Gallow said, holding a burning hand perilously close to Trouble's face. "You know me well, father. You know I would kill her gladly."

I gestured to Boom and the others. "He's right. Lower your weapons."

"Good," Gallow said. "Very good. Now I must leave."

"Let Trouble go," I said.

"Do you take me for a fool? No, she will come with me, and I will release her once we are a safe distance away."

"Talon!" Trouble said. "Don't listen to him! Don't . . ."

Gallow tightened an arm around her throat. "Don't be foolish," he hissed, "and you can continue to live." Then he began to drag her to the door, moving toward us.

"You will all move out of our way, if you want her to live," he said.

"Do what he says," I told the others. I got hard looks from Hammer and Sloane, but they were professionals and I was in charge, so they did as they were told.

"This is far from over," Gallow said to me as he passed, his smile twisting Garnoff's features.

"You're right about that," I said.

"Until the next time," the spirit said, dragging Trouble to the illusory wall covering the exit from the chamber.

He backed out through the wall, taking her with him, both of them passing through the illusion like shadows.

Immediately I turned to the others. "Where's Isogi?" I asked.

"Over here," a voice said from a corner of the room. Isogi's immaculate suit was spattered with blood and there was a gun in his hand, although it was lowered at the moment. He looked dazed as he realized events had spiraled out of his control long ago. "I don't understand . . ." he began.

"Garnoff's dead," I said. "And he played you for suckers. He wanted to free that fire spirit and now he's done it, but the spirit has taken control of his body. You've made a serious mistake, Isogi-*san*."

The sound of his name seemed to snap Isogi out of his confusion. He turned his eyes directly toward me for a moment, before lowering them toward the floor in shame.

"You are right. I must make amends."

"What can we do?" Boom asked.

"I'm going after them," I said. "Clear out of here and get back to the safe house. With luck, Trouble and I will see you there soon."

I started for the door when Boom put a large hand on my shoulder. "Wait," he said. "We can go with you."

I shook my head. "No, I have to do this alone. Gallow is a spirit. He can't really be hurt by physical weapons, but Trouble can. Starting a firefight just means more ways she could get caught in the crossfire. The only real way to handle him is with magic. I learned his true name on the metaplanes. It should allow me to banish him."

"If he gives you the chance," Boom said.

"I can't let him go," I said. "He'll kill Trouble as soon as he thinks he's safe. Now get going!"

I turned and stepped through the illusory wall into the tunnel beyond, Talonclaw clutched in my hand. I didn't bother getting a gun. Like I told Boom, mundane weapons weren't much use against a spirit, even one possessing a living body. Only magic and magical weapons like my mageblade could harm him. Gallow was like no other spirit I'd encountered, though, so there were no guarantees.

I kept my senses focused on the astral plane, looking for signs of Gallow's passing. He was a powerful spirit, and his presence left faint traces in the astral. They wouldn't last for long, but long enough for me to follow him, I hoped. I went down the tunnel and out into the main subway tunnel, deep beneath the streets of Boston. Gallow seemed to know the tunnels fairly well. *He's spent a great deal of time down here,* I thought, visions of the murders Gallow had carried out down in the underground more than a decade ago playing in my mind. If he wasn't stopped, those killings would start all over again, and Trouble would be the first.

*Gallow will head for the Catacombs,* I thought. He would seek familiar ground where he felt safe. I was fairly sure he would keep Trouble alive until then. She could still prove useful as a hostage. Only when he reached his home turf would he take the time to kill her. From what I knew about Gallow already, he didn't like to kill randomly or quickly. He was a sadist, drawing pleasure and power from the fear and pain of his victims, prolonging their deaths as long as possible.

*I enjoyed killing them so much,* Gallow had said. *Like you did.* I thought about the Asphalt Rats on fire and the spirit's words and shook my head. There was no time for that now. Gallow's astral traces beckoned me further down the tunnel.

It was well after midnight according to the chronometer on my visual display. That meant the trains were no longer running. The tunnel was dark and silent, lit only by the scattered emergency and maintenance lights along its length. The faint impressions left in astral space allowed me to follow Gallow's movements, although it wasn't difficult to figure which way he went.

For a moment, I contemplated using astral projection, sending out my spirit to track them and leaving my physical body behind. It would be a lot faster than trying to follow them physically. As a spirit, I could reach Gallow from the astral plane and Trouble would be safe from any conflict, being a mundane. I just as quickly dismissed the idea. Gallow was still a physical threat to Trouble and knowing the spirit's true name wouldn't help me fight it on its home turf of the astral plane. If Gallow did hurt Trouble, I wouldn't be able to help her as an immaterial wraith. Dragging Trouble along, Gallow wouldn't be able to move very quickly, so I should be able to catch up.

A short distance down the main tunnel, I found a maintenance hatch. The lock was melted into slag, still steaming in the cool air, the hatch slightly ajar. I opened it carefully, my mageblade in hand. There was a narrow corridor beyond it, faintly lit by green fluorescent strips placed along the walls near the ceiling. I stepped in and closed the hatch behind me. The astral traces and the physical evidence showed that Gallow had passed this way.

The corridor ended at the top of a ladder leading downward into darkness. Reluctantly, I sheathed Talonclaw and started climbing down the ladder. The maintenance shaft was old, the rungs of the metal ladder spotted with rust and corrosion. It wasn't visited or used often, from what I could tell. At the bottom of the ladder was a heavy

steel door with "CLOSED: KEEP OUT" stenciled on it
in white paint. The lock was melted through like the one
on the hatch above, and I could make out the faint marks
of fingertips in the softened metal.

Beyond the door lay part of the Catacombs, the abandoned portions of the underground sealed off after the 2005
quake because they were unsafe or simply too extensively
damaged to make repairs cost-effective or worthwhile.
The closed-off tunnels and stations in areas like the Rox
and South Boston were havens for outcast metahumans,
ghouls, and other creatures that preferred to hide from
the light of day. The door opened onto an old platform,
closed off for more than fifty years. Strange tracks criss-
crossed through the dust that lay thick over everything,
and the empty train tunnel yawned like a gaping black maw.

I drew Talonclaw and silently wished I had gone the
whole route and gotten cybereyes, or at least some retinal
modification like the Assets' cyberdoc had suggested.
The catacombs were dark and silent. It would be difficult
to see much of anything down here. Fortunately, I still
had my astral sight. The glow of the living earth was damp-
ened here, suffocated by thick layers of concrete and
metal, but I could still see the faint impressions left by
Gallow's presence, and the living auras of Gallow and
Trouble should stand out, clearly visible in the gloom. I
moved out onto the platform and looked out down one of
the tunnels.

There! I spotted a telltale glimmer of light, the light of
a living aura, shining in the darkness.

Unfortunately, there was no way to conceal the glow
of my own aura from Gallow's astral senses, either. He
must have spotted me at the very same moment, because

the tunnel was suddenly lit up with a hellish light as a stream of fire shot toward me.

I spun to the side and flattened myself behind a heavy concrete pillar as the flames shot past, feeling the wave of heat on my skin.

"Give up, Gallow!" I shouted, the words echoing strangely in the vast, empty tunnels. "You can't escape me! There's nowhere for you to go!"

"No!" the spirit shouted in Garnoff's voice. "You are no longer my master! I am free, and I will never become part of you again! You cannot stop me and if you do not leave, I will kill her!" I heard a gasp of pain from Trouble and a muffled cry as she tried to say something.

I didn't really expect Gallow to surrender, knowing that I couldn't allow it to go free. I gathered my power around me like a shining mantle and spun around the side of the pillar. Another blast of fire roared down the tunnel. This time, I rushed forward and jumped from the platform to the old train tracks below, the flames missing me by centimeters. When I landed, I raised my hands and called out an invocation, the words echoing down the tunnel.

"Avant, ye elemental! Avant, ye nature unbound! Begone from this place and trouble it no more!" The words echoed those Dr. Gordon had spoken to banish the fire elemental Garnoff sent against me. It seemed fitting somehow to use his formula. "By the power of the elements, I command you! By the power of your Name, I compel you! You are Talon's Hate and I, your maker, bid you begone!"

Gallow screamed in fury as streamers of light stretched out from my aura to touch his. His grip on Trouble weakened, and she was able to break free. The spirit, in Garnoff's body, could do nothing to stop her. We were both locked in magical combat until the struggle of wills was decided. Bright, fiery energies surged back toward me, and I could feel Gallow struggling against the banishment.

"You . . . cannot . . . destroy . . . me," the spirit cried. "I am your dark reflection, all that you longed to do, but feared!"

I ignored his protests and focused my will even stronger. "I am responsible for making you," I said. "Now I will unmake you. You will do no further harm." I felt Gallow's power begin to weaken as I fought with all my strength.

As the battle raged between us, I saw Trouble move out of the corner of my eye. She picked herself up along the tunnel wall and went for the weapon Gallow had dropped when she broke free. As she scooped up my Ares Viper, I tried to call out to her.

"Trouble! Don't! You can't . . ."

Gallow saw his opening and seized it, sending a massive surge of power against me. I gasped and staggered, nearly driven to my knees by it. I could feel my own strength buckling under the savage assault.

Trouble hesitated only a second before leveling the gun at Gallow and firing. A burst of high-velocity flechettes hummed through the air at close range, shredding parts of Garnoff's stylish corporate suit and the black over-robe. The needles tore exposed flesh and inflicted enough damage to bring down a man twice Garnoff's size, but Gallow did not flinch in his assault. The wounds immediately began to close, healing even as I watched. Gallow sent a final surge of power that dropped me to my knees before breaking off the contest. He turned toward Trouble, flames igniting in a blazing aura around his body.

"Have you learned nothing?" he said with a smug grin.

"Weapons of the physical world cannot harm me, woman. I am immortal, invincible!"

He lashed out with a hand, sending a jet of flames rushing toward Trouble. She screamed, a terrible sound in the tunnel, and fell back, her clothes burning. She dropped to the rough and rocky ground, rolling around madly, trying to put out the flames. I got to my feet and rushed toward her as Gallow gave a hideous grin and started off down the tunnel.

"If you want me destroyed, you can come after me now," he called over his shoulder. "Or you can try to save her useless life."

I cursed Gallow as his laughter echoed down the tunnel, but I stopped short at Trouble's side. The flames were mostly out, and I threw my long coat over her to snuff out the rest. Her clothes and skin were terribly burnt, most of the hair on one side of her hair shorn away by the flames. Raw, red burns stretched across her skin, already beginning to ooze a clear, shiny liquid. She moaned and writhed in pain, barely conscious. I was momentarily grateful for the banishing contest. If our battle hadn't depleted Gallow's strength, his attack probably would have killed her outright.

I knelt down beside her and placed my hands over her heart, calling the mana to me. I channeled energy into her weakening life force, pouring mana through my body and spirit like cooling water to soothe the angry burns. A bright glow surrounded her body in my astral sight, growing stronger as the power flowed. The mana burned like fire along my veins and my nerves. The struggle with Gallow had weakened me as well. I was drawing too much power, more than my weakened system could handle at the moment, but I had no choice. No one else was going to die because of my mistakes. Not so long as there was anything I could do about it. I ignored the pain and kept the energy flowing.

Before my eyes, Trouble's burns began to heal, angry red giving way to pink and then to pale new skin that grew in the damaged places. Blood and plasma stopped flowing and her skin firmed and strengthened beneath my touch. Her breathing became more regular and calm as the pain was washed away by the flow of life-giving mana.

My own pain was intense, but I gritted my teeth as I concentrated on maintaining the spell until Trouble's own life force was strong enough to maintain the healing itself. I could feel blood dripping down over my mouth and chin and felt the beginnings of a massive headache starting behind my eyes. My hands trembled as I lifted them gently from Trouble's chest, watching the spell start to stabilize. I was in no shape to go after Gallow, and in even worse shape to try and continue our battle.

"Talon!" a deep voice echoed in the tunnel as Boom and the others rushed toward us. I looked up weakly from where I knelt as the troll hurried over, combat shotgun at the ready.

"How . . ." I started weakly, "I told you . . ."

"Yeah, yeah," Boom said. "I know, but I never was very good at taking orders. Val tracked you down using your headphone link. You left the circuit open. How is . . . ?"

"She'll be okay," I said. "She just needs to rest a bit."

"You too, from the look of it," Boom said. He glanced around the tunnel. "Gallow?"

"Escaped," I replied. "I can't rest for long, chummer. I have to find him, have to stop him . . ."

I started to rise and Boom caught me under one arm as I wobbled. "Easy, easy," he said. "You're not going to be any good against anyone right now. Take a few minutes. We'll find him, Talon."

"Yes," Isogi said, stepping forward. He seemed in charge of himself again, his face an emotionless mask. "We will stop this spirit," he said.

*This is far from over,* I thought, repeating Gallow's earlier words to me. I had to find it and stop it, but now, all I could do was sink down beside Trouble and try to rest. I slumped on the rusting tracks. There was no way I could handle Gallow by myself right now, but fortunately, I had some help.

"Thanks," I said quietly. "Here's what we're going to have to do."

# 22

Trouble's eyes fluttered open. I stopped what I was do-ing and moved to help her sit up against the tunnel wall.

She looked up at me and smiled weakly. "Hi," she said.

I returned the smile. "Hi yourself. How are you feeling?"

"Tired, but okay. Did you get him?"

"No."

Trouble's face fell, the smile vanished. "Talon . . ." she began.

"It's okay," I said. "There was no way I was going to just leave you there. You were hurt pretty bad."

Trouble winced slightly. "The fire, I remember . . ." She hugged herself tightly. "My god, what was that thing? Where did it come from?"

"It calls itself Gallow," I said, "and I created it."

"What?" she said.

I held up a hand to forestall the question for a moment as I motioned to everyone else to gather around. I went back over to the partial diagram drawn in colored chalk on the cracked concrete of the old platform and began to explain what I'd pieced together so far as I continued to sketch symbols and runes around the edges of the circle.

"The creature from the Catacombs that is possessing Garnoff's body is a free spirit," I began. "It calls itself

Gallow, and it's a great deal smarter than I gave it credit for. It turns out that it played me for a sucker and that's not a feeling I'm fond of, especially since I discovered my own connection to this whole mess."

I took a deep breath, and continued. "I told some of you about how Mitsuhama tried to recruit me as a company mage years ago, how Garnoff was responsible for arranging Jason Vale's death, and how that convinced me to take MCT's offer and go to MIT&T on a corporate scholarship.

"The part I didn't tell you came between Jase's death and my taking MCT's offer. I loved Jase, he saved my life and gave it some meaning for the first time I could remember. When he died, it was like I died with him. I didn't really care what happened to me. All I could think about was getting the fraggers who'd done it.

"It wasn't hard to track them down. The gang was called the Asphalt Rats and they operated on the outskirts of the Rox. They were a small-time go-gang, running protection and playing errand-runner for some of the bigger fish in the pond. Mostly they just hit the streets doing as much random violence as they could. Having them hit Jase was smart. Nobody would connect another incident of 'random street violence' to a corporate hit, and it probably didn't cost Garnoff anything more than some new BTL chips for the gangers to fry their gray matter on.

"I knew a few spells back then, but nothing that would let me take on a whole gang by myself. I needed help, but I had nowhere to turn. I didn't have any real money, or any contacts. So I took the magical gear that was left in Jase's apartment and used it to perform a ritual, a rite of summoning. I conjured up the biggest, meanest, toughest fire elemental I could. Looking back on it, I'm amazed

I pulled it off without giving myself a stroke in the process, but I don't think I would've cared at that point. All I wanted was to see the Rats dead. So I called up the spirit and bound it to obey me.

"I went down to the turf where the gang usually hung out. It didn't take long to find them. They'd taken over an alley and turned it into their party zone for the night. The music was blasting, and most of the Rats were hitting the booze and BTLs pretty heavy. They never even knew what hit 'em.

"I called up the spirit and gave it one command: 'Kill them all.' And it did." I paused in my work and looked at the silent faces staring back at me. There was no judgment, no recrimination. All of them lived life in the shadows. Trouble had told me Hammer came from one of the toughest neighborhoods in New York City, and I knew Boom's early life hadn't been easy. Even Isogi remained impassive, inscrutable. They knew that the shadows forced people to do some hard things sometimes.

"I didn't really know what I was doing," I continued, drawing a set of symbols in the southern quarter of the circle with bold strokes. "When the elemental lit into them, it was like nothing I'd ever seen before. I was horrified, fascinated. I must have lost control over the spirit. The alley was a blackened ruin. I just turned and walked away, put that whole part of my life behind me and went to tell MCT I'd take their offer. I didn't give a second thought to what became of that elemental . . . until now."

"So, the elemental you summoned to kill those gangers was the same spirit down in the underground?" Trouble asked.

I nodded. "Mama said the answer was somewhere on the metaplanes. Dr. Gordon's map guided me to a place on the metaplane of fire where I saw visions of Gallow's past and learned how it was connected to me. I suspect Mama knew something about it all along, but I don't think Garnoff really knew what he was dealing with."

"But Garnoff was working with that . . . thing," Isogi said with a note of distaste.

"Yes, but I think Gallow was playing him as much as it was playing me. When Gallow escaped my binding and became a free spirit, something happened to it. I'm not sure what, but I think it had to do with the fact that it was summoned by my anger and need for revenge. The first and only command it received was to kill, so that was all it knew how to do. Its hold on this world is tenuous. It needs the energy of living beings to sustain itself and a physical body to channel its power. It possessed one of the dying gangers and used his body to commit murders to provide it with enough life force to keep going and start to increase its power."

"That was the hanged man?" Trouble asked, and I thought about my Tarot layout, *the Hanged Man,* reversed.

"Yes," I said. "The poor fragger Gallow possessed worked up enough willpower to try and kill himself. The spirit couldn't stop him, but it managed to sustain his body by using all its remaining power. That left it none to escape on its own or find a new body. It needed help for that.

"That's where Garnoff comes in. His metaplanar exploration must have touched on something that allowed Gallow to communicate with him. It offered Garnoff magical knowledge and power. All he had to do was kill a few victims to help Gallow build up his power again. Garnoff was a sick fragger. Deep down he probably enjoyed the whole thing. Gallow could never have done it if Garnoff hadn't gone along willingly. He probably hoped to find out enough about Gallow to eventually figure out a way to bind it and control it himself."

"That's why Garnoff wanted to sacrifice you?" Trouble said. "To give Gallow more power?"

"That's what he was told," I said. "Like I said, Gallow played us both for suckers. It probably told Garnoff that I was its summoner, and that my life force, my blood, was the most potent of all for increasing its power. It may have even told him that it wanted to use my body for a new vessel to channel its power. The magical symbolism works, the 'child' kills the 'father' and takes on his power. Garnoff probably never even questioned it. He probably figured he could use me as some kind of bargaining chip, or that he'd be able to bind Gallow once it was free of that body.

"I knew Garnoff wanted me, but I didn't know why. Mama's information as much as told me that. I also knew from the Manadyne run that we didn't have much of a chance of getting close to the real reasons without having to go through a lot of security. That's why I figured it was easiest to give Garnoff what he wanted, make him think he had me so I could find out why."

I finished up the southern quarter of the circle and moved on to the western quarter, sketching new signs and symbols there.

"You're so fragging lucky that worked," Boom said. "I mean, Garnoff could have killed you and Trouble both before we ever got there."

"It was a risk," I admitted, "but no bigger than a shadowrun against some of MCT's best security. Garnoff thought Trouble was under his control, thanks to his little suggestion spell."

"Are you saying she wasn't *ever* under Garnoff's control?" Isogi asked, glancing over at Trouble.

"She was for a while. What Garnoff said about her informing him about our run on Manadyne was true."

Trouble colored a bit at the reminder. She was so angry when I told her about Garnoff's spell that I wasn't sure she'd be able to pull off that act without trying the kill Garnoff herself.

"Garnoff didn't know that I'd performed a mind probe on Trouble when she was hurt after the Manadyne run. I noticed something strange while I was in her mind, and I found the spell and disabled it." I smiled. "And he thought I was drugged with something other than some harmless antibiotics. I was able to mask my aura well enough to make it *look* like I was helpless. Garnoff didn't look too deeply. He was overconfident and he figured he had me for sure. He was too busy gloating to notice anything wrong.

"The truth was, Gallow wanted me for a totally different reason. I summoned Gallow out of anger and commanded it because of a need for revenge. More than life force, Gallow feeds on those emotions, especially from me. It's almost like a part of my own psyche, impressed on the substance of astral space, a dark reflection of my personality.

"That's part of the reason it hates me. In a lot of ways, Gallow *is* me, or a part of me. It knew Garnoff couldn't resist telling me he was the one who had Jase killed, and it knew how that would make me feel—just like I felt when I first summoned it. I suspect that if Garnoff hadn't told me the truth, Gallow would have. Gallow penetrated my masking. It knew I was faking, but it didn't warn Garnoff. It didn't need my life force to give it the power it

needed. It needed my anger, my hate, the same murder-
ous rage that created it. When I killed Garnoff, I gave
Gallow just what it needed.

"Now it's got Garnoff's body to work through, and a
whole city full of victims," I said. "It's only a matter of
time before Gallow starts to kill again to sustain itself,
and I want to find it and stop it before that can happen."

"Can you do it?" Boom asked.

"I think so," I said. "Ordinarily, I know I could. I learned
Gallow's true name on my astral quest. I should be able
to summon it into my presence and try to bind it again,
but I have no idea if that'll work. Gallow isn't like any
free spirit I've encountered before. Since it's possessing
a physical body, it may not be drawn to summonings using its true name.

"But I do have an idea how to track it down. I've got a
spell attuned to detect specific individuals. I should be
able to do a quick ritual to allow me to figure out where
Gallow is, and sustain the spell so I can track him, no
matter where he goes.

"Gallow was weakened somewhat by our fight down
in the Catacombs, so it'll probably go to ground for a
while, then try to hunt down some victims for a recharge.
We need to find it before that happens. If I can get close
enough, I can try and banish it again."

"You will deal with this spirit, then?" Isogi said. I turned
to look up at him again. His immaculate suit was stained
with concrete dust and spattered with blood, although
very little of it his own, from the look of him. Despite
that, he retained his composure and regarded me coolly.

"One way or another," I said, "I will deal with it. I
have to."

Isogi nodded slightly, as if he understood.

"*So ka.* I must inform the oyabun of what has happened. He will be most displeased with Garnoff's faithlessness and deception." He fixed me with a dark stare. Isogi made no mention of the fact that the oyabun would probably be quite displeased with him as well.

He bowed slightly at the waist before turning and walking down the tunnel a short distance. He stood there, half-turned away from us, staring into space. I had no doubt that he was using some kind of headphone radio system to contact his people and tell Hiramatsu, the oyabun, of what was happening in the underground. His face betrayed no emotion and his jaw moved only slightly as he subvocalized through the link, far too quiet for anyone to overhear, even if they were standing right next to him. Isogi would also have to take whatever punishment was due for his own involvement in the affair and his support of Garnoff, assuming any of us got out of the tunnels alive.

"Get him," Trouble said a few moments after Isogi walked away. "You'd think he was in charge around here."

"Do you think it's a good idea having him around?" Sloane asked quietly.

"We don't really have much choice," I said. "We've got bigger things to worry about than one yakuza, and we could use his help."

"Wouldn't take much," Sloane continued, almost like he hadn't heard me. "Down here, it'd be a long time before the yaks figured out what happened to him. With all the ghouls in the tunnels, they might not ever find the body . . ." He cradled his gun in his hands as he contemplated the idea.

"No," I said, "he's better off alive. He'll tell the oyabun what happened and, if we can't stop Gallow, the yakuza might. At least someone else will know Gallow's loose and be able to do something about it."

Sloane looked over at me, the gaze of his cybereyes flat and emotionless, showing nothing of the man behind them. "We don't need his help," he said.

I looked into Sloane's eyes without flinching or backing down. I was tired, but I wasn't going to let the team start coming apart. "I say we do . . . for now." I turned back to working on the circle I needed for the spell. It was almost finished.

Hammer came over and hunkered down nearby, careful not to disturb what I was working on. "Sloane hates yaks," he said quietly, "but he's a pro. You don't have to worry about him."

"I'm not," I said. "I'm more worried about pulling this off."

"You think it'll work?" Hammer asked, his voice a little louder.

I shrugged. "I don't know. Trying to banish Gallow took a lot out of me. I also don't have the time to do this up right. The spell's going to have to be quick and dirty, and that means it's going to be pretty weak. I'm banking that I took as much out of Gallow as it took out of me. If its resistance is down, I might be able to make this spell work."

"And then?" Hammer asked.

"Then we find Gallow and finish this once and for all," I said.

Isogi approached us quietly. I could feel Sloane tense a bit from where he leaned up against a concrete post.

"I have spoken with Hiramatsu-*sama*," he said quietly. "You may deal with this matter as you see fit. But if the spirit escapes or overcomes you again and begins more killings that may threaten the underground, we may be forced to take action, and our response will be swift and merciless."

I nodded in acknowledgment of the pronouncement. It was no more or less than what I'd expected.

"I am to remain and assist you in whatever way I can," Isogi continued. As part of his punishment, no doubt, a way of at least partially redeeming himself in the eyes of his superior.

"Your help is welcome," I said, with a glance toward Sloane. "Do you have a weapon?"

"Of course."

"Good, because you're going to need it."

# 23

Once the circle was complete, I began the ritual. It was makeshift, even by my standards, but sometimes you have to work with what you've got. The circle I drew on the concrete platform was just wide enough for me to stand in, the bare minimum, worked with runes and signs of knowledge and protection. I incorporated symbols representing Gallow's true name in it, in hopes of achieving a better link with the spirit. The two of us were already connected, and I hoped that would allow me to find it, no matter where it might have gone.

A single candle—taken from the pocket of my coat—burned on the floor in front of me as I completed the circle and began the spell. I drew Talonclaw from its sheath and held the blade in the tiny flame of the candle. Garnoff's blood still clung to the blade from where I'd stabbed him. Normally the blood would allow me to cast my ritual on Garnoff, no matter where he might be. I was trusting, with Gallow possessing Garnoff's body, that the ritual would let me find the spirit instead.

The blood sizzled and burned, sending wisps of acrid smoke drifting up. I reached out with my magical senses, sending out a tendril of power, searching for a connection to make the link. I chanted in Latin, low and sonorous, and my voice echoed in the tunnels as the others stood and silently watched me work. I was only barely aware of their presence, all my attention focused on reaching Gallow.

The link held and I began the spell itself, building its energies slowly and directing them through our connection. There was a definite chance Gallow would sense what I was doing and try to protect himself. I was banking on the fact that Gallow seemed bound to its host body, that it couldn't travel through the astral plane to follow the link back and attack me. At least, that was what I hoped. It might try to hide from the spell, but it wouldn't be able to stop me before I was finished. If it tried, the others were waiting for it. If I could get Gallow to come to us, so much the better. But I knew the spirit wasn't that dumb.

The minutes ticked by as I patiently built up the energies of the spell. I wove a subtle web of power stretching across the distance between Gallow and me. Then I began focusing energy down through it to extend my senses and allow me to pinpoint the spirit's location, almost like a spider sensing movement by the vibrations in her web.

I held Talonclaw, point up, in front of me, the steel of the blade like a compass. The spell was nearly complete. I spoke the final phrases, the Latin words rolling off my tongue. I concentrated on the sound and flow of the spell, centering my attention and directing the final surge of energy needed to bring it into being. Images filled my mind and, for a moment, I was aware of the complete layout of the tunnels and catacombs of the underground. Gallow's presence shone like a beacon in the shadows, a flame burning in the dark maze of tunnels.

"I have it," I said quietly. "Let's go." Everyone quickly

fell into step behind me as I made my way down the darkened tunnel, lit only by the small flashlights we carried.

"Where is he?" Trouble asked me.

"Not far. I think he's trying to make his way deeper into the Catacombs. The trains don't run this late and there's nobody around the T stations, so Gallow must be trying to reach the old tunnels where there might be some people he can use to strengthen his powers, maybe a place to hide out."

"Does he know we're on to him?" Hammer asked softly, his gun already out and in his hand, ready for anything.

"I don't know," I said. "We have to assume he does. I couldn't really conceal the spell from him, and Gallow is astrally aware, so he probably noticed it. Either way, I suspect he'll be ready for us."

I guided the group through the tunnels, sticking to the older maintenance passages and sidings, going back toward the main tunnels only when necessary. It was quite late, and not a soul was around, save for the occasional devil rats that squealed when our light fell on them, scurrying back into the shadows or hissing at us from their nests. The size of our group seemed to dissuade them from attacking.

The tunnels we passed through were old and decrepit. Many showed signs of damage from the earthquake that had closed them down decades ago: rusting tracks, broken pipes and wires, deep puddles of black and brackish water, layers of faintly glowing mosses, slime molds, and piles of debris from places where the tunnel walls collapsed, exposing conduits, pipes, and bare earth.

We made our way through one access tunnel where the floor was flooded in calf-deep water.

"Careful, terms," Boom said. "Who the frag knows what's living in that drek."

"Is there any way around it?" Isogi asked me.

I shook my head. "The most direct way is through there."

Isogi looked at the black, stagnant water with an expression of disgust, but slowly made his way through it along with the rest of us. The water stained and soaked his expensive pants and shoes, and I was glad I was wearing my boots and a pair of battered jeans.

As he picked his way through the water, Isogi brushed against Sloane, who reacted by shoving the slighter Japanese man roughly away.

"Stay away from me, fragger," Sloane said.

Isogi pushed himself away from the wall, his eyes smoldering in anger. "Do not lay your filthy hands on me again, *gaijin*."

"I'll do whatever I damn well please, you piece of drek!" Sloane said, his rising voice echoing in the confines of the tunnel.

"Hey!" I said as quietly but as forcefully as I could. "Hold—"

"Shut the frag up, Talon!" Sloane shouted at me. "You don't know what they did . . ." He started to turn toward Isogi, and reached for the gun in his shoulder holster.

"Sloane, no!" Hammer shouted and moved to grab Sloane's arm. He wasn't fast enough for that, but he did manage to knock Sloane's aim off. A shot rang out, but missed Isogi, the bullet ricocheting off the tunnel wall. The sound of it echoed in the confines of the tunnel. Isogi brought his own gun up, his eyes burning with anger. Boom stepped in and grabbed his wrist and forearm in one giant hand.

"The man said hold it, term," Boom said, and Isogi spun on him and struck Boom in the throat. The blow wasn't enough to really hurt someone as tough as a troll, but it caught Boom by surprise and made him loosen his grip on the yakuza's arm.

Opening my senses to the astral, I confirmed my suspicions. Hammer tried to keep his hold on Sloane's arm as surgical steel blades slid out from under the street samurai's fingernails. I allowed my aura to flare visibly and called out in a loud and firm voice.

"Stop it! It's Gallow! He's doing this! Stop it right now and listen!" The bright glow of my aura in the dimness of the tunnel, combined with the sound of my voice, had the desired effect. Isogi and Sloane stopped struggling for a moment and looked at me. They seemed somewhat dazed.

"What?" Sloane said, like someone startled out of a daydream.

"It's Gallow," I repeated. "He's doing this. He's using his power on us, to heighten dislike into hate, to fan hate into violence. He wants to turn us against each other so we can supply him with the power he needs and he can be rid of us at the same time. We must be very close for him to be able to do this. It's what he wants. We have to focus. Put aside our differences and concentrate on getting to Gallow."

"But he . . ." Sloane began.

"If you can't handle it," I said, "I will personally knock you out and leave you here for the fragging devil rats to chew on for a while!"

Anger flared in Sloane's eyes and I forced myself to stop and take a deep breath. "We're all in this together," I said more calmly and, hopefully, more persuasively.

"We have to stick together if we're going to do this. We're a team, like it or not. Don't let Gallow do this. Fight it. Don't let your anger get the better of you."

Sloane slowly relaxed in Hammer's grip and the hand-razors retracted. He glanced over at Isogi, who straightened up and adjusted his tie as Boom stood warily over him.

"Okay," Sloane said. "We deal with Gallow first."

"Good enough," I said. "We must be pretty close. Let's go."

Drawing Talonclaw and feeling the magical blade come alive under my touch, its magic flowing into me, I led the way down the tunnel.

# 24

We came out near a station on the outskirts of the Rox. It was still operating, but closed down for the night. The platform was lit by pale fluorescent lighting above, washing out what little color there was. The blood staining the floor and parts of the walls was nearly black, gleaming wetly in the pale light.

"What the . . . ?" Trouble said as we rounded the corner. The bodies of two night guards lay on the platform in pools of blood, barely recognizable. It looked as if they'd shot each other, several times, with the guns that lay close at hand.

A flicker of light caught my attention from the ticket booth near the entrance to the platform.

"Get down!" I yelled and dove for the floor.

The booth exploded in a blast of orange flames that shot out across the platform. Fragments of molten plastic and burning wood and metal rained down as I threw up my arms to shield my face and head. The others managed to hit the ground or find cover, but we were all scorched by the blast. Sloane took a fragment of shrapnel in his shoulder, blood soaking his shirt, and parts of Boom and Hammer's exposed skin were burned.

Gallow stepped out of the burning booth, shrouded in

an aura of flames that cast Garnoff's features in an un-
holy light.

Everyone opened fire on him at once, guns roaring. I
saw the bullets impact, leaving red tears in Gallow's borrowed flesh and staining his clothes with blood. He showed
no signs of pain or injury and the wounds began to close
instantly, fading even as we watched. They fired until their
weapons were empty and they had to change clips, but
Gallow kept coming, with death in its eyes.

"Your weapons cannot hurt me," the spirit sneered. "I
am not this body. I can shape it to my will and protect it
against you. You're fools to attack me here." Gallow
raised one hand and a sheet of flames shot out from it.

"Get down!" Hammer yelled and hit the floor as the
flaming blast engulfed him. Sloane screamed as the fire
burned and blistered his skin. Boom and Isogi pulled
back around the corner of the tunnel while Trouble and I
stayed low to the ground. The flames cleared, and Sloane
fell to his knees on the concrete, skin charred and smoking. He struggled to rise, barely clinging to life, then fell
face-forward onto the platform, dead.

I picked myself up off the ground, stretched my hands
out toward Gallow and began the ritual of banishment.

"Avant, ye elemental! Avant, ye nature unbound! Begone from this place and trouble it no more! By the
power of the elements, I command you! By the power of
your Name, I compel you! You are Talon's Hate and I,
your maker, bid you begone!"

In response to my words, Gallow's aura flared brighter,
a white-hot flame, causing the floor under his feet to
smoke and smolder, hissing where it stood. It threw its
head back and laughed.

"By my Name, by the freedom I have won, and by the

power that is mine, I will never bow to any man's will again! Creature of flesh, father of spirit, I deny you! I will *not* be bound!" A malevolent grin twisted Garnoff's borrowed features. "You only get one chance, father, and you failed. You cannot banish me now. You have no power over me. The power is mine!"

It gestured again and a line of flame stretched out from its aura along the floor to either side, spreading out to become a ring of flames surrounding the two of us and leaping nearly a meter high, penning us in.

"Your weapons cannot hurt me. Your magic cannot stop me. I will kill you all, one by one, while Talon watches, then I will destroy him as well. What do you say to that, father? Your feeble powers cannot stop me!"

I leveled Talonclaw at Gallow and spoke a single word, channeling a powerful bolt of magical force at the mocking spirit. Gallow merely raised a hand and swatted the manabolt aside like a bothersome insect.

"Ha! Your spells are still weak," he gloated. "It seems you haven't fully recovered from failing to banish me before, have you? But I am as strong as ever. I grow stronger with every life I claim. Whose will be next, I wonder?"

His fiery gaze swept over the group. Hammer and Boom looked at each other and raised their weapons toward Gallow, firing off another volley of rounds. The spirit just stood there in the hail of gunfire that shredded clothing and flesh, but the wounds immediately began to close again, healing before our eyes. The spirit shook its head almost sadly.

Gallow pointed toward Hammer and Boom, and I tried to cast a counterspell, but too late. Another blast of flames shot out at them, engulfing Hammer as Boom dodged out of the way. Hammer hit the floor on fire and rolled to put the flames out as Boom threw off his burning jacket. Hammer groaned and moved a bit before lying still.

I spun toward the laughing devil and shouted. "Stop it! Leave them alone. Your fight is with me!"

"Make me," the spirit smirked. "If you can."

With a shout of rage I clutched Talonclaw and charged Gallow, heedless of the aura of flames surrounding him. The spirit didn't make a move to stop me as I slammed into it, tumbling us both to the ground. The heat was terrible and I could smell scorched cloth and hair everywhere, but I didn't care. I stabbed at Gallow, and Talonclaw bit into its shoulder with a hiss, like water thrown on a fire. Gallow cried out, either in pain or ecstasy, I couldn't say then. The flames around its body flared, and I pulled back to avoid getting burned. Gallow began rising into a crouch, the shoulder wound starting to close, although I noticed that it did so slower than before.

"You think you can stop me?" it taunted. "Is that feeble effort the best you can offer? Perhaps I should kill another one." It turned toward the others with a terrible smile and raised a hand toward Trouble.

"NO!" I shouted. No one else was going to die because of me. I threw myself in front of the blast, all my magical defenses ready, although I had no idea if they could ward off the blast. I saw Gallow hesitate for a moment before the blast of flames engulfed me. They flowed around me like water from a firehose, then just as suddenly vanished.

I stood in amazement for a moment. I was completely unhurt. My clothes were a bit singed, but otherwise not even a hair on my head was touched by the flames. It was then I noticed that my hands, face, and arms weren't burned from my tussle with Gallow, either. It was my magical defenses that stopped it. I hadn't even felt any pressure against them. I looked up at the spirit and saw something akin to fear in its eyes.

"Why?" I said. "Why didn't you kill me?"

Gallow hesitated for an instant. "Not yet," it sneered. "First your friends, then you, father."

"No," I said. "No. That's not it. You can't kill me, can you? You *need* me."

"Need? I need nothing from you, human!" it spat out the word with contempt.

"Oh, I think you do. I think you need me more than anything, more than you're willing to admit. You need my anger, my rage, you feed on that, don't you? Talon's Hate," I said slowly. "Your true name. That's what you are, an embodiment of my hate, my anger, my rage. Will you even exist without me?"

"Shut up!" Gallow screamed, "shut up or I will kill them all!"

"You don't know, do you? You don't know what will happen to you if I die! Will you even exist then?" I taunted. "My death might free you from your connection to me. Or it might kill us both. That's what you're afraid of." When Garnoff's features twisted in hate, I knew I'd struck a nerve. I had a weapon I could use against Gallow. I only hoped I could survive it.

"Why?" the spirit shouted at me. "Why do you plague me? Why?" His borrowed face was distorted in rage and pain.

"I created you," I said, "but you're out of control. This is going to stop. No one else is going to get hurt because of you!" I stepped forward again and Gallow fell back a step, the ferrocrete scorched and blackened beneath it.

"Why?" the spirit cried again. "Why did you create me, then? Do you destroy all that you make, father?"

In that moment, I looked into the depths of Garnoff's eyes and saw the spirit I summoned reflected there, and almost pitied it. In that moment I felt the hate and anger over what Gallow had done drain out of me. Garnoff may have been motivated by greed or madness, but Gallow was what it was; a spirit born of rage and hatred. It knew nothing else. It wasn't like a real person. It had no depth, no other feelings to call upon.

"You were a mistake," I said sadly. "A terrible mistake. You should have been summoned in the joy of learning and achievement. Instead I called you out of anger and a hunger for revenge. I used you to kill because I wasn't strong enough to do it myself, I made you a weapon, a tool of my hate and you've become something twisted and corrupt because of it. Now you must be stopped, and it's my responsibility to do it. I'm sorry."

"Sorry?" Gallow screamed, his flames roaring brightly. A blistering wave of heat drove me back a step. "I don't want your pity! I don't need your weakness! I don't need *you*! I am the fire of hate! The burning heat of anger! I will consume you and all the other weaklings in this city in a conflagration the likes of which you have never seen! You will fight, father, or you and your friends will die!"

Gallow's flames flared as it pointed one hand toward me. A roaring jet of fire shot out. I was too late to jump out of the way and, this time, I sensed that Gallow didn't care any more. It really wanted me dead. Fortunately, I was prepared this time. The flames roared around me, flowing over my clothes, hair, and skin as Gallow laughed madly. I clutched Talonclaw tightly as the flames cleared.

My clothes were singed and smoked a bit, but I was
otherwise uninjured by the blast.

"What?" Gallow cried. "But, but how?"

I gestured with my free hand. "I've learned a great
deal since I summoned you," I said. "I have other spirit
allies to protect me from getting burned." The air near
my shoulder shimmered faintly, like heat rising off a hot
roadway, as my fire elemental hovered close at hand, its
power protecting me from the heat and fire.

"Your feeble servants can't protect you," Gallow said.
"I'll tear your heart out with my bare hands!" With an ani-
malistic growl, it leapt at me.

"Not that way, you won't," I said as I stepped quickly
to the side.

The presence of the spirit made Garnoff's body inhu-
manly fast and strong. If it got me in its grip, it would
probably crush the life out of me. On the other hand, Gallow's rage made it careless, randomly violent. It was heedless of everything else in its desire to destroy me. I knew
the feeling. It was the same feeling Gallow tried to inspire
in me.

Rage was the source of his power, but it was also its
weakness, I hoped. I knew considerably more about hand-
to-hand combat than Gallow. Although I relied mainly on
magic and marksmanship, Ryan and a few other people
had taught me some martial arts moves. I also had Talonclaw, and its magic made me a far more skilled blade-
fighter than I had any right to be by skill alone. Gallow
had no such skill, allowing me to keep him off balance
while I stoked the flames a bit more.

"Did you hope I would kill you?" I said. "Maybe that I
would fall for the same trick you pulled with Garnoff?
Make you even stronger? Maybe strong enough to take

over *my* body?" Gallow was seething, but it made no effort to deny what I was saying. "It's not going to happen," I said. "You've failed.

"You can't beat me," I said, backing slowly away from Gallow as it spun toward me. "You haven't got a chance. You can't take my body. You know you can't kill me. I *made* you. You're mine. Talon's Hate, my slave, a part of me forever. You're a pale reflection of my power. Just admit it."

The flames burned brighter, hotter. "No!" it shouted. "You lie! I am bound to no one! I am FREE!"

It rushed at me again, even faster this time. I sidestepped once more, but only barely. This time I managed to connect with Talonclaw, leaving a long gash in its side that began to heal before my eyes. The pain of the wound further maddened the spirit.

"You, free?" I said with a laugh. "*Look* at you! Bound to a prison of flesh, bound in chains of hate! You'll never be free of me, Talon's Hate." I spit out the spirit's true name with contempt. "You'll *never* be free. We're bound together, you and I, until the end of time."

"NOOOOOO!" Gallow howled. "No! I *will* be free! I will destroy you! I will destroy you all! DIIIIIEEEEE!" All reason was gone. Gallow was nothing more than a mass of pure, seething rage. Its flaming form came charging at me, its only desire to see me destroyed.

I swung a leg out in a low sweep at Gallow's feet, one hand coming forward to grab his arm. Even my servitor elemental's power couldn't protect me completely from the terrible heat surrounding Gallow's host body. It felt like I was touching a piece of burning metal that had lain in the sun too long. I gritted my teeth and ignored the pain. Gallow's face was mere centimeters from mine, twisted in rage and madness.

"Here's your freedom," I said. I thrust Talonclaw into the spirit's chest, driving the blade in to the hilt. Then I twisted and dropped to the ground, using the force of Gallow's own charge to send him sailing over my head into the deep trench behind me where the train tracks lay. The blade slipped free and I grabbed the edge of the trench to keep from going over myself.

There was a loud cracking sound as Garnoff's body struck the charged third rail of the subway track. The body convulsed and stiffened as thousands of volts of electricity poured into it and the flames surrounding it flared, sending a massive pillar of fire roaring to the ceiling and filling the tunnel with the acrid smell of charring flesh. A loud scream was ripped from Garnoff's throat. Whether it was him or Gallow, or both, who made it, I couldn't say. I lay panting on the concrete and threw up an arm to shield my face from the terrible heat.

Finally the charred and blackened body lay still, blue sparks snapping and crackling occasionally around the smoldering form. The ring of fire on the platform flickered and died, leaving only blackened marks where it once was. I looked at the body with my astral sight and saw no living light, no aura whatsoever. It was truly dead.

Gallow was gone.

# 25

The alley was quiet and still at nightfall, broken only by the occasional distant sound of traffic or the wail of a siren. The broken and blasted remains of the Asphalt Rats and their machines were undisturbed except for the natural erosion of time and the ravages of scavengers. Only the four-legged kind. The locals called the place "Fire Alley" and said that it was haunted, so no squatter or gang was willing to claim it for their own. They gave it a wide berth.

I stood near the end of the alley and drew my fingers across one blackened brick wall. I used the soot to draw black lines under my eyes and chin, and across my forehead, then I raised my hands and bowed my head.

"Restless ones," I intoned, "spirits that dwell here, I call to thee. Samhain is fading fast. The door between the worlds is closing. I ask you to appear to me here on this morning, so you may find the rest you deserve."

As I called, they came, appearing out of the walls and the alley and the bleached bones and twisted metal. They were faint, even to my astral sight, translucent images of the bodies they wore in life, dressed in the colors of the Asphalt Rats. Their eyes were dark and hollow, sad to behold. I didn't have to tell them who I was. They knew. They drew closer and I stood my ground. I wasn't afraid.

"Please," I said to the assembled spirits, "forgive me."

They looked at me with their lifeless eyes for what seemed like a very long time. They seemed to be waiting for something else. I looked at each of them carefully, noticing their faces and features like I never had when they were alive. Each was a unique individual, each with lives and feelings of their own once. Like me. Like Jase. Tears stung my eyes and began running down my face.

"I forgive you," I said. One by one, the ghosts began to file past me out of the alley. As they passed, I felt the brush of a hand, a kiss, or a phantom embrace, one last touch of life before they left. The last to go paused and looked into my eyes. His features seemed familiar to me and I realized where I'd seen them before. On the body hanging in the depths of the underground.

*Thank you,* the spirit said silently. I nodded and he went past me, out into the street and into the world beyond.

I lowered my hands. The alley was silent and peaceful. Those ghosts had been laid to rest. The violence done here had been so pointless, two pawns struggling with each other on the edges of the board, unaware of the actions of the real players. Dawn was just beginning to creep up over the cityscape and its pale light stretched into the shadows. Frag, I was tired.

"Talon?" a voice said. I turned to see Trouble standing near the mouth of the alley. She was wearing a short leather jacket and under it a jumpsuit that clung to her curves like a second skin. Her hair was pulled back into a ponytail. I gave a wan smile to show I appreciated the fashion statement, if nothing else.

We talked after we got out of the alley. When I explained

things to her, Trouble just laughed and said, "Why is it all the good ones are either married or gay?

"I'm sorry," she continued. "I didn't mean to disturb you." She started to turn away.

"No, it's okay, it's okay, I'm done," I said.

"Boom said you'd be here."

I made a mental note to someday find out how Boom managed to keep tabs on everyone so well.

"I had some unfinished business to take care of," I said.

Trouble didn't comment. She only took a handkerchief from her jacket pocket and offered it to me. I took it and started to wipe the soot and tears from my face.

"You okay," she said, looking at me with concern written on her face.

"Yeah," I said. "I think I am. How's everyone else doing?"

"Hammer is going to be okay. Your healing spell saved his life. Isogi is back in business with the yakuza. I don't think the oyabun is too pleased with him, but he made up for a lot of it by helping us stop Gallow and bringing all the information about what Garnoff was up to back to the Hiramatsu-*gumi*. I think the yaks will be careful about expanding operations in Boston for a little while at least, which makes Don O'Rilley quite happy."

"That's good," I said. It was always nice to have the local Mafia don pleased with your work.

"I can't believe it's over," she said, looking around the ruined alleyway.

"Why? Wasn't that enough excitement for you?"

She smiled and laughed. "I'm just glad we were able to pull it off. In the underground I wasn't sure I was going to be able to keep up the act."

"You did great," I said. "You even had Garnoff convinced his spell was still working after I disarmed it."

Trouble shuddered a bit and pulled her jacket closer in the evening chill, hugging herself with her crossed arms. "Garnoff. That poor fragger. Knight Errant already recovered the body, you know. All burned like that. They have no idea what really happened to him."

"He was as good as dead anyway," I said. "Gallow isn't the kind of spirit who's likely to share a body with someone. Hopefully, Garnoff was beyond pain by the time his body finally died."

"Mitsuhama is claiming that Garnoff was involved in illegal chips," she said. "The press releases are already starting to go out over the newsnets. Knight Errant is blaming the serial killings on him, saying he was unbalanced, crazy, which is true, but there's nothing about Gallow in any of it. Seems the corp is not too happy. Their PR people must be working overtime. Manadyne canceled their partnership agreement with MCT and they're looking for a new partner. I hear Novatech is already planning to move in on it."

"That's how it works," I said. "One corp take a fall, and another one moves in to take its place."

"So, when are you going back to DeeCee?" she asked. "Hammer wants to get everyone together to raise a glass in memory of Sloane."

"I'm not going," I said.

"What . . . ?" Trouble began.

"I mean I'm not going back to DeeCee. I'm staying here."

"What do you mean? Garnoff's dead, Gallow's dead, there's no more danger."

I shook my head. "Gallow's not dead."

"What do you mean? They pulled his body . . ."

"*Garnoff's* body," I said. "Gallow was just a passenger along for the ride. I told you, mundane weapons can't really kill a spirit, especially not one as powerful as Gallow. Not even a few thousand volts of direct current. Only magic can kill a spirit permanently. The death of his host-body drove Gallow away from the physical world for a while, but he'll be able to come back, maybe soon."

"Oh, gods . . ." Trouble said. "But you know his name, right? Can't you use that to destroy him?"

"I don't know," I said. "When I broke off my first attempt to banish it, I lost most of the power Gallow's true name gave me. I can't try to banish it any longer and I sure as hell can't try to summon or control it. I may be able to kill it, but the trick is going to be finding it again."

"Well, with all of the resources Assets has . . ." Trouble began.

I shook my head. "Like I said, I'm not going back to DeeCee. I've decided to stay here."

"Because of Gallow?"

"Partly," I said. "Sooner or later, Gallow is going to be back. It's my responsibility. I have to find some way to keep it from hurting any more people. There's already been enough death over all this."

I glanced back into the blackened, silent alleyway. "I also made a promise to Dr. Gordon to continue his studies of the metaplanes. After my first run with Assets I thought we'd taken care of any dangers that could come from there, that the Dragon Heart would keep the world safe from anything like that. This has made me realize that the creatures we encountered during the Dragon Heart run are only a fraction of what's out there. The metaplanes are vast, maybe endless, and there's more there than we can imagine. The Awakening isn't over yet. In some ways it's only begun. We need to understand what's out there and we need to be ready for it. I think I've got some experience in that department."

"So, are you getting a research grant and a lab somewhere?" Trouble asked with a smile.

"Who, me? I don't think so. I like being in on the action too much. Jase taught me that life doesn't happen in school or in a lab. It happens right here, out on the streets where people live life. I didn't realize until I came back just how much I missed Boston, and these days the sprawl can certainly use some good shadowrunners. Boom's one of the best fixers and face-men on the East Coast, and I know a really wiz decker. That is, if you're interested."

"We do make a great team," Trouble said, smiling again.

"The best," I said.

"I don't know if Hammer will forgive you, though, stealing his team's best decker."

"I think I can work it out with him," I said. "In fact, I could definitely use someone with his kind of experience, if he's willing."

"I think he just might be," Trouble said. "What about Assets?"

"At this point they're used to losing mages," I joked, "and I rather like the idea of being the first magician to walk away from Assets, Inc. alive and in one piece. It's something I have to do. I still need to talk to them, but I think they'll understand. In fact, I know they will." That was just the kind of guy Ryan was.

"C'mon, let's go and raise a glass to Sloane, then we can talk about this new team. If I know Boom, he's already got some potential recruits and jobs lined up and waiting."

Together, we walked away from my past and into the future. When I'd left Boston, I was leaving my home behind. Now I had my home back again. I thought I'd severed my ties with the Hub back then, but life's connections are too complex to be broken so simply. They're the ties that bind us to our past and our selves, that make us who we are. I passed the crossroads and began walking down the path I'd chosen.

# Epilogue

Gallow appeared in the Citadel of the City of Gold and Brass with a burst of rage and pain. *Damn that accursed mage to an eternity of torment!* He'd underestimated how much Talon's magic had grown, how much he had changed, during his time of imprisonment. Talon had become wiser, more clever, but his "father" was a fool if he thought killing that flesh-puppet Garnoff would keep Gallow from the physical world. He was still free of the binding, and the time it would take to return to the mundane world would be little more than an eyeblink compared to the long years he'd waited to be free of his imprisonment.

Gallow paced the chamber of the citadel, which contained only a mirror, covered by a pale cloth. There was a flutter of wings and the black bird settled on the top of the mirror, looking at Gallow with glittering, dark eyes. It was a spirit the fire elemental had never seen before. It silently watched him, and he thought of how he would gain his revenge, against Talon, against all of them.

He brushed aside a thread of astral energy that hung like a cobweb from the ceiling as he plotted. It would have to be long and painful, so as to be properly savored,

yes, a true masterpiece, not like the work of the clumsy
fool Garnoff. Perhaps Talon would make a more suitable
host than Garnoff, provided the proper . . . arrangements
could be made. Yes . . . that would be ideal. Gallow
would enjoy forcing Talon to destroy his newfound friends
and make him understand what it felt like to be outcast,
alone, always alone.

Another astral thread draped across the spirit's path.
He angrily pushed at it and three more of them dropped
down. Then three more, then more, and more, until
the mass of threads began to grow into an enmeshing
web. The more Gallow thrashed and struggled, the more
entangled he became in them. Thin as gossamer, the
threads held as strong as steel. Gallow turned toward
the raven sitting atop the mirror, where it watched his
struggles impassively. What was happening? Who could
be . . . ?

"Tsk, tsk, tsk. Poor dear thing, beaten by a mere human in single combat. What is the world coming to?" The
mocking voice came from an astral form nearby. Gallow
had not sensed it before she simply appeared within the
Citadel; an ancient crone clad in black. She smiled and
bared her sharpened teeth, her aura dark as the deepest
night, filled with a triumphant malice.

"Still, you'll make a useful enough servant, I suppose,
once I've taught you some obedience."

The spirit shook with rage, but recoiled into whimpering as a burst of agony surged through the bindings holding him fast. How could this be? It was impossible . . .

"I have plans for you, my little Talon's Hate," she said,
using Gallow's true name. "It was so nice of Talon to come
back home, where he's so needed. Such a good boy, and

such an opportunity for me. Come now, my pet, and we'll begin your lessons."

With a thin, cackling laugh, Mama turned and made her way from the Citadel, with the helpless spirit drawn along behind her.

# ABOUT THE AUTHOR

*Crossroads* is Stephen Kenson's second novel. His first, *Technobabel,* was also set in the Shadowrun® universe and published by Roc Books. Fans of the Shadowrun® universe also know Kenson as the author of game books like *Portfolio of a Dragon: Dunkelzahn's Secrets* and the *Underworld* sourcebook. Talon the mage has previously made an appearance in Jak Koke's Shadowrun® novel, *Beyond the Pale,* and in game books like *Awakenings* and *Portfolio of a Dragon,* but this is his first novel-length solo adventure.

Steve Kenson lives in Milford, New Hampshire, and loves to hear from readers and fans of Shadowrun®. He can be contacted by e-mail at *talonmail@aol.com.*

Don't Miss the Next Exciting
Shadowrun Adventure!

**THE FOREVER DRUG**
by Lisa Smedman

There's a new drug on the streets, one that
provides a phenomenal—and deadly—high.
The drug isn't a substance, but a being: a
"corpse light" that gives you a euphoric rush
even as it drains your life away.

Will a shapeshifting freelance police agent
unlock the mystery in time?

Coming in June from Roc Books